THE HAT TRICK

Thanks for reading

Best wishes,

the HAT TRICK

a novel

TOM EARLE

Harper*Trophy*Canada™
An imprint of HarperCollins*PublishersLtd*

Published by Harper*Trophy*Canada™,
an imprint of HarperCollins Publishers Ltd.

First Canadian edition

Harper*Trophy*Canada™ is a trademark of HarperCollins Publishers.

HarperCollins books may be purchased for educational, business,
or sales promotional use through our Special Markets Department.

HarperCollins Publishers Ltd
2 Bloor Street East, 20th Floor
Toronto, Ontario, Canada
M4W 1A8

www.harpercollins.ca

Library and Archives Canada Cataloguing in Publication

Earle, Tom, 1966–
The hat trick / Tom Earle.

ISBN 978-1-55468-628-5

I. Title.
PS8609.A76H38 2010   jC813'.6   C2010-900814-6

Printed and bound in Canada
DWF 9 8 7 6 5 4 3 2

For Janet, my favourite hockey mom

THE HAT TRICK

Part One

CHAPTER ONE

As Ben McMillan walked to the podium, he was shaking perceptibly. He had just endured a high-stakes game of chicken and was about to cash in.

McMillan was the general manager and head scout of the Barrie Colts of the Ontario Hockey League. He and his brain trust, which included the head coach, two assistant coaches and three main scouts, had just suffered through an hour of watching other teams go to the podium and announce their selections in the OHL's Priority Draft. Since joining the OHL, the Colts had been a very successful team. Within five short years they had advanced all the way to the Memorial Cup final, where they lost a hard-fought game to the Rimouski Océanic led by future NHL star Brad Richards. But recently the Colts had fallen on hard times and missed the playoffs. Their reward for their futility was the fifth-overall pick in the Priority Draft.

It would be easy to overlook McMillan at an arena; he didn't seem like your typical scout. Most scouts looked like old athletes: giant hands that were too swollen to hold the

3

pen that they took notes with, stiff knees that told of long-ago battles, and outdated, ill-fitting suits. McMillan was tiny, with a bald head and round John Lennon glasses. He looked like he belonged in a library, not a rink. In fact, the former high school teacher had always approached scouting with a teacher's eye, looking for that student who, with the proper instruction, would learn the game and develop into a star.

This past season, McMillan and his scouts had scoured every arena from Kenora to Windsor, from Cornwall to Kirkland Lake. McMillan alone had watched more than two hundred games.

He thought about previous selections he had made. Daniel Tkaczuk proved to be a star in the Ontario Hockey League, or "the O," as insiders referred to it. Bryan Little was a late-round selection who had blossomed into the team's captain, an all-around leader and the franchise's all-time top scorer. But this year, for the first time in a long time, McMillan was questioning his ability to judge talent. He had stumbled across a kid that he felt was a bona fide can't-miss pick. Ironically, McMillan had found him right under his own nose, playing in Barrie's minor hockey system.

One night, McMillan was leaving one of Barrie's many arenas after watching the AAA midgets play the York Simcoe Express. It had been a particularly frustrating game to scout because neither team had a player he felt could jump in and help the Colts become a better team. As he scurried out of the rink, he almost collided with a man who was hustling just as quickly towards the entrance. It was Darryl Phillips, one of his former players.

"Coach McMillan!" Darryl exclaimed. "How are you doing?"

"Hi, Darryl. I haven't seen you for ages. What are you doing here?" McMillan asked.

"I'm just heading in to see my son play. What about you? Still scouting?"

McMillan nodded. "Just watched the midgets play York Simcoe."

"Huh. See anybody you like?"

McMillan shook his head. "No, nobody tonight." Then, in an effort to get his mind off his frustration, McMillan decided to swing the conversation back towards Darryl. "How old is your boy, Darryl?"

"Minor bantam," Darryl answered. "He's thirteen."

"Does he play like you used to?" McMillan asked jokingly.

"No," Darryl laughed. "He has a lot more skill than I had."

McMillan paused. He knew it would probably be a waste of his time, but given how much hockey he watched in a year, what was one more game? "Well," he said, "what are we waiting for? Let's go watch him play."

By the time that they got into the rink and got settled, the game had already started.

McMillan planned to stay only for a shift or two and was already thinking up an excuse so that he could make a polite exit when Darryl pointed out his son, who was skating towards the face-off circle. It was the moment the old scout had waited his whole life for. He shook his head in disbelief, not sure that he was really seeing what he thought he was seeing. McMillan stayed for the rest of the game and marvelled at what the kid could do. At five feet, eleven inches, he was big and strong, but he also skated beautifully and was a natural goal scorer. McMillan went back three more times that year to watch him play.

That had been two years ago. Since then, McMillan had watched the boy play close to forty games and was convinced he was the real deal. What he couldn't understand was why the other nineteen teams in the O weren't as excited as he was. For weeks, the team had followed the updates issued by Central Scouting, monitoring their boy's progress. They were convinced Phillips was a consensus number one pick and that the buzz surrounding him would rival that of the great Sidney Crosby. But each week, there he was: projected as a strong first-round pick, but by no means a clear number one. As the day of the draft drew closer, McMillan became more and more nervous. Was he a genius who was about to pluck a future superstar out from under the noses of the other general managers in the league, or were the rest of the GMs better judges of hockey talent than he was? Right or wrong, he was willing to stake his reputation on this kid, and he was determined to figure out a way to draft him.

When the day of the draft finally arrived, McMillan was left with a decision. Should he try to work out a deal with the Guelph Storm, who had the first pick, thus guaranteeing that he could pick his boy? Or should he gamble and hope that Phillips was still around for the fifth pick? A trade would be costly, and the Colts simply didn't have enough depth to try and swing a trade. Besides, McMillan was pretty sure that Guelph had their sights set on a big, mobile defenceman from the Toronto Young Nationals of the Greater Toronto Hockey League. That left the teams drafting second, third and fourth. Sudbury, scheduled to draft second, was on record as needing a scoring winger, while Belleville, with the number three pick, was after a defenceman. That left Sault Ste. Marie. The Greyhounds were a wild card—McMillan had no idea where they were headed. After much discussion and agonizing, the Colts decided they would gamble on the first four picks and hope their boy was still available. And if he wasn't, McMillan would go to the podium and announce that Barrie was taking a goaltender from Markham. Only the men at the table would know that the goalie wasn't their first choice, and the Colts' brain trust would smile and say how excited they were about the future.

"It's just like playing poker, boys," McMillan told his colleagues. He hoped he sounded more confident than he felt when he added, "you just have to have the balls to gamble a bit."

So here they were: seven very nervous men, trying to appear calm, yet growing more fidgety and nauseous with each selection. After three picks, their boy still hadn't been selected. It would be about fifteen minutes before the league commissioner called on Skip Daniels from the Soo to make his selection.

Suddenly, McMillan stood up and pushed back his chair.

Head coach Adam Graham looked at him quizzically. "Where are you going, Ben?"

"I'm going to ask Skip if he'll trade picks with us."

"But I thought this was just like poker!" Graham protested.

"It is. And I'm about to fold. I want that kid, damn it, and I can't stand the thoughts of Daniels getting him."

McMillan turned and marched over to the Greyhounds' table. He had a strong feeling this wasn't going to go well. During the season, the Greyhounds and Colts had engaged in a nasty little bench-clearing brawl. The Greyhounds thought the Colts were taking cheap shots with late hits. The Colts, of course, felt it was the Greyhounds' dirty stickwork that was to blame. As the Greyhounds left the Barrie Molson Centre after the game, Daniels walked past McMillan and sneered, "Are you teaching that crap to your boys, Ben?"

McMillan stiffened like he had been punched. There were very few times when he lost his composure, but when he did it was legendary. "What did you say, asshole?"

Daniels exploded. "You heard me! You're teaching those boys to be nothin' but a bunch of goons!"

McMillan lunged at Daniels and snarled, "Why don't you go and . . ." The rest of his brilliant verbal retort was lost in the ruckus as coaches, spectators and players rushed to separate the two middle-aged combatants.

McMillan smiled to himself, remembering that night, as he neared the Greyhounds' table. Sometimes it was fun to blow off a little steam. Helped to keep you young. "Ah, hey Skip. You got a minute?"

"Sure, Ben, what's up?" Daniels's cheerfulness seemed only slightly forced, so Ben decided to push on.

"I was wondering if you'd be interested in swapping picks?" he asked, as he looked at the floor.

"Well now, you must really be after someone if you're willing to swap a five for a four. Who are you hoping to get?"

McMillan had been around long enough to know you never reveal your pick to someone who's ahead of you in the draft. Especially if he was a prick like Daniels. He thought fast and responded, "Um, we like Charette, that goalie on the Waxers."

"Okay," said Daniels. "Well, we don't have a lot of time here, so let's see. I'll swap picks in exchange for Bibby."

Ben snorted. "Do you honestly think I'd swap a five for a four at the price of my top scorer?"

"Like I said, Ben, we don't have a lot of time. That's my offer. Take it or leave it," Daniels grinned. He was clearly enjoying having the upper hand.

Time to burn a bridge, Ben thought. "Skip, do you remember what I said to you last time you were in Barrie?"

"Actually, I couldn't hear you. There were too many people trying to keep me from kicking your sorry little ass."

"Well, let me refresh your memory." Ben was struggling to keep his voice down. "Go and—"

"Ladies and gentlemen!" the commissioner's voice boomed over the public-address system, drowning Ben out. "With the fourth pick in this year's draft, the Soo Greyhounds."

Skip stood and smirked at Ben. "Talk to you later, Bennie." And with that, he strode confidently to the podium.

"Arrogant bastard," McMillan muttered under his breath.

As Daniels stood at the podium, McMillan closed his eyes and held his breath. "The Sault Ste. Marie Greyhounds are pleased to select, from the Markham Waxers AAA Midgets, goaltender Michael Charette." Daniels looked directly at McMillan, smiled and winked at him. There was an instant buzz in the room as people applauded for Charette and the Greyhounds.

Ben was ecstatic. Daniels had taken the bait! He ran back to the Colts' table and grinned at Adam Graham. "Holy shit, we got him!" He slapped Graham on the back and then began to pace back and forth behind the Colts' table. Over the course of the next fifteen minutes, McMillan checked his watch thirty-seven times, punched Adam Graham repeatedly on the shoulder and gave a series of triumphant fist pumps. He was in the process of wearing a hole in the carpet when the commissioner finally stepped up to the microphone and announced, "And now, with the fifth selection, the Barrie Colts."

Ben took a deep breath and tried to calm himself down. He willed his hands to stop shaking, then he walked to the podium, turned and smiled to the crowd. "The Barrie Colts are pleased to select, from the Barrie Minor Hockey AAA Midgets, centreman Ricky Phillips."

The Colts had their boy.

CHAPTER TWO

On a warm summer day about a month before the Barrie Colts were scheduled to open their training camp, Ricky Phillips was lounging on the couch after his morning workout. His mom was out shopping and his dad was puttering around the house, enjoying a day off work. Ricky was engrossed in an offshore powerboat race on the Speed Channel when his dad walked in and flopped on the couch beside him.

"Whatcha watching, Bud?"

"Boat race from Miami," Ricky answered.

"Hmm," Darryl responded thoughtfully. "Do you think you could join me in the basement for a minute?" he asked.

Ricky, who really wanted to see the race, hesitated before answering.

"I'm a little pressed for time," his dad said, in a tone that made it clear it was more of a command than a request.

Reluctantly, Ricky shut off the TV and followed his dad to the basement. As they descended the stairs, Ricky looked around at the open space before him. When Ricky had first started to show an interest in hockey, his father decided not to finish the basement. On one wall he had tacked up several sheets of plywood, in front of which he'd placed a hockey net. Ricky could Rollerblade all over the basement and shoot pucks at the goal.

From his first house-league game at the tyke level, as a five-year-old, it was very apparent that Ricky was a special player. He was bigger, stronger and faster that the other players. He had an incredible pair of hands and a burning desire to win.

Ricky and his parents lived in Oro-Medonte, a tranquil little slice of central Ontario that is located between Barrie and Orillia. Ricky started playing his minor hockey in Orillia, but when he was nine and a minor atom, Darryl moved him to Barrie to play AAA. Even at the highest level, Ricky stood out as a dominant player. By the time Ben McMillan started watching him as a minor bantam, Ricky already stood five foot eleven and weighed 160 pounds. In the three games that McMillan watched that year, Ricky had nine points and controlled all aspects of the game. Two years later, McMillan pencilled him in as the Colts' top priority on his wish list.

At the bottom of the basement stairs, Ricky looked around at the tattered hockey net and the puck-marked plywood and thought fondly about the number of hours he had spent down here, honing his skills. He snapped out of his daydream when his dad called to him to put on his Rollerblades.

"Oh, and grab your helmet and gloves too."

Ricky was a little puzzled; it had been months since he'd Rollerbladed, and surely his dad knew that he didn't wear a helmet anymore. Ricky's curiosity continued to be piqued as Darryl sat down beside him and started to lace up his own Rollerblades. Ricky smiled to himself, assuming his dad was trying to connect with him in some sort of male-bonding-type way.

Ricky was still smiling to himself when his dad skated over and asked, "Are those straps tight on your face mask?"

Man, he's taking this safety thing a little too seriously, Ricky thought. "Yeah, Dad, they're tight."

Darryl nodded and skated around the basement. "Okay, Ricky, hurry up. We don't have a lot of time."

Ricky stood up and skated towards his dad. "Time for what?"

Without any warning, Darryl swung a roundhouse and caught Ricky square on the chin. Ricky landed with a thud on the concrete floor. Quickly he scrambled to his feet and yelled, "What the hell was that for?"

Darryl raised his hands apologetically and said, "I'm sorry, but I had to do this when your mother wasn't home. She'd kill me if she knew I was teaching you how to fight. Now get ready and we'll try that again."

"I can't believe you hit me!" Ricky said. His jaw ached and he was more than a little pissed off.

His dad laughed. "Do you honestly think some guy's going to ask your permission before he hits you?"

Ricky glared at him.

"Listen," Darryl said, "you're fifteen years old. You are going to be playing against twenty-year-olds who are big, strong and mean. Some of them have no talent other than the fact they like to fight and are very good at it."

Ricky had never really thought about the fact that he might have to fight in the O. He was suddenly nervous and a little bit scared. "You think I'm gonna have to fight?"

Darryl shrugged. "You're their first-round pick. They drafted you to score goals, not to fight. But you should know how to protect yourself."

13

Ricky took a deep breath and nodded. "Okay," he said. "Let's learn how to fight."

For the next hour, his dad passed on the tricks of the trade that he'd learned when he played junior hockey.

"When there's a scrum after the whistle and guys are pushing and shoving, the guy who wants to fight won't say anything. That's why I hit you—they'll do the same thing. Lesson number one is to beware of the quiet guy, because he's getting ready to swing.

"If a guy is chirping away at you, talking trash and calling your mother names, he doesn't want to fight," Darryl continued. "He's just trying to wind you up so that you'll take a penalty." He skated towards Ricky and grinned menacingly. "You're a loser, Phillips."

Instantly, Ricky's hands came up. They collided with his dad's hands and the two of them pushed each other away. Catching on quickly, Ricky decided to try and talk a little trash of his own.

"Is that all you've got, old man?" he asked.

His dad laughed. "Good one. Now listen, Ricky. If you want to send this guy a message, as your hands come up, open your glove and put the palm right in his face. Then kind of flick at his face like he's not worth your time. It's called a face wash, and that's lesson number two."

For the next few minutes, Ricky and his dad skated towards each other, colliding and trying to give each other face washes. Ricky was a fast study, and soon he was pushing Darryl back and controlling the tempo of each altercation. He was having fun, and he was hungry to learn more.

"What else you got up your sleeve, Dad?"

"Okay then, lesson number three. It's a simple one: He

who punches first, wins. The whole key to fighting is to decide whether or not you want to fight before he does. It's crucial to get that first punch in. It'll keep him off balance and give you an advantage. Now, then, drop your gloves."

Ricky did as he was asked; but, remembering the punch his father had thrown at him earlier, he did so reluctantly.

"Okay," Darryl went on, "now grab a big handful of my shirt with your left hand."

Ricky reached over and grasped his father's T-shirt.

"Good. Now drop your head slightly and tuck your face in tight against your left bicep."

Ricky did as he was told. His dad took a few half-hearted swings at him and said, "See how hard it is for me to land a good shot? Your face is protected by your arm. Now close your eyes."

Ricky closed his eyes and waited for the next instructions. His dad laughed. "I was just kidding, Ricky."

Ricky blushed and opened his eyes.

Darryl continued: "You know, you *could* close your eyes because all you do now is swing towards your left hand. His face will be slightly above your left hand. Go ahead and swing, but not too hard—I'm not as young as I used to be."

Ricky took a deep breath, grabbed his father, tucked his face in nice and tight and swung several times with his right hand. Most of the punches hit Darryl in the upper chest and had little effect on the big man. The last punch, however, caught him square on the jaw and rocked him back a step.

"Oh shit, Dad. I'm sorry!"

Darryl shook his head, rubbed his jaw and grinned. "That's okay, Ricky." Then his expression suddenly turned serious. "Crap . . . Is that your mother I hear?"

Ricky hesitated slightly, and Darryl grabbed him and before he knew what was happening, Darryl had pulled his T-shirt up and over his head and cinched it tight around his face.

"Ha!" Darryl laughed. "Your old man's still got it. You just got jerseyed—and that, my boy, is lesson number four."

●

Ricky chugged around the corner and jogged up the final small hill towards his house. As he finished his five-kilometre run he pressed the stop button on his watch. While he walked around his front lawn and waited for his breathing to settle down, he glanced at the time on his watch: twenty minutes and fifteen seconds.

Not bad, he thought to himself, but it was still ten seconds off of his best time. His goal was to break twenty minutes before the end of the summer.

His dad had been concerned that Ricky might get injured or be overtired when it came time to report for the Colts' training camp. So he suggested that he not work this summer, but concentrate instead on the workout regime the team had prepared for him. Ricky had thought it was a great idea. For the past two summers, Ricky had worked as a detailer at a local marina. He cut grass, pumped gas, washed and waxed boats and did anything else that needed to be done. The work was physical and the hours were long. Compared to that, working out and then relaxing seemed like a great way to spend his time.

Ricky was tall at six feet, three inches, but he was a relatively slight 180 pounds. The Colts felt that if he could add more bulk to his frame, he would be more likely to withstand the rigours of an OHL season. What Ricky hadn't bargained for was that, after a month of sit-ups, push-ups, core stability exercises, bench presses, jogging, watching TV and playing video games, he was incredibly lonely and bored. He played golf with his dad whenever he was free after work, but what Ricky was missing was someone his own age to hang out with. The only friends he'd ever had were his hockey teammates. At school, he was a good student, but he was very quiet and the demands of AAA hockey left very little time for friendships. He had begun to notice girls, but the thought of actually talking to one seemed more daunting than cutting through the neutral zone with his head down.

The only exciting thing that had happened that summer was that his dad had started to teach him how to fight. It was a lot of fun, but his dad was terrified that his mom, Haley, would find out what they were doing and put an end to the "lessons."

Ricky's breathing was almost back to normal when he noticed his mom coming out the front door of the house. She waved and smiled as she hustled for her car.

"Hi, honey," she called. "How was your run?"

"Okay."

"That's nice." She never broke stride. "I'm sorry, Ricky, but I'm late for work."

"That's okay," he said. "Maybe I'll ride over to the golf course and hit a bucket of balls."

Haley got in her car and started it up. As she backed out of the driveway, she rolled down her window and called to Ricky: "You can go to the course later, but right now your dad needs a hand in the basement."

Ricky waved at his mom as she drove down the road. Then he turned and walked towards the house. He was smiling when he opened the door. If his dad had stayed home from work, it could mean only one thing: it was time for another lesson.

Ricky hustled down to the basement, where he found his dad already in his Rollerblades.

"Is your mom gone?" he asked.

"Yup."

"Good." He threw a hockey jersey at Ricky. "Put this on."

"What's this for?" Ricky asked.

"It's part of today's lesson," Darryl answered. "It will be easier if we're wearing jerseys."

Today's trade secret was learning how to "tie up" an opponent. This was a particularly important skill when you were tired at the end of a fight, or if your opponent was stronger than you and you were worried about getting hurt. Essentially, this entailed grabbing as much jersey as you could, in both hands, under the biceps. This manoeuvre effectively limits your opponent's ability to punch because he can't free up his arms.

Wearing the jerseys really helped Ricky get the hang of holding on. Darryl had Ricky all tied up, and as Ricky fought to free up an arm, Darryl smiled and said, "This is where you hold on tight and hope the refs break it up fast before he figures out how to pull his arm out of the sweater backwards."

Ricky grinned when he recognized the escape route. You don't try to punch; instead, you pull your arm back out of the sleeve of the jersey. Ricky's arm was now free and Darryl was left uselessly holding the empty sleeve of Ricky's jersey.

"Oh, I've got you now, Dad," taunted Ricky, waving his arm menacingly as if he was going to throw a haymaker.

"Not so fast, kid. Don't forget lesson number five: If you're about to get your ass kicked, reach down and grab the front of his pants. Pick him up, take him to the ice and hold on tight until the refs come in." And with that, Darryl promptly knocked Ricky on his butt.

◉

As the month passed, Ricky's confidence grew. He was convinced that he was physically stronger than his father. He began to pester his dad to drop the mitts for real. Repeatedly, he would ask, "Hey, Dad. Do you want to go?"

Darryl just ignored him, except for the one time Ricky followed the question with, "What's wrong, Dad? Are ya chicken?"

That was simply more than Darryl's testosterone-fuelled pride could take. He turned and stared hard at Ricky. "What did you say, smart guy?"

Ricky instantly knew that he had crossed the line. Oh shit, he thought. But then, just as quickly, he had a surge of bravado and said, "You heard me. I asked if you were ch—"

Suddenly, Darryl threw his gloves in Ricky's face. Ricky was momentarily caught off guard by the flying distraction. In the same instant, Darryl grabbed Ricky with his left hand and threw wildly with his right. The punch missed, and Darryl's arm flew up and over Ricky's head. As he pulled his arm back, his hand caught the back of Ricky's helmet and it flew off as easily as a ball cap in a windstorm. Darryl then jerseyed Ricky and tied up both arms with the excess material. Before Ricky could react, Darryl had him defenceless, helmetless and completely at his mercy. Darryl pulled back his right hand and . . . stopped.

"I thought I told you to beware of the quiet guy," Darryl grinned. Then he mussed Ricky's hair and let him go. "So, do you still want to go, tough guy?"

Ricky, feeling rather humbled, smiled sheepishly. "Maybe tomorrow."

CHAPTER THREE

On the morning of tryouts, Ricky leaped out of bed and raced to the bathroom, where he promptly threw up.

"Oh great, that's not good," he muttered to himself. He ran his fingers through his hair and realized that his hands were shaking.

He grabbed a quick shower and went out to have some breakfast. His parents were already in the kitchen, and they both turned to smile at him. "Hey, kiddo, how was your night?"

"Great, great," Ricky muttered.

Haley looked at Darryl with a say-something-look on her face.

"Uh, hey, Ricky, I was wondering if you would mind if I came to your tryout?" Darryl asked.

Ricky took a deep breath and relaxed. "Yeah, Dad, that would be great."

"Well, I've been to every tryout you've ever had. I don't know why I'd stop now."

The whole way to the rink, Ricky was on edge. I hope I don't puke in the car, he thought to himself. When Darryl pulled into the parking lot of the Barrie Molson Centre, Ricky suddenly sat still and didn't move.

"You okay?"

Ricky nodded his head nervously but made no effort to get out of the car.

"Dad?" he finally asked.

"Yeah?"

"What if I'm no good?"

Darryl laughed gently. "Aw, Ricky," he said. "I've been around hockey my whole life. You're good."

Slowly, Ricky turned to face his dad. "Really?"

Darryl nodded. "Really. Now go get 'em."

Ricky reached tentatively for the door handle. He took a deep breath and sighed.

"Okay," he said. "Let's go get 'em."

The second Ricky stepped onto the ice he felt better. He knew right away that he could play as this level. In a one-on-one drill he completely undressed the defenceman and scored a nice goal. During the scrimmage he threw a thunderous body check that separated a defenceman from the puck, and then he set up a nice play in front of the net.

Driving home with Darryl that night, he talked the whole way. It reminded Darryl of when Ricky was small. He loved driving Ricky to hockey games because the two of them would talk about anything they wanted to. They even had a code: What's said in the car, stays in the car. After a game, Darryl would find the local McDonald's and the two of them would talk and munch fries and drink Cokes the whole way home. Each time they pulled into the driveway, Darryl would look at Ricky and whisper, "Don't tell your mother we ate junk food."

Darryl was still smiling to himself at the memory as he pulled onto Highway 11. "Hey, Ricky, would you like to stop at McDonald's?"

Ricky looked at him as if he was insane. "You know I can't eat that shit, Dad."

Well, there's a nice childhood memory shot to hell, Darryl thought.

❂

Each day during tryouts, Ben McMillan and Adam Graham would watch the practice from the press box. And each day, McMillan got a little more excited over Ricky's progress. By the end of the first week, he was convinced Ricky would carry the team in his rookie year. Graham was pleased with Ricky, but was somewhat more reserved than his GM. "We'll see how he does against Peterborough tomorrow night," he said.

The next night, the Peterborough Petes skated onto the ice at the BMC for the first game of the pre-season schedule. All the players were edgy, and Ricky, like the other rookies on both teams, was anxious to make a good first impression.

His first shift started with a face-off to the left of the Colts' goaltender. Ricky won the draw back to his defence-man, who fired an outlet pass up the wall. The Colts' left winger, Ronnie Cepuran, chipped the puck past one of the Petes' defencemen, who had pinched in to try to hem the Colts in their own end. Ricky was gone—a two-on-one with his right winger, Jimmy Kirton. He crossed Peterborough's blue line at full speed, coming down the left side. As a right-hand shot, he pulled his stick back behind him so the D-man would have to play the pass. From the moment Ricky got the puck, he knew he was going to shoot. He was counting on the D playing the pass, and that's exactly what he did. As he hit the top of the circle, Ricky unloaded a quick wrist shot. The goalie still hadn't moved when the puck hit the back of the net in the top right corner and sent the water bottle on top of the net flying. Ricky circled down behind the net and was met with a congratulatory hug from Kirton. Ricky was far too excited to realize that he had just scored on his first shift—on his first shot—of his OHL career.

As the teams took the ice to start the third period, Ricky had a goal and an assist and the Colts were ahead 4–1. His confidence was growing with every shift. Meanwhile, on the Petes' bench, a big twenty-year-old named Bill McDuffie was also anxious to make an impact. He had spent the last two seasons bouncing around from team to team. Last year he ended up playing more time in Tier II Junior A than he did in the O. He was desperate to make an impression so that, in a year's time, he might sign as a free agent with a pro team. He fully understood his role and he was very good at it. So far tonight, he'd been as physical as possible. And he'd decided that, if he got another shift, he would make something happen.

With two and a half minutes to go, the Colts dumped the puck into the Petes' zone and peeled to the bench for a change. Ricky's line hopped the boards. The three energetic rookies, sensing that it might be their last shift, flew into the Petes' end. After a quick shot by Ricky, the Petes relieved the pressure and dumped the puck for a line change of their own. As Ricky's line broke out of their end, McDuffie hopped the boards with two other twenty-year-old forwards.

Ricky gained the zone and dumped the puck harmlessly towards the Petes' net. The goaltender froze the puck as the three Colts converged on him. Ricky and Ronnie Cepuran peeled off towards the corner, but Kirton continued to the front of the net and stopped. McDuffie, who was trailing

Kirton, cross-checked him hard in the small of the back, sending him sprawling face-first across the ice. Ricky and Cepuran curled back and, without hesitating, rushed to the aid of their splattered teammate.

Before he had time to think, Ricky collided with McDuffie and their gloves came up. McDuffie shoved back and sneered, "Back off, rookie."

In a flash, Ricky's gloves were off and he grabbed McDuffie's jersey with his left hand. His right followed an instant later and caught the big Pete square on the . . . visor!

Oh shit! That hurt! Ricky thought as he instinctively buried his face in his left shoulder. Then he threw his next punch past McDuffie's head. As he pulled his hand back, it caught the back of the helmet and off it popped.

The crowd, which moments earlier thought that it would see Ricky receive an old-fashioned ass-whipping, roared its approval at this turn of events. McDuffie had clearly underestimated the rookie and tried to gain control of the situation. He had yet to land an effective punch, and the ones that did connect were bouncing harmlessly off of Ricky's helmet. Seeing the way that Ricky had his face protected, he knew that he needed to switch hands and swing with his left. He was in the process of doing so when Ricky caught him square on the nose with a solid right. McDuffie's head snapped back and the BMC crowd came unglued. Ricky's fist came again and again scored a shot on the end of McDuffie's chin. The big Pete's knees buckled and down he went, with Ricky right on top of him. The roar of delight that echoed through the BMC made it sound as if the game were a playoff sellout, not a preseason game played before just eight hundred fans.

The linesmen jumped into the fray and pried the combatants apart. Blood was pouring from McDuffie's nose as he tried to get at Ricky. "You're a dead man, asshole."

"Yeah, keep talking, Rudolph," Ricky yelled back.

The liney that was skating Ricky to the penalty box patted Ricky on the back and laughed, "Hey, rookie, the fight was good, but the trash talk was better. Way to go."

As Ricky sat in the box and the adrenaline rush started to subside, his hands began to shake. He looked at them and saw that his right hand was cut and starting to swell.

Dad didn't tell me about punching a guy with a visor on, he thought. I can't believe I bloodied his nose. He grinned.

By the time the game was over, Ricky had collected a "Gordie Howe hat trick"—a goal, an assist and a fight—and been named the game's first star, and the city of Barrie began to buzz with talk of a new superstar. The local news devoted more coverage to Ricky's fight during its sports highlight package than it did to the goals.

The next morning, the Peterborough Petes released Bill McDuffie.

CHAPTER FOUR

Ricky progressed well through the preseason. With each passing game, he gained more confidence, and his uncanny ability to get the puck to open teammates began to show. He was averaging a point a game, which was good for a rookie, but by no means awe-inspiring. What was catching people's attention was his variety. He delivered the puck to his teammates the way an effective centreman needs to do, and every once in a while he would make a Gretzky-like pass that left people wondering, "How'd he see him?" He had the hands of a small, skilled forward, but he was a big physical presence. As the regular season approached he was six foot three and was closing in on 200 pounds. He loved to separate the D from the puck, usually with a bone-jarring hit, and once he had the puck there was no way you would get it back. But the facet of his game that was drawing comparisons to Eric Lindros was the fact that he fought his own battles. After the dust-up with McDuffie, he had fought two more times. Both were against the other team's "puncher"—an older, more experienced, one-dimensional player. Both times he had held his own.

In fact, the only early-season speed bump that Ricky encountered was off the ice. The Colts wanted Ricky to move to Barrie and be billeted with a family that lived close to the Molson Centre. His mom and dad wanted Ricky to stay at home. Ricky didn't know what he wanted. Staying at home would definitely be easiest, but the last thing he wanted to do was make waves for the organization or look like a mamma's boy.

His father, Darryl, had been around hockey all his life and knew that the one thing a coaching staff couldn't stand was an overbearing parent—the kind who thought their kid was better than he really was and that any disciplinary action or decrease in ice time was a deliberate attempt to prevent the boy from being scouted. And this was in novice! Parents like that got worse as their kids got older. But Darryl felt compelled to do what he felt was best for Ricky, and in his opinion that meant staying at home.

As the preseason wore on, the Colts got more anxious to have Ricky move in with a billet. They wanted him enrolled in his new school and settled in before the season started. Darryl felt like he was being pushed into a corner, while Ricky felt like he was caught in the middle. As they drove down to the BMC for a practice one day just prior to the start of the regular season, Darryl told Ricky that he would be meeting with Mr. McMillan and Coach Graham afterwards.

Ricky felt like he was going to be sick. "Aw Dad, do you have to?"

"It'll be okay, Ricky," Darryl answered.

"No it won't. They'll think I'm a big pansy. Dad, if they want me to billet, then I'll billet. I just don't want to make waves."

Darryl gripped the steering wheel and stared straight ahead. Finally, he spoke.

"Don't you think you'd be better off living at home, sleeping in your own bed, eating your mom's home cooking and going to your own high school?"

Of course that made sense, but looking like a coddled first-rounder didn't sound too appealing.

"Just promise me you won't embarrass me—please, Dad?"

His dad laughed nervously. "I'll do my best."

When they had pulled into the parking lot of the BMC, Ricky made Darryl promise that if the Colts insisted that he be billeted, his dad would agree to it. Darryl smiled and promised that he would.

●

After practice, Ricky changed quickly and hustled up to the main concourse of the arena. Waiting outside McMillan's office, he felt just as queasy as he did on the first day of try-outs. He told himself that his dad wasn't the type who would yell and scream, and he certainly wasn't going to make demands like "We're going to do things this way or that way or I'll demand a trade." That would be stupid, because then Ricky really *would* need to be billeted.

After what seemed like an eternity, the office door opened and the three men walked out. Instantly, Ricky jumped up out of his seat and turned to face them. He stood nervously and waited for the verdict.

Darryl shook hands with McMillan and Graham. "Thanks for your time, guys. You have my word that he'll never be late for a game or a practice."

"No problem, Darryl," McMillan answered. "We'll see how it goes." Then he turned his attention to Ricky and smiled. "How are ya, Ricky?"

"Good, sir," Ricky answered nervously.

"Did your old man ever tell you that I used to be his coach?" McMillan asked.

Ricky nodded.

"Tough son of a bitch. Actually had to tell him to stop fighting and start playing," McMillan added. Then he turned back to Darryl. "Listen, I've got to fly. We'll talk later, okay? Ricky, Adam, I'll see you guys later."

Driving home, Darryl filled Ricky in about the meeting. The Colts had agreed to let Ricky stay at home on a trial basis until Christmas. Darryl assured Ricky that he hadn't made any waves for him or made him look like a mamma's boy.

Slowly, Ricky began to relax. As they pulled into the driveway, Ricky said, "Thanks for the ride, you ole tough son of a bitch."

His dad laughed. "No problem."

"Dad?" Ricky asked.

"What's up?"

"Were you a goon?"

Again Darryl laughed. "No, I wasn't a goon. I was a fourth-liner."

Ricky wasn't sure he knew what his dad meant and said so.

"A fourth-liner does what needs to be done. I never went looking for a fight, but if I needed to, I fought. Kind of like what I did for you today."

Ricky nodded his head. "Well, thanks for fighting for me."

"No problem. Now let's go see what Mom has cooked up for dinner."

CHAPTER FIVE

The Colts opened the season well for a team that had been struggling as badly as they had for the past few years. In their first ten games they were 5–4–1 with a shootout win and a shootout loss. Early in the season, Ricky celebrated his sixteenth birthday. Jimmy Kirton was the only other sixteen-year-old to make the opening day roster and he was assigned to Ricky's right wing. On Ricky's left side, the Colts pencilled in Johnny Parker, a big, strong twenty-year-old. In three years with the Colts, Johnny had seven goals and twenty-three assists—and 250 minutes in penalties. When Coach Graham had had his meetings with each player before the start of the season, he had made it very clear to Johnny that his job was to look after the two rookies.

Ricky, Johnny and Jimmy started the season as the fourth line. However, through their first five games, Ricky had two goals and three assists, Jimmy had three goals and two assists and, most surprisingly of all, Johnny had a goal and two assists. The boys took the ice for game six as the third line.

Over the next five games the line continued to impress. Jimmy had four more points and Johnny chipped in another goal and two more assists. Remarkably, after ten games he had been assessed only three minor penalties. Ricky added seven more points, plus he scored the winning goal in the shootout of game ten. He gave the goalie a nifty little head fake and then took the water bottle off the top of the net with a sweet backhand. Number 16 jerseys with PHILLIPS on the back were starting to pop up throughout the crowd at the BMC. And the boys were moved up to the second line.

As Christmas approached, the Colts were the talk of the league. They were eight games over .500 and in second place in their division. Ricky was cruising along at a point-per-game pace. His only competition for rookie of the year was Jimmy, who was ten points behind him, and Michael Charette, the goalie from the Soo.

Johnny was easily the comeback player of the year. In the thirty-fourth game of the year, he notched his thirtieth point, equalling his total for his first three years. He had fought only three times and had spent only twenty-six minutes in the penalty box. Johnny had not been selected in the NHL entry draft, but now he was starting to generate some free-agent buzz. Some of the more cynical, and perhaps wiser, scouts had already decided that his two rookie linemates were making him look good. Nevertheless, Johnny was thrilled to be thought of as a player and not just a puncher.

●

The Colts' last game before the Christmas break was scheduled for December 23. The players were looking forward to heading home for four or five precious days of family and home-cooked meals before resuming the season—and what was now becoming a realistic push at the playoffs.

After practice on the twenty-second, one of the trainers, named Scooter, came over to Ricky's stall. "Ricky, Mr. McMillan wants you to stop by his office after you've showered."

Getting called to the GM's office was never a good sign, and several of the players near Ricky suddenly went very quiet. He tried to appear calm. "Yeah, no problem. Did he say what he wanted, Scooter?"

Scooter just shook his head. "No idea."

After showering, Ricky headed up to McMillan's office. There's no way they'd trade me three days before Christmas, he told himself. Just stay calm. Ricky knocked on McMillan's door. It flew open, and McMillan greeted Ricky with a big smile.

"Hey, Ricky, how are you? Come in and sit down."

Ricky, still a little apprehensive, sat down.

"So Ricky," McMillan began, "I can't tell you how pleased I am with how you're playing. How are you enjoying life in the O so far?"

Ricky had no idea where this conversation was going, but he smiled and said, "I'm really enjoying it, sir."

"Great, great," McMillan responded. "Now Ricky, I was wondering if I could ask you to do me a favour?"

Oh, shit, I *am* being traded, Ricky thought. He could think of nothing to say, so he just stared at his GM.

McMillan went on. "You see, Ricky, tomorrow night's game against the Soo is . . . well, let's just say that their GM and I don't have a great history together. At the draft this year, he thought I wanted Charette, so he took him one pick ahead of me—thought he'd really screwed me. But I really screwed *him* because I wanted you instead. Now the thing is, this kid Charette, he's been playing really well and there's even been talk of him winning rookie of the year. What I'd like from you, Ricky, is to fill the net on this kid tomorrow night. Can you do that for me?"

Ricky was so relieved to hear that he wasn't being traded that he had difficulty answering. He finally stammered out his response. "I'll do my best, sir."

McMillan grinned. "That's great, Ricky. This is personal for me. There's only one team I can't stand losing to, and that's the Soo."

Mr. McMillan was such a small, quiet man. Ricky never would have dreamed that he had a ruthless side. He walked out to the car where his dad was waiting and smiled to himself. I like it, he thought to himself. Tomorrow night's going to be fun.

●

There was an electricity in the air at the BMC that accompanies all big games. The Colts had been drawing well since early in the season, when it was obvious that they were going to be a good team. The one thing they hadn't had yet was a sellout.

When the Colts took the ice at 6:45 for the pre-game warmup, there were close to 3,500 people in the stands. They greeted the Colts with a boisterous cheer. Jimmy skated past Ricky and smiled. "Big crowd."

By the time warmup was over the place was sold out and packed to the rafters. In his pre-game speech to the team, Coach Graham challenged the boys to respond. "This is *our* barn and it's full. Let's not let these people down." Then he said something that he hadn't said all year: "Jonsie, you and Popo start on D. Ricky, your line's up front."

Ricky and Jimmy grinned at each other and then high-fived Johnny, who was trying to look like it was no big deal. But it *was* a big deal. When the Colts took the ice at the start of a game, they skated through an inflatable archway, atop which sat the figure of a giant horse holding a hockey stick. The starters were announced one at a time with their names, heights, weights and hometowns bellowed through the public address system. The other players came out together to the rather anticlimactic call of "and the rest of your Barrie Colts." If any of the boys had said that they didn't care about starting, they would have been lying.

An arena attendant called for the players to line up in order—the starting goalie, two D-men, left wing, right wing and centre. Ricky listened to the crowd cheer as the goaltender was introduced. The noise got a little louder when Jonsie and Popo went out. By the time Johnny and Jimmy were announced, the place was hopping. Then he felt the hair on the back of his neck stand up as he heard the PA announcer yell, "And at centre, from Oro-Medonte, at six feet, three inches and 200 pounds, *RICKY PHILLIPS!!!*"

Ricky came through that archway like he was on a clear-cut breakaway, and the crowd rose to greet him. When he stopped at the blue line and took his spot beside Johnny, the winger asked, "How come you get a standing O?"

"I'm better looking than you are, that's why."

"Oh, that must be it," Johnny grinned as he took off his helmet for the national anthem.

When the game started, the boys came out flying. Johnny dumped the puck into the Soo's end with Ricky at full speed and right on the defenceman's tail. The D-man had barely touched the puck when Ricky hammered him into the end wall, then cycled the puck behind the net to Jimmy, who fired a perfect pass to Johnny cutting through the slot. Johnny fired a quick shot that was labelled for the top corner, but Michael Charette flashed his glove out and made an incredible save.

As the boys came off on the line change, Johnny muttered, "Okay, so we've established that he has a glove."

The Colts dominated the first period, throwing twenty shots at the net, but Charette turned every one aside. The Soo only mustered one chance, but they scored on a fluky bounce. The period ended with the Greyhounds up 1–0.

In the dressing room during the intermission, the Colts were still upbeat, feeling that the next shot would burst Charette's bubble and the floodgates would open. But after another aggressive period, the Colts were still trailing. Ricky scored partway through the period, but the Soo scored again to lead 2–1 after forty minutes—even though Barrie had outshot the Greyhounds 35–12 in the two periods. The dressing room during the intermission was somewhat more subdued. Chris Popovich, the Colts' captain, sensed the feeling of dread and tried to rally the boys. "Hang in there, guys. The energy's been great. We'll get to this guy! Who's got the next one?"

It was a question that every team asks in a tight game. A coach will usually look up and down his bench and implore his players, "Come on guys, who's got the next one?"

Usually, the entire bench will respond with a confident "I do!"

But tonight, only one person answered, "I got it, Popo."

Nineteen players turned and looked to see if Ricky was joking, trying to lighten the tension in the room, but one look at his face and they knew that he was serious. "What?" he looked around the room at his teammates. "I got it."

Five minutes into the third, Ricky thundered down the right side and unloaded a slap shot that beat Charette high on the glove side. On his next shift, he held off two Greyhounds behind the net long enough to spot Jimmy, who had an easy tap-in to give the Colts the lead. With five minutes to play, Popo sprung Ricky on a great pass. Ricky had a clear-cut breakaway and made no mistake. It was his first hat trick in the O.

On their last shift, Ricky dumped the puck in on Charette and raced to the net. The goaltender smothered the puck just as Ricky arrived on his doorstep. A Greyhound defenceman shoved him and growled, "Leave my goalie alone, numbnuts."

Ricky shoved him back. "I never touched him, asshole."

The Soo D-man shoved again, and the other eight skaters on the ice arrived to join the scrum. Four players on each team squared off, and soon enough it looked as though the moment would defuse itself, but Ricky was bursting with adrenaline from his four-point night. He didn't know what to do next, but he knew he wanted to fight. He smiled at the Greyhound D, looked him square in the eye and, through clenched teeth, snarled, "Pussy."

That had the desired effect, and the defenceman dropped his gloves at the exact instant that Ricky's came off. Ricky grabbed with his left, tucked his face in his shoulder and swung with his right. He was now very adept at getting his opponent's helmet off, and in no time he had removed the helmet and landed four good shots. However, something unusual happened. He was experiencing some intense pain. Ricky's helmet was also off, and he was absorbing some hard shots of his own. It took him a moment to realize that he was fighting a lefty. The only thing he was accomplishing by burying his face in his left shoulder was to leave the whole right side of his face open to this guy's left-handed bombs. The two players continued to trade punches and the crowd roared its approval. Ricky's face was really starting to hurt when he remembered one of his dad's lessons; when you're getting your ass kicked, take him to the ice and hold on and wait for the lineys. Ricky reached down and grabbed the defenceman by his pants and lifted as hard as he could. The D landed on his back and Ricky crashed down on top of him. The two rolled around like a couple of toddlers having a scuffle.

Why aren't they breaking it up? Ricky wondered. Out of the corner of his eye, he caught the reason. The ice was completely covered with gloves, sticks and helmets. All ten skaters had paired off and were involved to varying degrees in fights. Some guys were pounding each other senseless, while others were merely holding on to their dance partners. Even the goalies had grabbed each other and were comically trying to throw punches from under their cumbersome equipment. The referees, badly outnumbered under the circumstances, were doing their best to get the situation under control and get guys off the ice.

Ricky looked at the Soo defenceman, whose left eye was already swollen nearly shut. The D looked back through his one good eye, smiled and asked, "Have you had enough?"

"Yeah," Ricky answered. "I'm done."

"Okay, here's the deal," said the D in an authoritative tone. "We'll both get to our feet and just hold on to each other and try to make it look good."

Ricky had the feeling that this big, tough kid had been here before. "Sounds good to me," he responded.

The two of them got to their feet and stood there and

held, rather lightly, onto each other's jerseys while they watched the goings-on on the ice, each a little leery that the other might end their verbal entente with one quick swing.

Ricky felt something warm dripping into his right eye. The Soo D noticed it too and said, "You're cut above your eye. It might need a stitch. Tell you what: why don't we let go and you can go back to your bench and get looked at?"

"Sounds good," Ricky answered.

"Hey, rookie?"

"Yeah?"

"You played a hell of a game tonight."

"Thanks."

Then the defenceman grinned. "Nice fight," he added.

Ricky laughed. "Yeah, you too."

"Merry Christmas."

"You too."

❋

Ricky was still bleeding when he came out for his curtain call as the game's first star. The Colts won 4–2 and Ricky had four points and a monumental punch-up. He had given the home-town fans a game they wouldn't soon forget. They cheered him heartily in appreciation.

After the game, Ben McMillan made sure he was visible right in the middle of the main concourse. He knew the Grey-hounds would have to pass by him on their way to the bus. He was in a great mood and he couldn't wait to share his feelings with his old pal Skip Daniels.

Eventually, the Greyhounds started to filter out and head for the bus. Finally, Daniels appeared. He tried to pretend that he didn't notice McMillan, but Ben wasn't about to let him off that easily.

"Merry Christmas, Skip," McMillan called in an overly friendly, enthusiastic voice. He was grinning wildly, clearly enjoying the moment.

Daniels looked up and tried to appear calm, as though it had been just another game. "Yeah, Merry Christmas, Ben."

Ben couldn't let it go; he was having too much fun. "Boy, Charette sure played well."

"Thanks, Ben," Daniels replied cautiously.

Ben waited until Daniels was almost at the bus before he yelled, "Yeah, he was great all right . . . for forty minutes! Right until Ricky lit him up. Hey, Skip, you should get your boy a watch. Games are sixty minutes long. And stop by the drug store on your way out of town. Maybe they'll have something for that sunburn on the back of his neck from that goal light going on so much behind him!"

McMillan roared with laughter as he watched the door of the Greyhounds' bus slam shut, almost taking off Skip's hand, which he'd extended towards Ben to give him the finger.

❂

Near the entrance to the Colts' dressing room, a table was set up where kids could get autographs from the players. After the game, Ricky patiently signed posters, hats and programs. Secretly, he loved it; who wouldn't get a thrill from being asked for an autograph? Darryl had told Ricky that it was an honour to be a role model and that he must always treat the fans with respect. In one of their car rides to the rink, he'd said, "You know what I hate?"

"What?" Ricky had asked.

"When a guy from the visiting team is named a star and won't come out on the ice to acknowledge the fans. I think it's arrogant and rude. If you are named a star when you are on the road, you damn well go out there and acknowledge those fans. They paid good money to see you play, the least you can do is say thank you. Wave your stick and smile."

Ricky had laughed when his dad said this, but the first time he was named a star on the road, one night in Owen Sound, he went out and waved to the crowd. It was something he would never forget to do for the rest of his career.

While he was signing, Scooter came up behind him and said, "Ricky, Mr. McMillan wants to see you when you're done."

"Okay, Scooter."

After Ricky signed the last ball cap, he headed over to McMillan's office and knocked on the door. McMillan ushered him in and told him to take a seat.

"Whoa, that's quite the eye," McMillan noted. "Any stitches?"

"Yeah, five, right in the eyebrow," Ricky replied. He was sore and tired, the adrenaline rush having long since subsided, and he just wanted to go home. "That guy kicked my ass pretty good," he added.

"Well, no wonder. Do you have any idea who he was?"

"No clue," Ricky said.

"That was Nicholas Hansbrough. He's the toughest guy in the O. First-round pick of the Calgary Flames last year." McMillan smiled and patted Ricky on the back. "And from what I saw, you held your own pretty good. His eye was closed too."

Ricky was starting to stiffen up and his head was throbbing. Suddenly, an idea came to Ricky and he blurted out the

question before he had a chance to think about the conse-
quences. "Mr. McMillan, is it okay if I continue to live at home
with my folks?"

McMillan clearly had no idea what Ricky was talking
about.

"Remember?" Ricky continued. "At the beginning of the
season, you said I could stay at home until Christmas?"

McMillan laughed. "Son, the way you played tonight, you
could live with the Queen of England for all I care."

Ricky got stiffly to his feet and said, "Thanks a lot, Mr.
McMillan."

McMillan smiled and held out his hand. As Ricky shook
it, McMillan grinned. "No, thank *you,* Ricky. That was the
most fun I've had in years. Now go on home and enjoy your
holiday. You deserve it."

CHAPTER SIX

Ricky used the time over the holidays to heal his bumps and bruises, to stock up on lots of home cooking and to catch up on some school assignments he was behind on. It was a low-key holiday, but that suited Ricky just fine.

After the Christmas break, the Colts picked up where they had left off. They finished the 68-game schedule in second place with a record of 38–25–5. Ricky had a tremendous year with 33 goals, 38 assists and 71 points. He had 63 minutes in penalties, which included five fights. Both Ricky and the Colts had high expectations for a long playoff run as they prepared for their first-round matchup with the lowly Kingston Frontenacs.

The Colts had dominated their season series with Kingston, four games to none. Ricky's line had scored eleven times in the four games. On paper, the series was going to be a laugher. Unfortunately, no one told the Frontenacs. They upset the Colts in a brutally rough five games. Ricky and Jimmy both got their first taste of playing against a shadow, a player from the other team who gives up all thoughts of offence. The shadow's job is to follow his mark, as closely as possible, and check him as soon as he touches the puck.

Neither Ricky nor Jimmy coped well with this strategy. Both were held scoreless in the five games.

The loving relationship that the boys had enjoyed all year with the Barrie fans and media quickly turned sour. As the clock ticked down to end game five, the team was serenaded with a loud chorus of boos. The media postmortem was particularly harsh. The majority of the criticism was directed at Ricky and his failure to produce in the playoffs. He was shocked to hear the boos in the BMC, and he was deeply hurt by the venomous attack of the media.

Early in the summer, the league announced its annual awards. Ricky was selected as rookie of the year in a close vote over Michael Charette, the goaltender from the Soo. The phone rang constantly that day at the Phillips house, as Ricky fielded calls from teammates and friends congratulating him on the award. Ricky chatted happily with each, and he was clearly enjoying the accolades.

Mixed in with these calls were reporters from the Barrie newspapers and radio stations asking Ricky to comment on the award. With the reporters, Ricky's tone changed. He was polite but subdued and he ended the calls as quickly as possible.

His father happened to walk through the kitchen just as Ricky was getting off the phone. He heard Ricky say, "Thanks, have a good day," then hang up the phone and mutter "asshole."

Dad looked at Ricky. "You okay?"

Ricky's face was red, and he was straining to keep his composure. "Two months ago, that jackass tore me apart in the paper. Blamed the entire playoff loss on me. Now he's calling to congratulate me on rookie of the year. Wanted my comments. It took everything I had not to tell him that my comment was for him to go and screw himself!"

Dad laughed. "Welcome to the big time, kiddo."

Ricky was stunned. "Are you on his side?"

"Not at all," his dad reasoned. "Look, Ricky, it's like this: when things are going well, the media will love you; when it's not going well, they'll lay blame. Sometimes it will be off base, and sometimes the truth will hurt."

"So what do you think, Dad? Was it my fault?" Ricky wasn't sure that he wanted to hear the answer.

Darryl smiled and put his arm around his son. "Last time I checked, hockey was a team sport." Ricky relaxed a bit, and Darryl continued: "But you *were* held scoreless."

"I was shadowed," Ricky protested.

"Yeah, you were shadowed, but you need to learn how to deal with that, and you will. But the big thing is that you were polite to those media guys. Remember, you're a role model and nobody likes—"

"I know," Ricky interjected, finishing his dad's sentence: "Nobody likes an arrogant athlete."

CHAPTER SEVEN

Word spread through the league like wildfire that the way to deal with the Colts' two young studs was to shadow them. The formula was successful, as both boys struggled out of the gate in their sophomore season. Ricky and Jimmy were both frustrated by the tight checking on the ice. Off the ice, they were adjusting to life without Johnny Parker, who'd signed as a free agent with the Ottawa Senators. His chances of ever playing for the big club were small, but as the season started he had earned a spot on the Senators' American Hockey League roster in Binghamton.

Ricky was thrilled for his friend, but felt an emptiness in the Colts' dressing room and on the ice. Through the first five games of the season, Ricky and Jimmy had yet to develop any chemistry with their new left winger. Worse still, neither boy had registered a point. Going back to last year's playoffs, they were now scoreless in their last ten games.

After each practice, Coach Graham would "volunteer" two players to stay late and work with Ricky and Jimmy. They would play games of two-on-two keep-away, but the volunteers were directed to ignore the puck and play like shadows. The extra practice helped, but any player who's ever been shadowed knows that you have to figure things out for yourself. Wayne Gretzky used to skate towards a member of the other team, then shadow that player. Gretzky's shadow would stay right with him, so now Gretzky had two players occupied, leaving one of his teammates unchecked and wide open.

Ricky's "aha" moment came during the sixth game of the season, against Owen Sound. He learned that if the puck was in his end and he left the zone, the shadow would follow. Ricky skated to the red line and went to the boards, where he stopped with his back to the wall. The shadow stopped, too, but his back was to the play because he had to keep an eye on Ricky. If the remaining four Colts chipped the puck out into the neutral zone, Ricky saw it before the shadow. One stride was all it took to give Ricky the head start he needed.

The first time the Colts dumped the puck out of the zone, Ricky beat his check, picked up the puck and scored on a clear-cut breakaway. The next time it happened, the shadow had to hold Ricky and was flagged for interference. Ricky scored on the power play.

During the intermission, the visiting coach made an adjustment: if Ricky left the zone, one Owen Sound defenceman would fall back to his own blue line. It worked well until the Colts realized they were now playing four on three, with Ricky being covered by two players. Coach Graham reacted by telling Jimmy to go and stand in the neutral zone on the opposite side of the ice to Ricky. His shadow followed and this put the Colts up three men to two and allowed them to leave their own zone virtually unchallenged. They penetrated the Owen Sound zone with ease. Both Ricky and Jimmy noticed that if they held back in the neutral zone, it would give the Colts a mini power play. Then, at the last second, they would bolt for the front of the net, a stride or two ahead of their desperate checks. If the puck popped loose or a teammate could hit them with a pass, they would rarely miss. The Colts won the game 7–2, Ricky had a hat trick and Jimmy had two goals. The monkey was off their backs.

❦

In Ricky's second season, the Colts' success tended to mirror Ricky's. He had another great year, scoring 42 goals and adding 67 assists. His 109 points placed him tenth in the league in scoring. The Colts once again finished second in the division, but this time they didn't collapse in the playoffs. For the second straight year they drew the Kingston Frontenacs in the first round. Kingston's game plan was to once again shadow Ricky and Jimmy, but this time the boys were ready. Ricky had eight points in the series, which the Colts swept in four straight.

The Colts then defeated Oshawa in five games to advance to the division final against the Ottawa 67's. Ottawa had finished first in the regular season and taken three of their four meetings with the Colts. But Ricky elevated his game to another level, registering eleven points—including the series-clinching goal, in overtime—as Barrie won the series in six games to advance to the league championship against the vaunted London Knights.

In Ricky's two years in the league, the best the Colts had managed against London was a tie. So it was no surprise that the Colts met their match in this series and were defeated in five games. London went on to represent the O at the Memorial Cup. But Barrie gained immeasurable respect and experience.

They would be returning fifteen players for next season, including Ricky Phillips, the leading scorer in the OHL playoffs. The same reporters that had ripped the team the year before were now speculating about a Memorial Cup run for the team next year.

●

Ricky started his third year with the Colts like a man on a mission. Right before the season opener, the National Hockey League's Central Scouting Bureau released its rankings of players eligible for the NHL Entry Draft. Among players from the OHL, Ricky was ranked third, but when the rest of the North American skaters were factored in, he was ranked thirty-second. He was the only Barrie player judged to have a chance to be a high draft pick, and the guys on the team congratulated him. Ricky, however, was furious.

"Thirty-second isn't even in the first round," he growled.

His response on the ice was even louder: five points in the home opener. He recorded his thirtieth point of the season in the ninth game. He was running away with the scoring race and was on pace for a two-hundred-point season. He didn't have to fight anymore, either. On his reputation alone, he was universally regarded as the toughest player in the league.

As Christmas approached, the Colts were in first place and Ricky was clearly the league MVP. He was rewarded with an invitation to try out for Canada's team at the World Junior Championships. Ricky was ecstatic, but his father warned him to be realistic. He knew that, every year, players who had never been cut in their lives got cut from the World Junior team.

"You'd have to be one of the top four centremen in the entire country to make that team," his dad tried to reason.

Ricky's response surprised Darryl for both its candour and its confidence. "Dad, I think I'm the best player in the O. That only leaves the Western league and the Quebec league. So the way I look at it, I should be in the top three."

Ricky made the team and centred the second line. He was one of only three eighteen-year-olds on the team. The other seventeen players were nineteen or twenty and had already been drafted by NHL teams. Ricky didn't look at all out of place against the best junior-age players in the world. Both his offence and his physical play helped Canada to yet another gold medal.

Despite missing nearly ten games with the Colts while he was with the national team, Ricky was still leading the league in scoring when he returned to Barrie. The Central Scouting report that came out in January had him ranked second. He had moved up thirty spots in four months.

●

The Colts ended the season in first place. Ricky had completely dominated the league, leading in all the offensive categories—goals, assists, points, shots on net, face-off percentage and ice time for a forward. The Colts rolled through the first three rounds of the playoffs to set up a rematch with London, and this time it was the Knights who were outclassed as Barrie won the series in six games. For the second straight year, Ricky was the league's leading scorer in the playoffs.

The Colts made a valiant run at the Memorial Cup. They advanced to the final against the Calgary Hitmen, who won a thrilling game 4–3. Ricky had two goals and an assist in what would prove to be his last game ever as a Barrie Colt.

●

About a week after the Colts' season ended, Ricky got off the school bus and walked briskly towards his house. He was in his second year of grade twelve, the victory lap as his friends called it, and he was three credits short of his diploma. He had an essay due in English and a test coming up in History and he was hustling home to face a long night of studying. He almost didn't notice that the flag was up on the mailbox as he turned in the laneway. Absently, he flicked the flag down, grabbed the mail and headed back up the driveway. He glanced quickly at the stack of envelopes and wouldn't have given them a second thought, except that there was a letter addressed to him—with the seal of the National Hockey League next to the return address. He stopped dead in his tracks and dropped everything else. He tore open the envelope and pulled out the letter. His eyes flew past the salutation and came to rest on the only line that mattered:

You are cordially invited to attend the National Hockey League Entry Draft.

He let out a whoop and ran for the front door.

Ricky found his dad out on the deck, newspaper balanced on his lap, glass of wine in his hand.

"How's it going, Dad?" Ricky asked as he sat down in a Muskoka chair.

"Good, Ricky. You?"

"I'm okay."

"What's on your mind?" Darryl asked, cutting right to the chase.

"I was just wondering if you and Mom would like to go to Vancouver with me next week?"

"Why? What's in Vancouver?" his dad asked as naively as possible.

"Shopping," Ricky replied dryly.

"Oh, I love to shop," Darryl responded. "Besides, I should have something new to wear so I'll look good when I'm watching my kid get drafted. Do you think Toronto will get you?" Darryl was a diehard Leafs fan and had been hoping all year that Ricky would be selected by them.

"I hope not, Dad." Darryl looked crestfallen, so Ricky added quickly, "It's not that I don't like the Leafs, Dad. I was just hoping to be selected early and they don't pick until number eleven."

Darryl smiled. "Well, whoever gets you will be lucky to have you, and they'll become my new favourite team. You don't think it'll be the Habs, do you? I don't think I could ever cheer for them."

Ricky laughed, "Just drink your wine, Dad."

●

Vancouver was a whirlwind. A debate that had been brewing since Christmas had gathered momentum as the regular season drew to a close. Ricky's play in the playoffs turned a friendly debate into a hotly contested question: who would go number one in the draft?

While Ricky had rocketed up the Central Scouting rankings, the consensus surrounding who would be the number one pick had never truly wavered. The scouts and other observers liked Nikolai Petrov, a big Russian kid who was a mobile, offensive defenceman. He was seen as a cross between Chris Pronger and Nicklas Lidstrom. His number one ranking hadn't come close to being challenged until late in the season, when it became obvious that the Ricky Phillips phenomenon wasn't just a passing occurrence. As the draft approached, the Los Angeles Kings, who had the first-overall pick, were suddenly being coy about whom they were going to select.

The media was everywhere that week, and Ricky found himself being whisked from a radio interview with the CBC to a television interview with ESPN. Ricky also went for interviews with the teams that had the first five picks. Like all the draft hopefuls, he found these meetings terrifying, but he did his best to appear calm and poised. Both the players and the teams' management knew how important the draft was. A successful pick could improve a team significantly for the foreseeable future; a bad one could have negative repercussions that the franchise would feel for years to come. Teams were terrified of making a bad pick, and the players certainly didn't want to become known as the guy who didn't pan out.

Darryl, on the other hand, was in his element. "What's Gretzky like?" he asked Ricky as they rushed between meetings.

"He's really nice, Dad. He said to say hi to you."

"Really?" Darryl beamed.

"No Dad, I'm kidding. But he *is* really nice, though." Ricky rolled his eyes at his mom, and Haley tried not to laugh. That was Darryl's only disappointment of the week.

Darryl and Ricky were both surprised when the San Jose Sharks asked to set up an interview. They were also the only team to invite Darryl and Haley into the meeting. As they walked back to the hotel that night, Ricky couldn't help but hide his confusion and disappointment. "The Sharks don't pick until seventeen. You don't think I'll go that late, do you, Dad?"

For once, Darryl was at a loss. "I don't know, Ricky."

"Well, why else would they have asked to interview me? And it was weird; the owner was there too, along with the whole coaching staff and the GM."

Finally, the day of the draft arrived. The anticipation was agonizing, but finally the NHL commissioner opened the proceedings. After what seemed like an eternity to Ricky, the commissioner called on the general manager of the Los Angeles Kings. The GM walked to the podium and Ricky, Darryl, Haley and several thousand other people held their breath.

"The Los Angeles Kings are pleased to select, with the number one pick, from Moscow Dynamo, defenceman Nikolai Petrov."

The look of absolute disappointment on Ricky's face was obvious. Darryl tried to cheer him up. The Florida Panthers picked second, so he smiled and said, "I hear Miami's a great town. Maybe you'll go second. Lot less pressure than being number one anyway, Bud."

Ricky gave his dad a weak smile.

When the commissioner returned to the podium he delivered a bombshell. "Ladies and gentlemen, the Florida Panthers have traded their first-round pick, second overall, in this year's draft to the San Jose Sharks for two players who will be named later, the number seventeen pick in this year's draft, and the Sharks' first pick in next year's draft."

A buzz swept through the crowd at General Motors Place. Ricky, who only moments before had looked like he was going to cry, turned to his dad and asked excitedly, "You don't think . . ."

Darryl could only grin.

The general manager of the Sharks walked to the podium and smiled. "Ladies and gentlemen, the San Jose Sharks are pleased to select, with the second pick, from the Barrie Colts of the Ontario Hockey League, centreman Ricky Phillips!"

Part Two

TWO AND A HALF YEARS LATER

CHAPTER EIGHT

The Toronto Maple Leafs were mired in another slump. Head coach Howie Neely was at his wits' end. He'd yelled, screamed, benched his star players, started his backup goaltender, tried extra practices, and still the Leafs lost. To make matters worse, they were scheduled to play the mighty San Jose Sharks tomorrow night. He was running out of ideas as to how to end the losing streak. As a last resort, he had reached into the very bottom of his bag of tricks and pulled out . . . a day off. "Maybe we're putting too much pressure on ourselves," he'd told the team. "Friday's practice is now optional."

Two defencemen who were trying to work themselves back into shape after injuries attended, along with three members of the Black Aces—players who were sitting out as healthy scratches. The rest of the team had gratefully taken the coach up on his offer of a day off.

With only five players showing up to skate, Neely didn't even bother to go out onto the ice. He let the guys stretch their legs and shoot some pucks, and then they were free to go. An hour later, only two of the Black Aces were still at the rink. Geoff Green and Charlie Davidson had stayed behind to work out. Geoff was itching to get back into the lineup. He'd been scratched for the last three games.

"Be careful what you wish for," Charlie joked.

"What do you mean?" Geoff asked.

"I'm just thinking that it might be easier to be in the press box than to try and take on the Sharks tomorrow night."

Geoff laughed. "Maybe you're right."

Charlie nodded. "Who wants to be humiliated on national TV?"

Geoff smiled and headed off to look for the team's physiotherapist while Charlie climbed aboard a stationary bicycle. Charlie had just started to ride when the room began to spin hideously and he fell off of the bike. He scrambled to his feet and gripped the bike's handlebars for balance. As he fought the urge to throw up, he looked around the room. Thankfully, no one had noticed his little spill.

●

The chartered plane had just levelled off and already it was starting its descent. After all, the flight from Ottawa to Toronto was only a forty-five-minute hop, skip and jump. On board, the San Jose Sharks were almost finished their longest trip of the year—the eastern swing. In the last twelve days they had made stops in eight different cities and amassed an impressive 5–2–1 record. They had beaten Florida, Atlanta, Carolina and Boston, lost close games to Tampa and Pittsburgh and lost a shootout to Philadelphia. Earlier tonight, they'd played the Ottawa Senators, the best team in the Eastern Conference, and beaten them soundly, 5–1.

Seated in the middle of the plane, with the team fanned

out around him, was the Sharks' star, Ricky Phillips. Ricky was in great spirits. Tonight, he'd had two goals and an assist and been named the game's first star. He had accumulated seven goals and thirteen points on the road trip. He was living the dream and he was very appreciative of his good fortune. He was twenty-one years old and was a multimillionaire with endorsement deals with Coca-Cola and Under Armour. At the end of the season he was going to shoot a commercial for McDonald's, something that thrilled his dad. After that he planned to spend a few days at home with his parents before heading up to Muskoka to spend the rest of the summer at his cottage. There, he would divide his time between wakeboarding and golfing. Tomorrow night, he was going to face the Leafs on *Hockey Night in Canada*. He was still young enough to get excited about playing in Toronto.

From the back of the plane, the sound of his teammates talking wafted quietly towards his ears. As the landing gear engaged and the engines whined to slow their approach, he smiled.

I love my job, he thought to himself and looked out the window as the lights of Toronto came into view.

●

Darryl Phillips's car rocketed down Highway 503. He rubbed his eyes and fought the urge to close them. It was 2:30 in the morning and he was hoping to be home by three. He was exhausted. Earlier today, he had cut work early, jumped in his car and driven the four and a half hours from Oro-Medonte to Ottawa. He had arrived just as the warmup ended and thus missed a chance to talk to Ricky. Having a son in the NHL was a thrill, but you sure didn't get to see him much. After the game, Darryl had jumped in his car and headed back towards home.

When he reached the house, he pulled into the driveway and parked the car. He decided not to put the car in the garage because the noise of the opener might waken Haley. He snuck through the house without turning on any lights. He brushed his teeth and then slipped into bed beside his wife.

A quiet, sleepy voice came out of the darkness. "How'd he do?"

Darryl gave her a kiss and smiled. "He was great—two goals and an assist and first star."

"I know, I watched on TV. You know, you could have saved yourself thirteen hours and stayed home and watched with me," Haley admonished.

"Yeah, I could have, but I wanted to see him," Darryl replied.

"Well, you better get some sleep, you crazy old fool, because we're going to see him again in a couple of hours."

●

The charter taxied to a stop, where it was met by two large cargo vans. Immediately, the team's equipment manager and his assistants disembarked and began loading the players' equipment into the vans. Then they would drive downtown to the Air Canada Centre. Their night wouldn't end until all the gear had been hung up to dry and all the supplies—tape, sticks, practice jerseys—were organized for tomorrow's pre-game skate.

The players were hustled through the airport to another bus, which whisked them downtown to the Westin Harbour Castle, just around the corner from the ACC. Ricky and his left winger, Eric Rollins, headed quickly towards their room.

Eric and Ricky had met at Ricky's first training camp with the Sharks. Eric was two years older than Ricky, but after drafting and signing him, the Sharks had returned him to his junior team in each of the next two years. During this, his third NHL camp, Eric had been put on Ricky's left wing and they had instantly hit it off, both on and off the ice. They were the only two rookies to make the team, and they quickly became inseparable. Eric had an impressive rookie campaign, posting fifty-seven points, while Ricky had ninety-three and won the Calder Memorial Trophy as the NHL's rookie of the year. They roomed together on the road and moved into an apartment together. The only time they didn't see each other was during the off-season, when Ricky went home to Oro and Eric returned to his hometown of Halifax. Eric considered Ricky to be not only his best friend in hockey but his best friend period. Their teammates called them "The Odd Couple" because Ricky was shy and quiet while Eric was friendly and outgoing. Ricky collapsed thankfully onto his bed as Eric reached for the TV remote. It was 1:45 A.M. The pre-game skate was scheduled for eleven o'clock.

●

Charlie Davidson's alarm went off at 7 A.M. He silenced it quickly so that he wouldn't wake his wife. He sat up and swung his feet onto the floor. Suddenly the room gave a violent lurch and he had to fight hard to control the nausea. He waited a moment or two before he stood up to walk to the bathroom. The room was still spinning, but he managed to make it.

He slapped cold water on his face and slowly the dizziness began to subside. Charlie was on his fifth concussion. He was terrified that a sixth would end his career, and he was doing his best to hide the symptoms. The trainers didn't know, and he was pretty sure that his wife didn't know, but he hadn't felt good since being rocked by a solid hit two weeks ago in a game in Edmonton.

"Okay, Charlie," he muttered to himself, "if it doesn't get better soon, you'll have to tell someone."

After brushing his teeth, he threw on his Toronto Maple Leafs warmup suit and headed out to the car. He moved quickly through the streets of his upscale neighbourhood in suburban Oakville, jumped onto the Queen Elizabeth Way and headed east towards the ACC. He arrived at the rink just after 8 A.M. and, as usual, was the first player there. He greeted the trainers and equipment guys with a smile. At thirty-two, Charlie had been around long enough to know that a smile and a little bit of respect would be paid back a hundred times over by the support staff.

An older, grey-haired man came into the room and smiled. "Hey, Charlie, how are you?"

Charlie smiled back. "I'm good, Big Joe. What's the word, anyway—am I playing tonight?"

Joe was a trainer, but the players called him the assistant GM. He'd been with the Leafs since Darryl Sittler was the captain, and he had the uncanny ability for knowing information before anyone else. Charlie had been a healthy scratch for the last three games. It had sure helped his headaches, but he was itching to get back in the lineup.

Joe paused as if in deep thought, then responded, "My guess is you'll be playing, Charlie."

Charlie smiled. "That's great, Joe. Do you know for sure?"

"Well, Coach will tell you after the skate, but Duke's ribs are too sore to play, so you'll be dressing."

"Bad for him, good for me, eh, Big Joe?"

"I guess that's right, Charlie."

❂

At 9:30 A.M., Haley Phillips pulled her car into the underground parking lot on the Queen's Quay. It was located across the road from the Harbour Castle and about two blocks from the ACC. Once she was parked, she leaned over and nudged Darryl. After his marathon yesterday, he had grudgingly agreed to let her drive this morning. They had barely hit Highway 11 when she could hear him snoring.

They walked up Bay Street to the rink and entered at Gate Two. A large security guard looked up from his computer monitor and asked politely if he could help them.

"Are there any tickets for Darryl Phillips?" Darryl asked.

The guard looked through his stack. "Wow, these are impressive. All access for the morning skate and platinums for the game. Are you related to Ricky or something?"

Darryl grinned. He never got tired of the rush he felt when people realized who he was. "Yeah, he's my son."

"No shit." The big security guard smiled. "I hope he doesn't play like he did last night."

Darryl laughed. "Me neither. I'm a Leafs fan too."

The guard laughed and then escorted them to the door that led to the lower bowl of the ACC.

Since San Jose had played last night and the Leafs hadn't, the Leafs took their pre-game skate first. At exactly 10 A.M., Charlie Davidson took the ice. He was greeted by a polite cheer from the thousand or so people in attendance. Darryl looked at Haley and smiled. "Remember when I drove down to New Jersey to see Ricky play the Devils last year?"

"Uh-huh," Haley responded.

"They had a smaller crowd than this at game time. Only in Toronto would you get a crowd like this for a game-day skate."

For several minutes, Charlie had the ice to himself. He skated slowly, stretching his legs and warming up. Occasionally he would grab a puck and shoot it effortlessly from one end of the rink to the other. If it hit the glass, the crowd would cheer. Then Charlie would take a puck and flick it up into the crowd, much to the delight of the Toronto faithful.

Eventually, the rest of the Leafs joined Charlie, and when Coach Neely came out, they ran through a series of drills. Each drill had a little more intensity than the one before as the players found their legs and the goalies got warmed up. After twenty-five minutes the practice wound down. Several players stayed on the ice. One, who was trying to get back into shape after an injury, did laps at three-quarter speed with an assistant coach hot on his tail to pace him. Two other players worked with the backup goalie, firing shot after shot high to his glove hand. The last player to leave the ice was Charlie Davidson. He shot several more pucks up to a team of minor hockey players who were at the practice, all dressed in their team jerseys. As he came off the ice he passed his stick up to a young boy who clutched the stick like it was the Stanley Cup itself.

Darryl smiled and said, "That was a classy thing to do. You've got to love those fourth-line players—they always seem like such great guys."

Haley frowned. "He's so big, I just hope he doesn't hurt my Ricky tonight."

Darryl dismissed that possibility. "Don't worry, Haley, he hasn't even dressed for the last few games. He probably won't be playing tonight."

At 11 o'clock, the Sharks took the ice. They were a relaxed, confident group. The road trip had been good to them and they were having fun. They went through a spirited skate that lasted about twenty minutes. One defenceman stayed out with an assistant coach, who would dump the puck into a corner while the D would backpedal, pivot, find the puck, look up, find the coach and blaze an outlet pass right onto his stick. They did this over and over again. Darryl marvelled at how effortlessly he moved and how crisp his passes were.

Haley nudged him in the ribs. "Come on, let's go see Ricky."

By the time they got down to the dressing room, most of the players had already changed. One of the trainers came out of the room carrying an armload of sticks. He grinned when he saw Darryl. "Hey, Mr. Phillips, Mrs. Phillips, how are you?"

"Just fine, thanks, Donnie. Is Ricky still getting changed?"

"No, he's gone to do an interview with *Hockey Night in*

Canada. Supposed to air between periods tonight. I'll tell him that you're here, though," Donnie replied.

Darryl and Haley mingled with the players while they waited for Ricky. Darryl was one of the more frequent visitors to the team, and he was on a first-name basis with most of tho playcrs. IIe thought nothing of jumping in his car and driving ten hours to a game in Pittsburgh or New Jersey. He considered Detroit, Buffalo, Montreal and Ottawa to be easy drives. Once a year, Ricky would fly his folks out to San Jose, and Darryl would attend every practice and game. He loved it. Because he was around so much, he had gotten to know everyone in the Sharks organization. He was polite and courteous, and he was equally at ease chatting with the trainers as he was talking to a suit from upper management.

Finally, Ricky came strolling around the corner. He smiled when he saw his folks. He hugged and kissed his mom, then turned to his dad and said, "There was a guy at the game in Ottawa last night that looked just like you."

Darryl smiled sheepishly. "Well, he must have seen a hell of a game."

Ricky laughed. "Hey, Coach says I can take you guys out for lunch. Let's go."

They decided to go to Wayne Gretzky's Restaurant—which, in hindsight, probably wasn't the best idea. Being a sports bar, which attracts sports fans, only about eighty per cent of the people in the restaurant recognized Ricky. However, they were very polite, and his time with his folks was only interrupted a few times while Ricky signed autographs.

After lunch, Ricky caught a cab back to the hotel so that he could take a nap before the team meal. Darryl and Haley walked around downtown Toronto and browsed in a few shops before Darryl convinced Haley to head over to the Hockey Hall of Fame. As they walked back to the ACC, Darryl asked Haley, "Wouldn't it be awesome if Ricky was in the Hall of Fame someday?"

Haley gave her husband an indulgent smile. "Yeah. That would be great. Now hurry up or we'll miss warmup."

●

At three o'clock in the afternoon, Julie Davidson was just finishing making Charlie's pre-game meal when she heard his alarm go off. Charlie and Julie had met in Kamloops, when Charlie was playing his junior hockey for the Blazers. The day they met, Charlie had eaten a grilled cheese sandwich before the game and gone on to score a hat trick. He had also fallen madly in love, at first sight, with Julie. Not being one to mess with a good thing, Charlie had continued the tradition of a pre-game grilled cheese. That was sixteen years ago. Since then, he had made it to the NHL and carved out a good living for himself. It hadn't been easy, though; he'd had to fight, literally and figuratively, for everything that he had. He didn't know if it was Julie's love or the grilled cheese that had brought him success, but he still wasn't about to mess with a good thing.

Julie was flipping the grilled cheese when she heard, ever so faintly, the sound of retching. Fifteen minutes later, Charlie came into the kitchen wearing a very nice Armani suit.

"Well hello, sailor," Julie purred. "You're looking good. I take it you're dressing tonight based on the fancy getup."

"Yeah, Duke's ribs are too sore, so I got the green light."

Julie handed Charlie a plate and he fumbled it slightly while he tried to lean forward for a thank-you kiss. He walked calmly to the kitchen table while fighting a wave of nausea. As he did, Julie noticed he looked a bit like a drunken sailor.

"You okay, honey?" she asked.

"Yeah, fine. Why?"

"I dunno. I thought I heard you throwing up a few minutes ago. Is there anything you want to tell me?" Julie asked.

"Yes, there is," Charlie said, getting to his feet. "I love you. Make sure you come to the game tonight." Then he kissed her and headed for the door.

After he was gone, Julie noticed the untouched grilled cheese still sitting on the table.

●

While the Sharks were out on the ice taking their pre-game warmup, head coach Ron Lester sat in the team's dressing room, filling out the lineup card. He was deep in thought and didn't even look up when he heard the dressing room door open.

"I hope you're starting Ricky's line," came the voice from the doorway.

Lester looked up to see the team's general manager, John Crichton, standing there.

Lester smiled. "What are you doing here, Johnny?"

"I'm here to check up on you, Coach," Crichton replied. "The way the team is playing, I may have to make some changes."

Lester looked shocked. "The way we're playing, we're second in the league."

Crichton let out a laugh. "Relax, Ronnie. I just wanted to see the boys play. Are you pleased with the road trip?"

"I would think that if we win tonight it has been incredibly successful," Lester answered.

Crichton walked over to a row of hockey sticks and picked one up. Leaning on the stick and flexing it, he said, "Is there anyone in this league who can touch Ricky?"

Lester smiled. "He's had a hell of a trip."

Crichton stickhandled a wad of tape and flicked it effortlessly into the garbage pail. "Hell of a trip," he repeated. "He's twenty years old and he's already won rookie of the year and most valuable player. I'll eat my shirt if he doesn't win MVP again this year."

Lester smiled and nodded his head in agreement.

"I watched your game on TV last night," Crichton continued. "He's like a man against boys right now."

"He's playing really well," Lester agreed.

Crichton placed the stick back in the rack and headed for the door. "Well, good luck tonight, Ronnie. I'm gonna head up to the box—I want to get something to eat before the game starts."

Lester laughed. "Tough job you've got there, Johnny."

Crichton smiled. "It's a burden, no question." Then he tugged on the door and headed out into the hallway.

CHAPTER NINE

There are certain events the diehard sports enthusiast should witness at least once in a lifetime. For the golf fan, it would be to watch Tiger Woods at St. Andrews or Augusta National. For the baseball junkie, it would be to watch the Yankees take on the Red Sox at Fenway. For the hockey fan, it would be Toronto or Montreal (ideally, Toronto *versus* Montreal) on a Saturday night. The mystique of the Rocket cutting in off the wing at the Forum, or Johnny Bower, bare-faced in front of a Bobby Hull slap shot at the Gardens, may be gone but there is still something magical about *Hockey Night in Canada* live from the Air Canada Centre.

Ricky could feel the excitement in the building when he stood at the blue line for the national anthems. He was wound tightly. From the moment the puck dropped, he was in the zone. He was just a hair quicker than everyone else on the ice. Before the puck came to him, he already knew where he wanted to move it. The result was that he opened up the ice for his teammates and generated chances in a seemingly effortless way. On nights like this, when things were really clicking, Ricky was clearly the best player in the league.

The first period ended 0–0, but even the most novice hockey fan could tell that the Leafs were in way over their heads. Toronto didn't muster a shot until the ten-minute mark, and at the end of the first period the shots were 18–3 for the Sharks. The only saving grace for Toronto was the outstanding play of their goaltender.

Charlie watched the play and waited for the call from the coach. Like everyone else in the building, he knew the Leafs were being manhandled. If the game stayed close, it dramatically limited his chances of getting on the ice. Goal scoring had never been in his repertoire; scaring goal scorers was his forte. Charlie had carved out a ten-year career for himself by being an intimidating presence. He fought when he had to and he threw his weight around. Even at his peak, Charlie had never been better than a third-liner, and for the last several years he had been on the fourth line. The fear of being replaced and sent to the minors was always foremost in his mind.

Halfway through the first period, Charlie's line had got the call. It was always tough to jump into the game and be effective when he had been sitting that long. The first few strides were always tough because his legs were stiff. Charlie's line had two tasks: create some energy and don't get scored on. The shift proved to be effective. The Sharks had difficulty breaking out of their own end, and Charlie even managed a shot on net. That shift led to a second, and at the end of the first period, Charlie had played a grand total of fifty-seven seconds.

As the team headed back to the dressing room, Charlie accepted a towel from Big Joe. He was breathing heavily, even though he hadn't been on the ice since the five-minute mark, and he was pale.

"You okay, Charlie?" Joe asked.

"Yeah, yeah, I'm good, Big Joe," Charlie replied as he walked past.

"You want me to get you anything?"

Charlie stopped and looked at the old trainer. "A couple of Tylenol would be great, Joe. But only if you promise not to tell anyone. I've just got a bit of a headache, that's all."

Joe hesitated. "Charlie, if you're hurt—"

Charlie cut him off. "Joe, I'm good. Stop acting like my wife."

Joe laughed and raised his hands in surrender. "Okay. Two Tylenol coming up."

●

The second period tended to mirror the first. The Sharks controlled the play and the Leafs were lucky to be able to clear their zone, dump the puck and get a line change. Then the fresh line would quickly exhaust itself trying to weather the next Sharks onslaught.

Partway through the period, as the Leafs were once again dumping the puck to alleviate the pressure, they had the good fortune of dumping it on net. The Sharks' goalie was forced to freeze the puck. This brought a sarcastic cheer from the knowledgeable home crowd, who realized that a dump-in was about as much offence as the Leafs could muster.

Ricky's line hopped the boards and got ready for the face-off, to the right of the Sharks goal. As Ricky came into the circle, he skated past his right defenceman and gave him a tap on the shin pads with his stick. Then he nodded at Eric. It was a set play the Sharks used. If Ricky won the draw cleanly, they would generate some instant offence.

Ricky moved to the face-off dot and got ready. He watched the linesman the way a cat watches a mouse. He was poised to strike, yet calm at the same time. The instant the liney's arm moved, Ricky slashed hard at the Toronto centreman's stick. By the time the puck hit the ice, Ricky's stick was blocking the Leaf player's stick. Instantly, he pulled it back and won the draw smoothly to his right defenceman.

The D hesitated, like a quarterback standing in the pocket, and waited for something to open up. There it is, the defenceman thought to himself as he saw Eric breaking hard for the left wall. He took one stride to his left and fired a hard snap shot that whizzed behind his net and around the boards.

Like a finely tuned watch, Eric arrived in time to corral the outlet pass. He barely had time to look up and see the Leafs' right defenceman closing hard to hem him in. He waited until the last possible second, then deftly banked the puck off the wall, past the D and into the neutral zone.

Ricky, who had watched the play develop, had waited just a few seconds longer than Eric, then bolted at full speed for the neutral zone. He arrived at the same time as the puck and picked it up at full speed.

The Leafs' left D had backpedalled when he saw the Sharks ring the boards, and now he was frantically trying to pick up enough speed to angle Ricky off and rub him out along the boards. Unfortunately for him, Ricky was carrying too much speed and beat him wide to the left side. Ricky flew down the wall and began to cut to the net. The Leafs' D, knowing that he was beaten, turned and tried to catch Ricky going forward. At the last second, he dove and swung a hard slash at Ricky's leg.

As Ricky cut to the net, he spread his legs wide and dropped his right hand down to his side to guard the puck from the slash that he knew was coming. The slash hit his hand and then bounced off his leg. He was balanced so well that it barely slowed him down.

To everyone in the building, including the Leafs' goalie, it appeared that Ricky had one play left: to cut hard across the crease and try to beat the goalie with a deke to his forehand. The goalie waited until the last second, then dove out and threw a hard, Johnny Bower–style poke check.

It would have been a great play except that Ricky jammed on the brakes, pulled the puck to his backhand and flicked it effortlessly over the prone goaltender. It was a beautiful goal by a highly skilled player. Ricky raised his stick and grinned as his teammates arrived to congratulate him.

In the Sharks' private box, John Crichton let out a whoop and jumped to his feet. He gave a fist pump and accidentally sent his caramel corn flying over the ledge of the box and down onto the heads of some unfortunate Leafs fans who were seated below him. Now they were disappointed *and* sticky. Crichton was so excited that he didn't even notice his snack was missing until the end of the period. When Ricky was in the zone, like he was tonight, he was a lot of fun to watch, and Crichton congratulated himself once again for his brilliance in drafting such a gifted player. The Sharks continued to dominate the play, and the period ended 1–0. Charlie Davidson did not have a single shift.

When a team is constantly chasing the puck, being reactive instead of proactive, they tend to become fatigued more quickly. The more tired a player gets, the less he moves his feet and the more he tends to clutch and grab. The Sharks continued to press the attack in the third period and the Leafs continued to scramble. With five minutes to go, the Sharks were buzzing in the Leafs' end. An outmatched Leaf defenceman had no choice but to grab a Sharks forward to prevent a scoring chance. The ref flagged him for holding.

Ricky hopped the boards and skated out to start the power play. The face-off was to the left of the Leafs' goalie. Ricky won the draw cleanly back to his right defenceman, who immediately passed across the ice to his partner. The Leaf penalty killers did a nice job of taking away the shooting lane, so the D continued to skate across the blue line to his left. Ricky skated through the Leafs' box and set up on the left half-board. For the next thirty or forty seconds, the Sharks made a series of pretty passes around the Leafs' box. The passes seemed to do little to create a scoring chance. However, while Ricky and the two D were engaged in a game of tic-tac-toe, Eric Rollins quietly slipped behind the Leafs' net and popped up on the goal line to the right of the goal. The second he arrived, Ricky faked a slap shot and drilled a bullet pass through the box right to Eric's stick. As a left-handed shot, he could easily redirect the puck past the startled Toronto goaltender.

Even though the outcome had never been in doubt, the crowd was shocked into silence by the goal. The Leafs had managed only fourteen shots in the first fifty-six minutes of the game. The final four minutes would appear to be a formality.

With a minute and a half to go in the third period, there was a face-off in the Sharks' end. Ricky's line came out for their last shift of the game. On the Leafs' bench, Coach Neely called out for Charlie's line. As they hopped the boards, he yelled after them to make something happen.

For one of the few times that night, Ricky lost the draw. The puck went back to one of the Leaf defencemen, who pounded a slap shot at the net. The Sharks' goaltender kicked out his left leg and directed the puck into the corner. Then the Sharks' left defenceman chased the puck and narrowly chipped it past a Leaf forechecker. The puck bounced along towards Rollins on the half-board. It looked as though he would corral the puck and dump it out into the neutral zone, but because the puck was bouncing, he mishandled it and momentarily lost it in his feet.

Wingers learn early in their careers to be aware of when they are going to be hit and when they have time to make a play. Most guys call it "Spidey sense," and Eric's should have been tingling, because Charlie Davidson had him in his bombsights. For whatever reason, fatigue or lack of concentration, Eric didn't see Charlie coming. Worse still, he didn't sense him. Instead of bracing for the impending hit, he made two glaring mistakes: first, he put his head down to look for the puck; then, when he couldn't find the puck, he turned to look for it against the boards.

At the exact moment that Eric turned, Charlie labelled him. What should have been a nice hit became a vicious hit from behind. Eric's head snapped back as Charlie propelled him into the boards. His face then slammed hard into the glass and he crumpled to the ice in a heap. Even the partisan Leaf crowd groaned in reaction to the hit.

Charlie cursed under his breath and spun around to prepare for the retaliatory onslaught that he had unintentionally unleashed. He had barely turned around when Ricky checked him hard into the boards. Three Sharks and four Leafs rushed to join the fray and suddenly nine big, strong, angry men were pushing, shoving and yelling at each other. A very entertaining, well-played game was about to turn ugly.

"What the hell did you do that for, Charlie?" Ricky yelled as he pinned Charlie against the glass.

"I didn't do anything . . . he turned his back!" Charlie shot back.

Ricky's left forearm was pressed hard against Charlie's chest. He was about to say something about Charlie being a cheap-shot artist when something caught him hard on the left cheek. Ricky flinched as a shot of pain seared through his face. Instinctively, in one motion, he pulled back his right arm and dropped his glove. Then he threw a hard right hand at Charlie. The punch caught Charlie square on the chin. Because Ricky had Charlie pinned against the wall, the punch had the added effect of slamming the back of Charlie's head off of the Plexiglas.

What happened next was that Ricky was driven hard to the ice under a fourteen-hundred-pound pile of elbow pads, shin pads and skates as players from both teams jumped on top of him and Charlie. Ricky's first reaction was to fear being cut, and he instinctively tried to "turtle" to protect his face and his exposed right hand from all those menacing skate blades. After an eternity of rabbit punches to the back of the

79

head, guttural sounds and curses, the linesmen finally succeeded in pulling the remaining players off of Ricky. One of the lineys pulled Ricky to his feet and grabbed him by the jersey under both arms.

"Take it easy, Ricky. It's over. You okay?" the liney asked.

Ricky, dazed and bloodied from the dog pile, only nodded.

As the liney skated him over to the door that led to the visiting team's dressing room, Ricky got the sense that something wasn't quite right. He wasn't being sent off to a round of jeers from the hostile crowd, as he might have expected. The entire arena, filled with more than nineteen thousand people, was absolutely silent. At the ACC, the hallway to the visitors' dressing room is right beside the visitors' bench. As Ricky stepped through the gate, he looked over at the bench, where not one of his teammates seemed to even notice that he was leaving the ice. Their eyes were all focused, with morbid fascination, on something across the ice.

Ricky turned and followed the gaze of his teammates. He suddenly remembered the hit from behind that Eric had taken, and he searched the ice to see if his friend was still down. He could see several trainers, medical staff and paramedics attending to a player.

Oh no, Ricky thought. Eric's hurt bad.

The paramedics had strapped a player onto a backboard and carefully lifted him onto a stretcher when Ricky finally noticed that the player was wearing a Leaf jersey. Now he was really confused. He leaned out of the door and called over to Tony Jamieson, the Sharks' backup goalie.

"Hey, Jamer. Where's Eric?"

Jamer's eyes never left the commotion on the ice. "He's

in the room. Cut his face pretty good and knocked out a few teeth, but he'll be all right."

Ricky looked back to the ice. "Then who are they working on?"

Jamer turned slowly and looked at Ricky. "Charlie Davidson," he answered.

A cold shiver ran down Ricky's back. He turned and ran for the Sharks' dressing room.

❧

When all the commotion had settled down and the refs had finally worked out all the penalties, the game resumed to play out the final thirty-seven seconds. Neither team seemed particularly interested. Perhaps they both sensed that they had crossed the line and that the injury to Charlie was more important than the outcome of the game.

At the end of the game, the three stars were announced. For the second night in a row, Ricky was named the game's first star. Unlike last night, however, Ricky didn't come out for his curtain call. His absence was greeted by a chorus of boos from the Toronto faithful, but they probably would have booed him even if he had appeared.

Only one person in the rink noticed anything amiss about Ricky not taking his bows. Darryl turned to Haley and said, "Let's go. Something's wrong."

Haley began to protest, but Darryl cut her off. "Ricky has never missed the three stars. Something must have happened."

Darryl and Haley's seats were on the opposite side and at the far end of the rink from the fight. All they had seen was Eric getting hammered, followed by a large scrum. They knew that Ricky was involved, but they couldn't see much else. Darryl's first guess was that Ricky had been hurt during the fight, so he wanted to get down to the dressing room to check on him.

What Darryl didn't know was that Ricky had already left the room. After the fight, he had raced back to the dressing room and quickly changed and showered. He was already dressed when the Leafs came off the ice at the end of the game. He quietly left the Sharks' room, pushed his way through the throng of fans leaving the lower bowl and walked over to the Leafs' room. A security guard stopped him and asked for his credentials.

Ricky gave him a look that said "Are you for real?" and announced: "I'm Ricky Phillips. I want to see Charlie Davidson."

The guard looked taken aback, then he stammered an apology. "I'm sorry, Ricky . . . one second." Then he disappeared through the door.

Ricky stood outside the Leafs' room and wondered to himself if he was overreacting. He was thinking about heading back to the Sharks' room when the door opened. Standing there, looking very angry and very menacing, was Stu Porter, the Leafs' goon.

"What the hell do you want?" he snarled.

Ricky's back instantly went up. What's with the tough guy act? he wondered. "I just wanted to check on Charlie," he said.

"You might have been a bit more concerned about him before you sucker-punched him!" Stu yelled.

"I didn't sucker anybody," Ricky protested. "Now, are you going to let me see Charlie or not?"

Porter took a step towards Ricky. "I'll tell you what I'm going to do . . ."

"Stu! That's enough!" bellowed an authoritative voice from behind the two men.

Stu and Ricky both turned to see an older looking man in a trainer's outfit.

"You stay out of this, Joe," Stu growled.

Joe's eyes flashed and he snapped, "Don't you take that tone with me, Junior. Now get back in that room and mind your own business."

Porter hesitated, as if he was about to say something, but he thought better of it and headed back into the room.

Joe turned his attention to Ricky. "Sorry about that, Ricky. The boys are a little freaked about Charlie, that's all. Here," he nodded with his head, "follow me."

Ricky followed Joe into the Leafs' dressing room. They headed for the trainers' room, where Joe closed the door after Ricky. Ricky looked around, confused. "Where's Charlie?" he asked.

"He's been taken to Toronto General Hospital," Joe answered. "Now calm down," he said when he saw the look on Ricky's face. "I'm sure he's going to be fine."

Ricky could think of nothing to say except, "Are you sure?"

Joe looked at him and had to remind himself that this was Ricky Phillips, professional hockey superstar. What he saw was a confused and frightened kid. He decided Ricky needed the truth, but how it was delivered would be critical. He sat down in a chair and spoke very softly.

"Ricky, I'll be honest: when we treated him on the ice, he was unconscious, but I'm sure he'll come around. Charlie's a tough guy. The EMS guys were being super-cautious. There's something else you should know, too. Charlie's had a series of concussions over his career and this will probably prove to be another one."

Ricky looked like he was on the verge of tears. "That's great. So I'll be responsible for ending his career."

Joe smiled a fatherly smile. "You don't know that. I'll tell you what: it was a good thing you did, coming here to check on him. You guys are staying in Toronto tonight, right?"

Ricky nodded. "Yeah, we fly home tomorrow around noon."

Joe grabbed a piece of paper and a pen and wrote something down. Then he handed it to Ricky. "Here's my phone number. If you want, why don't you call me tomorrow and I'll give you an update on Charlie."

Ricky took the number, thanked Joe and headed for the door. He didn't notice the surprised looks on the faces of the reporters who were waiting to get into the room to get their post-game sound bites from the Leaf players. He headed back towards the Sharks' room at a complete loss as to what he should do next. As he rounded the corner, he saw his parents waiting outside the door to the Sharks' dressing room.

"You okay, buddy?" Darryl asked. "Everybody's been looking for you."

"I went to check on Charlie Davidson," Ricky mumbled.

"We couldn't see from our seats. Is he the one that went off on the stretcher?" Darryl asked.

Ricky nodded, then added, "Could you guys give me a ride up to Toronto General?"

"I guess so, Ricky, but I don't understand . . ."

Ricky was beginning to panic, and he didn't have the patience to deal with a lot of stupid questions.

Haley stepped towards him and put her arms around him. "It'll be okay," she said and hugged him tight.

"Aw, Mom, I've got a really bad feeling about this," Ricky said. For the first time in his life, he felt genuinely scared.

Haley smiled at him and patted his shoulder. "It's going to be okay," she said. Then she led him down the hall. "Come on. I'll drive."

CHAPTER TEN

The Phillipses worked their way up University Avenue, which wasn't easy with all the traffic letting out of the ACC. They found a place to park and then wound their way through the cavernous Toronto General Hospital until they found the emergency unit. Ricky went up to the window and told the nurse at reception who he was. She didn't seem to know, or care, who he was and directed him to the waiting room. Ricky and his parents went and sat on a row of hard plastic seats.

About ten minutes later, Darryl nudged Ricky and motioned towards the reception desk, where two well-dressed young men were making inquiries. Ricky knew they played for the Leafs but didn't know their names.

"Who's that?" he whispered to his dad.

Darryl, still a Leaf fan, whispered back, "Geoff Green and Robbie Padgett; they play on Charlie's line."

Geoff and Robbie seemed to be given the same information as Ricky, because they headed towards the waiting room. As they entered, they noticed Ricky. Robbie stopped and hesitated, but Geoff came forward and extended his hand. Ricky shook his hand and introduced his parents. They engaged in some awkward small talk when it was clear that there was still no word on Charlie. Robbie asked how Eric was doing, and Ricky realized that he had forgotten all about his roommate.

"Ah, I think he's okay. Knocked out a few teeth and I think he might have a concussion."

A few minutes later, Geoff noticed an attractive woman pacing nervously in the hall. He nudged Robbie and nodded towards her. "Julie," he said.

The two men stood, excused themselves and politely said goodbye to Darryl and Haley. Ricky stood and shook their hands, then asked, "Is that Charlie's wife?"

They nodded.

Ricky felt a knot forming in his stomach. "I wonder if I should talk to her?" he wasn't sure whether he was asking them or himself.

Geoff cleared his throat. "I'm not sure that's such a great idea, Ricky. Why don't you let us talk to her first?"

Ricky nodded sadly and returned to his plastic seat beside his parents. He watched them go out into the hall and hug Julie. He could tell that she was putting on a brave face. Ricky felt like a little kid sitting outside the principal's office waiting to be punished.

Let's get this over with, he thought after some time had passed. He stood up and told his parents, "I'll be right back," then walked over to Julie Davidson.

Julie had her back to him and was talking quietly with Geoff and Robbie when Geoff noticed Ricky standing behind them. Julie turned around and looked Ricky square in the eye.

"Mrs. Davidson," Ricky started, but then the words failed him.

Julie smiled kindly and held out her hand. "Thank you so much for coming, Ricky."

Ricky shook her hand and tried to smile. He tried to apologize. Suddenly he realized that he had no idea what to say. Julie, still holding his hand, led him to some chairs and the two of them sat down.

"Listen to me, Ricky. This is not your fault."

Ricky was having trouble looking Julie in the eye. He sheepishly said, "Ma'am."

"Julie."

"Uh, Julie, I hit him, tonight, during the fight."

"I know," Julie replied quietly.

"I'm so sorry."

"I know you are. Charlie would understand too. And he'd tell you the same thing. Charlie's been in hundreds of fights. I'm sure you have too."

"I've been in a few," Ricky answered softly.

"You need to know, Ricky, that I have no hard feelings and Charlie doesn't, either. Everyone who plays hockey knows that there are risks involved. If you're a fighter, the risks are multiplied that much more. When Charlie's feeling better, you come see him and he'll tell you that there's no ill will."

A doctor approached them. "Mrs. Davidson? I'm Dr. North."

"I'm Julie, this is Ricky Phillips." She motioned with her hand to where Robbie and Geoff were standing and introduced them as well.

Dr. North's expression didn't change. He shook hands quickly and added, "I'm sorry, I don't follow hockey too much. Are you guys teammates of Charlie's?"

Geoff and Robbie nodded, but Ricky grimaced. "I play for San Jose. I'm the guy that hit Charlie."

Dr. North maintained his poker face and said curtly, "I see." Then he turned to Julie and said, "Mrs. Davidson, I need a word, please—in private."

Ricky watched as Julie and Dr. North disappeared around a corner. Reluctantly, he returned to the waiting room and resumed his uncomfortable vigil on the hard plastic chairs.

❂

Dr. North showed Julie to an empty exam room and offered her a seat. Julie looked at him expectantly, and he cut straight to the chase. "Julie, Charlie's in surgery as we speak."

Julie gasped as the doctor continued speaking. "He had severe swelling on his brain when he arrived. We had to operate to relieve the pressure."

Julie felt like she was standing on the edge of a cliff and was about to fall.

"One of our top neurosurgeons was on call tonight. Charlie has the best care possible."

Julie was slowly regaining her composure, and now the questions were coming faster than she could ask them. She decided to ask the most important one first: "Dr. North, he's going to be okay, though, right?"

Dr. North answered slowly and sympathetically. "Julie, I don't think you understand. Charlie has suffered tremendous damage to his brain. We're doing all we can for him, but his chances of surviving through the night are slim at best. I'm very sorry."

Julie felt as if her insides were tearing apart. "No . . . no. This can't be happening."

Dr. North watched Julie kindly as the tears came. He had learned over the years that people who have received horrible news respond best if you can keep them talking.

"Julie," he asked gently, "how many concussions has Charlie had?"

"Five," Julie answered, adding softly, "that I know of."

"I'm sorry?"

Julie looked at the floor and answered guiltily, "Charlie threw up this afternoon. He told me that he was fine, but now I'm wondering if he was hiding his symptoms from me." She looked imploringly at Dr. North. "He wanted to play so badly."

"I see," said Dr. North.

Julie suddenly felt herself getting angry. "I don't understand how someone as big and strong as Charlie could be hurt this badly from one punch."

Dr. North nodded. "Well, all I can tell you right now, Julie, is that when someone suffers a concussion, what is really happening is that the brain bounces off of the inside of the skull. Damage, sometimes minor and sometimes major, occurs to the brain. Subsequent injuries can dramatically exacerbate the damage. Charlie has had five documented concussions. He was possibly playing with a sixth one tonight. Compound that with the blow to the head that he took tonight and we have a very serious situation."

Suddenly, Dr. North's pager vibrated and he glanced down at it. "That's the OR," he said. "Charlie's out of surgery."

Julie felt her chest tighten. "Can I see him?" she asked.

Dr. North smiled. "Of course. They'll take him to recovery. I'll show you where that is."

Ricky had lost all sense of time. He wasn't sure whether it had been just a few minutes or several hours since he'd talked to Julie. He looked up at the big clock on the wall and realized that it was almost two in the morning. Slowly he stood up and tried to stretch the kinks out of his legs and back. He walked stiffly over to the reception desk, but was once again told there was no word on Charlie. He walked over to the window and looked out at the lights of downtown Toronto. He felt numb with fatigue and fear. Not knowing what else to do, he returned once again to his chair beside his mom and sat down to wait.

CHAPTER ELEVEN

Charlie died at 3:52 on Sunday morning. He was only thirty-two years old. He left behind a grieving widow, shocked teammates and a stunned city. Charlie had, unfortunately, gained the dubious distinction of being the first National Hockey League player ever killed as a result of a hockey fight. In a town as obsessed with its hockey team as Toronto, the news hit hard. In the summertime, it is not uncommon for the Maple Leafs to usurp the baseball Blue Jays as the top sports story simply by re-signing a player. During the hockey season, even on days when there is no game, the team's practices will often garner the top spot on sportscasts. To the sports world this story was a firestorm.

◉

After leaving the hospital, Ricky holed himself up in his parents' basement and watched the game film. He saw Charlie hit Eric, then watched as Eric's head snapped back. He saw himself pinning Charlie against the glass. Then a hand came out of the scrum and caught Ricky in the face. He saw himself hammering Charlie with an overhand right.

He leaned forward, riveted by the film, his mouth dry. Charlie's hands had never come up from his sides. He didn't throw the punch that Ricky had absorbed. Ricky realized with a chill that Charlie didn't want to fight. His eyes welled up and a tear coursed slowly down his cheek. He brushed it away with the back of his hand, then rewound the footage and watched it again.

❀

By Monday night, the story was in every newspaper in North America. In Canada, it led the national news on the CBC and CTV networks, and it dominated every sports-talk radio show from St. John's to Victoria. The radio hosts were almost unanimous in their support for Ricky. They were saddened by Charlie's death, offered their condolences to the family and felt that Ricky was simply playing the game the way it had always been played. The overwhelming sentiment was to let him get on with his life and continue to play.

The mainstream media wasn't so kind. There were calls for inquests and inquiries into what was wrong with the game. There were demands for a ban on fighting and a complete overhaul of the game. Public opinion outside of the sports-radio world was about seventy per cent in favour of banning Ricky from hockey for life, and some newspaper editorials called for criminal charges.

The Ontario Provincial Police did visit with Ricky. They also conducted extensive interviews with the players and coaching staffs for both the Sharks and Leafs, and spent hours viewing tape of the game. Rumours spread that Ricky would be charged with manslaughter, but the police couldn't determine with any certainty whether it was Ricky's punch, the dog pile that formed afterward, or the fact that Charlie was playing hurt that had been the deciding factor in his death. Eventually, they announced that no charges would be laid.

The National Hockey League was in a very awkward position. Despite the loud calls for severe punishment, there appeared to be little it could do. In terms of the epic punch-ups that the league had witnessed over the years, this one would barely register as a skirmish. It just happened to have a tragic ending. Most of the league's top brass didn't want to suspend Ricky at all—not because he was a marquee player, but because he had fought and been assessed the proper penalty: a five-minute major for fighting. However, they also knew that if there were no further disciplinary action, the league would be perceived as not only condoning violence, but encouraging it. After all, hockey and lacrosse are the only professional sports in the world that allow bare-knuckle fighting. Even the promoters of the wildly popular mixed martial arts require that their athletes wear protective gloves.

Therefore, a few days after Charlie's death, the NHL reluctantly announced that Ricky would be suspended for the remainder of the season and the playoffs. At a press conference, a league spokesman made the announcement and quickly left the room before the group of startled reporters could even ask a question.

If the Sharks were to reach the Stanley Cup final, this would prove to be the longest suspension in league history. But after the game in Toronto, the Sharks were a different team. The bravado and swagger of a Cup contender was gone, replaced by confusion, disappointment and remorse.

The suspension suited Ricky just fine. The last thing he wanted to think about was going back out on the ice and playing hockey as if nothing had happened. He'd spent the entire night of the accident at the hospital, waiting for word, and when he finally learned of Charlie's death, he simply didn't know what to do.

The Sharks flew back to San Jose that Sunday, but Ricky refused to go with them. He wasn't sure what he should do, other than stay close to Toronto. The Sharks' public-relations director always travelled with the team, and he was ordered to stay behind with Ricky. In anticipation of the media frenzy that they knew was coming, and to deal with any legal action that might arise, the team flew in a lawyer from San Jose. The lawyer hunkered down in the room beside the PR man, and the two of them were kept busy with a constant stream of media requests. Ricky, on the other hand, went home with his parents to Oro-Medonte. He left town without once checking to see how Eric was doing.

Darryl Phillips had taken a leave of absence from work so that he could be available to help his son. However, with Ricky spending all his time in the basement, all Darryl had been doing for the past few days was to work his way through a huge onslaught of mail. Most of it was positive—letters of sympathy and encouragement for Ricky to hang in there. However, some of the letters were terrifying. They ranged from venomous attacks on Ricky's character to actual death threats. Darryl didn't share any of these with Ricky or Haley, but he did show them to a golfing buddy who was a cop. He was told that there was nothing the police could do unless someone actually came to Darryl's house. That didn't do much to reassure him.

On one of the rare occasions when Ricky emerged from the basement, he found his dad in the kitchen, reading the newspaper. He pulled up a chair and got right to the point. "I want to go to the funeral," he announced.

Darryl put down his newspaper and looked at Ricky. "I figured you'd be saying that sooner or later."

"Well, I'm going and that's that."

Darryl paused for a moment before answering. "If you really want to go to the funeral, then I'll go with you, but you need to think about a few things first."

Ricky could feel his back getting up. "Dad, don't treat me like a baby . . ."

"Look, Ricky. I know you feel bad but—"

"*Feel bad?*" Ricky snapped. "I killed a man! A man who didn't want to fight, and I killed him."

"It was an accident! A hockey fight."

"Yeah, and you're the one who taught me how to fight, and now look what's happened!"

Darryl jumped to his feet, sending his chair sprawling behind him. "You think this is my fault?"

Ricky stood up so that he was nose to nose with his father. "It's got to be somebody's fault, Dad. You were the one who taught me how to fight, and now a man's dead."

"You were fifteen years old. All I did was teach you how to protect yourself. This is not my fault, and don't you ever take that tone with me again!" his father shot back angrily.

Deep down, Ricky knew that it wasn't his dad's fault, but he wasn't about to back down. "You taught me to fight," he repeated.

Slowly, Darryl put his hands on Ricky's shoulders. "Ricky," he said softly, "the reason things are called accidents is because they're no one's fault. You hit Charlie, but he was already hurt. Then he ended up on the bottom of the dog pile. It was just bad luck. It wasn't supposed to end like this."

Tears welled up in Ricky's eyes. "Well, it did." He angrily brushed the tears away with the back of his hand.

Darryl sighed. "Yeah, you're right. It did end that way. But here's a question for you."

Ricky sniffed. "What's that?"

"Did you mean to kill Charlie?"

"What the hell kind of question is that?"

"Just answer it."

"Of course I didn't mean to kill him," Ricky snapped.

Darryl smiled kindly. "All right then. I guess it was an accident after all." Ricky didn't respond, so he continued: "Ricky, you're a good person. You didn't do anything wrong."

"I hit him," Ricky interrupted.

"Yeah, you hit him. And guys have been hitting each other in hockey games for a hundred years now. Your situation just had a horrible result. I read in the paper that the Leafs think Charlie had been playing hurt since a game in Edmonton a couple of weeks ago. Do you know how many concussions Charlie had?"

"No."

"Five," Darryl answered. "So tell me, Ricky: Why would a man with five known concussions play when he was probably suffering from a sixth?"

Ricky looked at the floor and didn't answer.

His dad answered for him, "Because he loved the game. I never made it to the NHL. Thousands of guys like me, who got close, would do anything for one day in The Show. I completely understand why he didn't want to lose that. Charlie knew the risks, Ricky, and he was willing to accept them because he just wanted to play."

Ricky found that he couldn't lift his head to meet his father's eyes. He was suddenly feeling very tired.

"Ricky, look at me."

Slowly, Ricky raised his head.

"I can't begin to imagine what you are going through, but you've got to find a way to forgive yourself, or this thing is going to tear you up inside. The radio shows, the sports shows on TV, all of them feel bad for you and think you should be allowed to play. The league says you can play again next year. Even the OPP ruled that it was an accident. So now there are only two people whose opinions matter."

"Who's that?" Ricky asked.

"You and Julie Davidson."

"Yeah, and that's why I want to go to the funeral," Ricky answered.

"Okay, but hear me out. I've been thinking a lot about this, and the way I see it, you're in a no-win situation."

"Tell me about it," Ricky replied sarcastically.

"Seriously, Ricky, it's a no-win. If you go to the funeral, people will say that you're distracting from the Davidson family's time of grief and drawing attention to yourself."

"And if I don't go?" Ricky asked.

"If you don't go, people will say that you're callous and heartless," Darryl answered.

Ricky sighed in agreement. "Sounds pretty much like a no-win. So what do you suggest I do, Dad?"

Darryl didn't hesitate. "You do what's best for Julie. I think going to the funeral would detract from her family's time together because the media would focus on you. I think you should go and see her privately. If you get ripped in the media, so be it. You'll know that you did the right thing."

Ricky looked at his dad. "My options suck."

Darryl smiled sadly. "Yeah, they do."

"Will you come with me?"

"Yeah, I'll come. Mom will, too."

"How do I get in touch with Julie . . . to see what's a good time?"

"We're going tomorrow at noon."

Ricky looked surprised. "I don't get it."

"Mom phoned Julie yesterday. We're going to go and see her tomorrow."

Ricky wanted to laugh, but he was also a little annoyed at his dad's presumption. "What if I hadn't agreed to your little plan?"

Darryl shrugged. "Then I guess your mom and I would have gone without you. This is the right thing to do, Ricky."

"I hope you're right," Ricky answered grimly.

●

The next day, Ricky and his parents pulled into the driveway of a beautiful, sprawling ranch-style bungalow in Oakville and parked their car. They walked to the front door and rang the bell.

A large man, who was clearly Charlie's father, opened the door. He didn't smile, speak or extend his hand.

Ricky's mother seized the moment and stepped forward. "Mr. Davidson, I'm Haley Phillips."

"I know who you are," he said curtly. He never took his

eyes off of Ricky. "My daughter-in-law is more forgiving than I am. If you think that coming here is going to make everything all right, then you've wasted your trip."

Ricky was surprised to hear himself answer, "We didn't come here to make everything right."

"Then why did you come?" Mr. Davidson demanded as he took a step towards Ricky.

"They came here to see me," said Julie as she came to the front door. "Hello Haley, Mr. Phillips, Ricky. Please come in." She glanced at her father-in-law and gave him a look that said, "Don't push your luck."

Julie led the Phillipses to the family room and offered them a seat. They made small talk for a few minutes, and when it was established that the drive down was fine and that the Phillipses didn't want anything to drink, Julie finally said, "I really appreciate your coming down."

Ricky wasn't used to being the one to carry a conversation, but after a moment he responded, "My dad felt that we'd be taking away from your family's time to grieve, if we attended the funeral."

Julie smiled sadly. "If you want to attend the funeral, you would certainly have my blessing. This is Toronto, the hockey capital of the world. It's going to be a media circus whether you're there or not, Ricky."

"Well," Ricky replied, "I want to do what's best for you. If you want me at the funeral, I'll be there. If you don't, I'll respect that too."

Julie thought for a moment and then said, "I think that a visit today is more important."

Ricky tried to smile. "Then a visit it is."

"Ricky?" Julie asked.

"Yes?"

"You remember what we talked about at the hospital?"

Ricky felt a lump forming in his throat. "I remember."

"Well, make sure you believe it. I bear you no ill will. And if Charlie was here . . ." Julie's voice quivered, but she smiled and wiped aside a tear. "If Charlie was here, he'd tell you the same thing. Hockey is a tough game and there are risks involved."

Ricky tried to smile. He stood and offered his hand, "I appreciate that, Julie."

Julie rose, strode past his outstretched hand and gave him a hug.

●

The next day, the Phillipses watched the news for coverage of Charlie's funeral. In spite of the circus-like atmosphere with the media, it was a very moving service. As Darryl predicted, the talk shows around Toronto buzzed with talk of the funeral. The main topic of discussion was why Ricky had not attended. Several callers took the opportunity to phone in and rip him. "Coward" was a frequent label.

But that sentiment changed the next day, after the CBC broadcast an interview it had managed to arrange with Julie.

"Why do you think Ricky Phillips didn't come to the funeral?" the reporter asked.

"Because I asked him not to," Julie replied.

The reporter's face fell. He'd clearly been hoping to play up the Ricky-as-villain theme.

"I'm sorry?" he said.

"I met with Ricky and his parents yesterday. We had

a good visit. Ricky is a good person, who, like me, is in the middle of a very difficult situation."

The TV story set the talk shows buzzing once again. But within the span of twenty-four hours, Ricky had gone from coward to class act. Ricky would always be grateful to Julie for her kindness and her understanding.

CHAPTER TWELVE

The days slipped by and Charlie Davidson and Ricky Phillips were quickly forgotten by the mainstream media as they invariably turned their attention to other pressing stories.

Three weeks after the fateful game at the ACC, Ricky was still living at his parents' place in Oro. During the day, he slept for hours on end. He hadn't been to a gym or gone for a run. When he was awake, he watched a lot of television, but his dad noticed that he never tuned in to a sports show. He seemed to have forgotten that he was a professional athlete and that he was still employed by the San Jose Sharks.

On one of the many occasions when his parents were trying unsuccessfully to get some sleep, Haley sat up and rubbed her eyes. "I'm really worried about him," she said. "Do you think I should call a doctor?"

"What for?" Darryl asked. "So some shrink can tell him he's depressed and he needs to face his problems? Then they'll prescribe a bunch of drugs. No, I don't like that idea at all."

"Well, what do you suggest, Dr. Phil?" Haley asked.

Darryl ignored the jab and answered, "He needs to go back to San Jose. He needs to be with his teammates. Work out, stay fit."

"Do you think he's ready to be on his own?"

"I think that the longer he stays with us, the more depressed he's going to get," Darryl said. "His life's in San Jose. It's not here, hiding in our basement."

He got up and grabbed his housecoat and put it on.

"Where are you going?" Haley asked.

"I'm gonna go and talk to him," Darryl said.

Darryl shuffled off to the basement, where he found Ricky in front of the TV, flipping aimlessly through the channels. He brightened at the sight of his dad.

"Ricky, it's three o'clock in the morning," his dad prompted.

Ricky shrugged. "Couldn't sleep."

Darryl took a deep breath and let it out slowly. "Ricky, what are your plans for the rest of the season?" he asked.

"Season?" Ricky responded. He wasn't sure what his dad meant.

"Season, Ricky. Remember, the *hockey* season?"

To be honest, Ricky didn't remember the hockey season. He had forgotten about it. He didn't know what to say, so instead he just pretended to be interested in some old black-and-white movie.

Carefully, his dad said, "Ricky, you still play for the Sharks."

"But I'm suspended," Ricky answered.

"Yeah, you're suspended, but that doesn't mean that you shouldn't be in San Jose supporting your teammates," Darryl reasoned.

Since Charlie's death, Ricky really hadn't thought much about the Sharks—his teammates or his coaches. He had completely blocked them out of his mind.

"Have you called Eric yet?" Darryl asked.

Ricky looked down at the floor and shook his head.

"He called the other day. He's worried about you."

Ricky was worried about Eric too, but for some reason he couldn't bring himself to call his friend. "You think I should go back to San Jose?" he asked his dad.

Darryl nodded his head. "Yeah, I do."

Ricky had no idea what he wanted to do. He was content to sit in the basement and watch TV, but he nodded his head and said, "Okay, I'll go and see the guys."

Darryl smiled and patted Ricky's knee. "That's good, kiddo. Get back to your own apartment and re-establish your routines. You'll be back in the groove in no time."

Ricky smiled indulgently at his dad. Darryl, feeling that the issue had been solved conclusively, wished Ricky a good night and headed back up the stairs to bed. Ricky waited until he was gone, then resumed his channel surfing.

●

Three days later, Ricky's flight landed in San Jose. He wasn't upset about being sent back; rather, he was simply ambivalent. For his whole life, he'd been told what to do: when to be at the rink, what position he would play, when to be at the team meal, what he should eat and how often he should exercise. For the first time in his life, he felt like he had no direction. It wasn't just that he was suspended and couldn't play—after all, he could still be with the guys, could still practise and travel with the team. He just had this nagging feeling that he didn't care about any of that anymore.

The Sharks were playing that night. He had no idea what to do; he guessed that his options were to go to his apartment or to go to the rink. He decided to head to the rink. He was about two hours early for the game, and when he arrived he found a welcoming scene of familiarity. Trainers were bustling about, preparing sticks, filling water bottles, taping wrists and knees. Players were stretching, riding the exercise bike or kicking a soccer ball around.

When he walked into the dressing room, he was greeted warmly by his teammates and the support staff. Most of the guys kept it simple and talked about the weather and the Sharks' losing streak. Some of the older guys knew enough to ask Ricky how he was feeling and to express their condolences for both Ricky, and what he was going through, and for Charlie. Ricky was surprised to realize that it felt okay to talk about it.

At game time, Ricky went up to the team's private box and watched the Sharks get absolutely pasted by Detroit. The team's play seemed to mirror Ricky's mood. They just didn't seem to care about the game. And it wasn't that they played poorly; they just lacked the heart and aggression necessary to be successful at the professional level. Since the Toronto game, the Sharks had managed just one win in nine games and were in a major tailspin as the playoffs approached.

After the game, Ricky headed back to his apartment with Eric. The two had watched the game from the team box. Like Ricky, Eric was also finished for the season, but his season was over thanks to the fallout from Charlie's hit. He had a concussion, a broken jaw and he had lost three teeth. His jaw was wired shut, but it would heal. He would have dental work done over the summer. What was really worrying him was the concussion. He knew that he would not be allowed to play until he received medical clearance.

At the rink, the two young men had watched the game in silence. Conversation is not easy when your jaw is wired shut, especially given the roar of noise from the crowd. It was easier for Eric just to sit and watch. Eric could tell that Ricky was quite content to stay silent, but he felt the need to talk. He was worried for his friend and was more than a little pissed off at him. In the three weeks since the accident, Ricky hadn't even bothered to check in and see how he was doing. Oh sure, he knew Ricky was going through a lot with Charlie's death and all, but he was really hurt by the fact that Ricky hadn't called.

After the Toronto game, Eric had spent two days in hospital before the doctors would allow him to fly. He then returned to San Jose with his mom, who had flown to Toronto to be with him after the injury. When the jaw was wired up, there was no arguing—Mrs. Rollins was staying to look after her boy. Like any good hockey mom, she knew that it would be next to impossible for him to keep the weight on with a liquid diet. She would see to it that he was fit and strong when he was finally cleared to play. So she started whipping up power drinks and shakes that were both delicious and full of nutrients. In the three weeks since his injury, Eric had only dropped two and a half pounds.

A few days after he got back to California, Eric wrote a series of questions on a piece of paper and handed it to his mom. He was worried about Ricky and wanted to know how he was doing. She placed the call to the Phillips house. The conversation was surprisingly short, and when she got off the phone, she said, "That was Darryl. He said Ricky's not available right now but that he'll call you later." Three weeks went by, and Ricky never returned the call.

Now here they were, sitting together in their apartment. Ricky seemed oblivious to the silence. He flopped down on the couch and immediately reached for the TV remote.

Eric looked at his mom and gave her a look that clearly revealed both his anger and his confusion. Mrs. Rollins took the hint and quietly disappeared into the guest room.

Eric looked over at Ricky, who was scanning the channels, oblivious to the fact that Eric was even in the room. "Icky, urn at ing off. I ahnt to talk to oo," Eric mumbled.

Ricky flicked off the TV and looked at Eric. "What's up?"

Eric couldn't believe his casualness, "Ut's up? My oddam aw's usted!"

Ricky's expression didn't change; he just continued to stare at Eric. He had no idea where Eric was going with this. The less he reacted, the more upset Eric got, "On't oo even air? Oo ever even eturned my all."

It quickly dawned on Ricky what Eric was getting at, but he didn't react by feeling guilty. Instead, he suddenly felt very angry.

"Are you kidding me?" he snapped. "You wanted me to call to check in on how your jaw was doing?"

Now it was Eric's turn to be confused. "Ee, ess," he stuttered.

"Here's a news flash for you, Eric," Ricky yelled as he jumped to his feet. "Your bloody jaw is broke, you're missing three teeth and you have a concussion! Well, guess what? Your jaw is going to heal. This summer, you'll go and see some fancy dentist who'll fix your teeth, and long before next season, you'll be cleared to play with your concussion. So what the hell's your problem?"

Eric looked baffled. "Ut's my oblem?"

"Yeah, what's your problem?" Ricky yelled. "You're going to heal and you'll get your life back." Suddenly, everything he'd been trying to get his head around for the last month became crystal clear. Tears welled in his eyes, but this time he wasn't ashamed of them. "You're going to get your life back. Charlie David . . ." His voice caught, but he took a deep breath and continued, "Charlie Davidson won't." Ricky flopped back down onto the couch. Tears continued to glide silently down his face.

"I'm sorry I didn't call to see how you were doing, Eric."

Eric, who was shocked by Ricky's anger, but completely dumbfounded by the tears, merely mumbled, "At's okay."

"No it's not," Ricky continued. "I should have called to check on you. And I'm sorry I yelled at you about your jaw. I know you're going through a tough time. But it's true: you are going to be okay. And you know what?"

"Ut?"

"I killed a man, Eric."

"It us an accident, Icky."

"I know, I know. But I hit him, and four hours later he died. He was just a hard-working guy who was trying to hang on in The Show for as long as possible. His wife, Julie, she's an incredible person. She forgave me and told me it wasn't my fault."

Eric smiled awkwardly with his wired jaw. "I ess all at's eft ow is or oo to orgive ore self, Icky."

Ricky smiled sadly. "Yeah, Eric, people keep telling me that."

●

The Sharks continued to sputter as the regular season wound down. But for Ricky and Eric, this was an important time. Caring for each other helped them to heal their own injuries. Mrs. Rollins taught Ricky how to make healthy shakes, and in no time his were almost as tasty as hers. Mrs. Rollins's maternal instincts told her that it was time for the boys to start fending for themselves, and about a week after Ricky arrived she headed back home to Halifax.

Ricky threw himself into the role of Eric's caregiver, and he found himself shopping for healthy ingredients for his milkshakes. When Eric suggested that Ricky come to the gym with him, Ricky hesitated, but then told himself that it was a way to help Eric stay fit while he waited for next season. It didn't occur to him that he, too, needed to get back in shape for hockey.

One night, almost two months to the day from the infamous game in Toronto, Eric and Ricky were sitting in the Sharks' private box at the HP Pavilion, watching the Sharks once again take it on the chin. It was the final game of the regular season. Ricky stared blankly down at the ice surface. He showed no emotion and didn't react, even when the Sharks rallied late in the game and the arena was hopping.

Eric, who had watched his friend sit this way through several games now, knew that it was time for Ricky to get back on the horse.

"Icky?"

Ricky looked over at Eric, "What's up?"

"Why on't oo ate with the eam, oomorrow?"

The question seemed to catch Ricky completely off guard.

"Skate?" He repeated the word like it was a concept that was completely foreign to him.

Eric persisted. "Eah . . . *ate.* Oo eed to et ack on the ice."

Nobody on the Sharks had pushed Ricky. They knew he was still an emotional wreck and wanted him to take his time. Eric felt differently. He knew his friend was avoiding the ice, and it was time to change that.

"Skate," Ricky said the word again.

"Ate," Eric repeated.

Ricky looked back down to the ice as the final seconds ticked down on the Sharks' regular season, "We'll see," he said.

Ricky didn't skate the next day, or the next. But Eric was relentless. Whenever Ricky would make him a milkshake, he'd say, "Anks. Oo eed to ate."

Ricky would shrug his shoulders and reply, "We'll see." He didn't know how to explain it, but he had no desire to get back on the ice.

One day at the gym, Eric tried a new approach.

"Icky," he said. "I'll et oo I can ench ress ore than oo."

Ricky laughed. "What are you talking about, Eric?" It was known around the NHL that Ricky was, pound for pound, the strongest guy in the league. Not only was he highly skilled, but his strength made it almost impossible to knock him off the puck.

"Ou erd me. I et I can ench ress ore than oo."

"Eric, I press close to a hundred pounds more than you. Besides, you shouldn't be lifting hard with your concussion."

Eric looked his friend square in the eye. "If I ift ore an oo, oo ate oumorrow."

Ricky laughed. He admired Eric's spirit. "You're on."

Eric put 215 pounds on the bar. This was about fifty pounds below his best, but his head still hurt when he worked out too hard. He still had trouble riding the exercise bike without feeling nauseous.

111

Ricky got behind him and got ready to spot. Eric pushed the weight up off the bar and brought it down to his chest. Then he grunted hard through his wired jaw and pushed the weight back up. Ricky helped him replace the weight on the bench. Eric sat up and grabbed his head with both hands. A sound like that of an injured animal came out of his mouth.

"Eric!" Ricky yelled. "Are you okay?"

Eric waved him off. "I'm ine! Oh it, at urt!"

"You idiot, you shouldn't have done that. You could've really hurt yourself."

Eric stood up shakily. "Ore urn."

Ricky looked at his friend and shook his head. His best lift was 375 pounds. He routinely did reps of ten with three hundred. So 215 pounds was nothing to him.

"How much do you want me to lift?"

"Ooh ifeen. Ooh imes."

Ricky laughed as he sat on the bench. "Twice? That's it? Hey, what do I get when I win?" He popped the bar off the holders and was instantly shocked at how heavy it felt. He lowered it to his chest and tried to lift it back up.

What the hell? he thought. The weight was about half-way up when his arms started to shake.

Eric reached in and helped him push it back up.

Ricky sat up on the bench and looked at his friend, "I don't get it. That's a light weight for me."

Eric sat down on the bench beside Ricky. "I'm ot uh octor, Icky, but ore mind and ore ody are utting down."

Ricky looked at his feet.

"Icky?"

Ricky looked up.

"It's ime oo ate."

Ricky sighed. "We'll see."

●

The next morning, Eric sat in the Sharks' dressing room while Ricky finished lacing up his skates. Ricky was as nervous as that first day of tryouts with the Barrie Colts all those years ago. He kept looking over at Eric, who would smile at him awkwardly through his wired-up face and nod encouragingly. The Sharks, who were already trailing two games to none in their first-round playoff series against Calgary, were getting ready for a game-day skate. Most of the players said something positive when they realized that Ricky was suiting up.

As soon as the ice was ready, Ricky headed out and skated hesitantly around. He had the ice to himself and he moved around it cautiously, not at all like someone who had been on skates since he was barely more than a toddler.

Eventually, the rest of the team joined him, and he seemed to relax a bit. Guys skated by him and gave him friendly whacks on his shin pads with their sticks. When the coach took to the ice and blew his whistle, Ricky immediately went and sat on the bench. No one, other than Eric, seemed to notice. Eric came over and sat down beside him.

"Oo okay?"

Ricky nodded nervously. "Feels weird."

Eric patted him on the shoulder. "Ore oing rate."

Ricky tried to look positive. "Thanks."

As the skate wound down and the guys started leaving the ice, Eric called Tony Jamieson over and whispered something to him. Jamer nodded, then headed back out onto the ice. He did a lap of the rink before skating over to the bench.

"Hey, Ricky," he called. "Do you think you could shoot on me for a while? I need to work on my glove hand."

Ricky looked over at Eric, who was trying to act casually, but Ricky knew that he'd put Jamer up to this. Ricky was more than a little ticked off with Eric. He thought his friend was acting like an overly protective mother hen, but he also knew that it would be rude to not help Jamer out by shooting on him. Finally, he answered, "Sure, Jamer, no problem."

Ricky went out and lined up twenty pucks across the hash marks. "Where do you want them?" he asked.

"High glove side," Jamer answered.

Ricky nodded. He took a deep breath and cradled his first puck, aimed . . . and fanned. His first four shots never got off the ice. Pucks went everywhere—Jamer's pads, his chest, the glass—but not one hit the glove. Ricky tried to make light of it.

"Sorry, Jamer. I guess I'm a little rusty."

"No sweat, Ricky."

"Can we shoot another round?"

"Sure."

This time, Ricky found the target on thirteen or fourteen of the shots, but Jamer stopped each one easily.

As Ricky moved to collect the pucks, Jamer smiled. "That's better. I think the hands are coming back."

Ricky smiled. "Thanks. Can we shoot one more set?"

"Sure."

"Only this time can I shoot anywhere?"

"Sure."

"Jamer?"

"Yeah, Ricky?"

"Will you try your hardest?"

"Sure, Ricky."

Ricky lined up behind the first puck and took a deep breath. Then he blistered a snap shot low to the far corner. He beat Jamer cleanly and rattled it off the post with a loud *ping*.

I forgot what a beautiful sound that is, Ricky smiled to himself.

Three shots later, he put one past Jamer on the stick side. For the first time in two months, he started to relax. When he had five pucks left, he stopped and called out to Jamer. "The last five high to the glove, okay?"

Jamer nodded and got set.

Even though Jamer knew where Ricky was going to shoot, Ricky scored twice and hit the crossbar once.

Back at the bench, Eric smiled. Ricky still had the magic hands. All that was left now was to see if he still had the heart to play.

●

The Flames finished off the Sharks in four lopsided games, ending, mercifully, a bizarre season in San Jose. On the fateful night they took the ice in Toronto, they were in first place in the Western Conference, second overall, and were a legitimate Stanley Cup contender. Their season really ended that night. They lost their two best players, including the best player in the league, and they never recovered from the fallout from Charlie Davidson's death. They fell from first to eighth in the conference and barely scraped into the playoffs. They simply weren't prepared, mentally or physically, to play Calgary.

After Eric managed to cajole Ricky onto the ice, he skated with the team twice more. On the morning of game four, he even took part in some breakout drills and acted as a penalty killer so that the power play could work on maintaining possession of the puck. Eric couldn't be sure, but he thought he saw Ricky smile when he made a good outlet pass.

The day after the Sharks were eliminated, the players came to the rink and cleared out their stalls. They said their goodbyes and headed off to their summer homes scattered around the United States, Canada and various parts of Europe. Ricky and Eric flew back to Toronto together. As they got ready to disembark, Eric, who would be continuing to Halifax, was feeling very protective.

"Icky, do oo ant me to ay ith you for a ew ays?"

Ricky smiled at his friend. "I'm good, Eric. You go home and see your folks. I'll call you this week." Then, remembering the last time he said he'd call, he added, "I promise." Part of Ricky wanted Eric to get on the damn plane and head off to Halifax so that he'd stop coddling him so much. But there was another part of him that was completely terrified about spending the summer on his own. This had been an extremely difficult time, and Eric had proven himself to be an incredibly caring and loyal friend.

Eric smiled his goofy wired-jaw smile, then hugged his friend. "All me any ime, ay or ight, if oo eed me."

"Thanks, Eric." Ricky found he was getting misty-eyed. "For everything."

"Ore elcome. I'll ee oo at amp, right?" he asked nervously.

It was the one question that Ricky was hoping he wouldn't ask. He smiled and answered, as honestly as he could, "We'll see." Then he turned and walked quickly away before Eric could protest.

❦

Darryl and Haley greeted Ricky warmly as he walked through the doors that led from customs to the arrivals area. Several people noticed Ricky, and he suddenly found himself surrounded by autograph seekers. It always amazed Ricky that he was recognized more in the Canadian NHL cities than he was in San Jose. A middle-aged man waited patiently while Ricky signed the last few autographs, then introduced Ricky to his son. The boy couldn't have been more than five years old and he was wearing a San Jose Sharks T-shirt.

Ricky knelt down and said, "I hope that doesn't say 'Rollins' on the back."

The little boy smiled and turned around to show Ricky the name PHILLIPS emblazoned across his tiny shoulders above a large number 16.

Darryl obligingly took a picture of Ricky with the man and his son. As the Phillipses were walking away, the man thanked Ricky for his time and added, "Good luck next year, Ricky. Everyone's pulling for you."

❦

Ricky went home with his folks and stayed for three or four days in Oro. But he was getting bored and restless, so he decided to head up to Muskoka. The year before, Ricky had spent a million and a half dollars on a stunning log home on Lake Muskoka. He also bought a little ski boat, which he used to get from his cottage to the golf course, the grocery store and the local bar.

One of his most frequent companions in Muskoka was Chris Popovich, his old captain from his Barrie Colts days. Popo was living in Gravenhurst and making a good living selling insurance. Popo had been drafted by Detroit and played for five years in the American league, but never once got a sniff of the big time. Like a lot of guys who get close to The Show, he knew he could either keep trying to chase the dream or wake up and face reality. His heart wanted to keep up the chase, but his left knee was ready for reality. So at twenty-four, Popo hung up his skates. His family had a nice cottage on Lake Muskoka, and Popo moved in when he got the job in Gravenhurst. For a young guy, it was a good life. He worked his tail off in the winter because there wasn't much else to do. When summer—and the cottagers—returned, he would reduce his work schedule to one or two days a week. This allowed him more time to wakeboard and play golf.

Most mornings, Ricky would pull up to Popo's dock and they would head over to the golf course for eighteen holes. Most nights, Ricky would pull up to his dock and they would hit the local bar.

People in Muskoka are used to celebrities and they're used to money. A lot of hockey players from south central Ontario who made it to the NHL bought cottages in Muskoka. So did a few movie stars. The majority of the non-celebrities came from old, established Toronto families with lots of money. They were the people you'd see at Leaf games, in the lower bowl of the ACC, wearing the expensive suits. Therefore, when the boys went to the bar, the locals didn't fawn all over them. To the regulars, they were known simply as Ricky and

Popo. They could order a beer, shoot a game of pool or hit on pretty girls and no one made a fuss. It was when someone who wasn't a regular noticed Ricky that things could sometimes get interesting. Often, they were well-meaning, but slightly drunken guys who were about Ricky's age and wanted to talk hockey. They'd ask him if he remembered a certain goal or a hit from a game that he had long since forgotten. If one of them was taking up too much of Ricky's time, Popo would come over and start talking to the guy. Then he'd discreetly lead him over to the bar and buy him another drink. Invariably, the drunk would forget all about Ricky, and Popo and Ricky could carry on with their evening. Ricky was always sure to reimburse Popo for any costs he incurred to dispense with the drunks.

❀

This summer, the routine was different. Ricky still picked Popo up every morning for golf. In the afternoon, he went to the gym to work out. His strength was coming back: he was up to sets of ten with 250 pounds on the bench press. But it was his mental strength that still had a long way to go. Not once in the first two weeks that he was up north did he pick Popo up to go to the bar. He was quite content to sit in his giant cottage by himself and watch TV. Often, he would sit on the end of his dock and watch the sun set. When the bugs got too bad, he'd call it a night.

Popo was worried about his friend and thought he needed to get out and have some fun. He was a firm believer in the concept that chasing a pretty girl would cure just about any ailment. Eventually, after several days of being pushed by Popo, Ricky agreed to go to the bar. "Ricky, you live a nice life for an eighty-one-year-old guy. Only problem is that you're twenty-one. It's time that you got out and lived a little," Popo goaded.

That evening, Ricky pulled up to Popo's dock and his buddy jumped into the boat.

"This'll be good for you, Ricky," he smiled.

The boys went to the bar, drank some beers and shot some pool, and Ricky found he was actually having a good time. Many of the regulars smiled and welcomed him back. A few even mentioned Charlie and how sorry they were that Ricky had been involved in such an awful situation.

Ricky was relaxed, and he even laughed when Popo jumped the cue ball clean off of the table. Ricky turned to pick up the ball when he saw three twenty-something guys standing behind him. They were clearly drunk and looked to be in a foul mood. Ricky didn't recognize any of them.

The largest of the three stepped towards Ricky and sneered, "What kind of a place would allow a sucker-punching murderer to come in for a game of pool?"

Ricky was so shocked by the question, and the hatred radiating from the three men, that he simply stood there, dumbfounded.

The big guy shoved Ricky hard in the chest and snarled, "I asked you a question."

Before Ricky could react, Popo was beside him. He grinned wildly at the three men and said, "How ya doing, fellas?" Then, before anyone could answer, he swung his pool cue as hard as he could at the big guy. It dropped the goon like a large tree, and the sound of the cue cracking was enough to attract the attention of the bouncers.

They came flying over just as the other two guys were about to join the fray. Four bouncers grabbed them and slammed them up against a wall. A fifth bouncer looked at Popo and his broken pool cue and asked, "What happened?"

"They called Ricky a murderer," Popo answered.

The bouncer turned to his colleagues. "Get these losers out of here."

The three drunks were roughly shown the door.

Ricky finally gathered himself enough to tell the bouncer, "Thanks, guys. I'll pay for the pool cue and any other damages."

The bouncer smiled. "That won't be necessary, Ricky. But you and Popo might want to call it an early night. If the police come around later to investigate a complaint of a swinging pool cue, I'll tell them you guys were never here."

Driving back in the boat, Ricky tried to make light of the situation. "I guess being a regular has its privileges, eh?"

Popo laughed. "Ricky, all five of those bouncers play hockey with me in the winter. We were in good hands."

After Ricky dropped Popo off, he headed home and tied up his boat. By the time he got to his living room he was already shaking. He didn't know whether he was more upset about being called a murderer or the fact that Popo had reacted before he had—in fact, he'd never really reacted at all. He stared out at the water and watched the moon dance on the lake.

What's wrong with me? he wondered as the tears started to glide down his face. He wiped his face with the back of his hand and went over to his easy chair. He flopped down and tried to take his mind off of the three guys at the bar by watching some TV. He flipped through the channels until fatigue took over and he eventually fell asleep in his chair. He had spent many nights this summer all alone in this chair, with the glow of the television and his own haunted feelings as his only companions.

●

One of the happier moments of the summer was marked by the expiration of Ricky's rookie contract with the Sharks. When Ricky was eighteen, he had signed a three-year deal with San Jose for $850,000 a year. The contract had been loaded with bonuses, for achievements like winning rookie of the year, that put his income well above the million-dollar mark.

However, that was small potatoes compared to what he was now worth. In spite of his suspension, and the fact that his confidence had been severely rattled by the Charlie Davidson incident, Ricky was about to become a very rich young man. He and his agent flew to San Jose to meet with John Crichton. Crichton knew that Ricky was still very fragile emotionally, and he hoped that a generous contract extension would show him that the team still had tremendous confidence in him. Over dinner at San Jose's finest restaurant, Ricky placed his signature on a three-year extension worth twenty-four million dollars.

●

The rest of the summer passed uneventfully. Ricky's bench press got back up over three hundred pounds. He skated in Gravenhurst with the other local NHLers and was feeling pretty good about his play.

Eric came and spent two weeks at the cottage, and he and Popo managed to talk Ricky into going out again at night.

This time, they didn't encounter any drunks, and Ricky had a good time with his two friends.

Ricky's parents were frequent visitors to the cottage, and they were pleased with the improvements that they saw in his demeanour. Only Darryl seemed to remember that Ricky had been scheduled to shoot a commercial for McDonald's this summer. But after Charlie's death, McDonald's had cancelled its contract. Ricky's agent had had three other deals pending with large companies for endorsements. All three had pulled out.

As the summer wound down, Ricky's life seemed to be getting back on track. He was definitely stronger, both mentally and physically. He wasn't acting as reclusively. In social settings, he appeared to be more in tune with everyone around him. Conversations were holding his attention longer, and he wasn't spacing out and tuning people out as often. He even smiled and laughed occasionally. He appeared ready to report to the Sharks training camp. Of the people closest to Ricky, only his father still had reservations, but he kept his thoughts to himself.

After their last trip to the cottage, Darryl and Haley were returning to Oro-Medonte in their car. Darryl was unusually quiet.

"All right, let's have it," Haley said.

"Have what?"

"Whatever it is that has you brooding."

"I watched him play today, in Gravenhurst."

"Yeah?"

"I dunno. Something's missing from his game, but I can't tell what it is."

"Oh come on, Darryl," Haley protested. "It was just a pickup game."

"It was a pickup game with a bunch of pros. Those guys don't play half-hearted. The pace was incredible."

"And?"

"And . . . I don't know. It's not that he played badly. He just didn't stand out."

"I'm sure he'll be fine."

"Haley, six months ago he was the best player in the world. In that pickup game today, you wouldn't have been able to pick him out if you weren't watching for him. Hell, Popo played better and he's only got one knee."

Haley stared straight ahead at the oncoming headlights. "It was just a pickup game," she repeated.

Darryl didn't answer, but he was convinced something was wrong with Ricky's game.

CHAPTER THIRTEEN

Ron Lester sat in John Crichton's office and watched his boss pace back and forth. Crichton couldn't believe that it had been less than six months since he had been at the ACC and watched, like a proud parent, as the team that he had assembled completely outclassed the Toronto Maple Leafs. He had been certain that the Sharks were a legitimate threat to win the Stanley Cup. Then, suddenly, in the blink of an eye—or, more accurately, the throw of a punch—it had all come crashing down.

The team had completely disintegrated, which was understandable considering that they had lost their two best players. But now Crichton was desperately hoping that they would be able to start fresh and put the nightmare of last season behind them. Tomorrow night they were scheduled to play their first exhibition game of the new season. The game would undoubtedly answer a lot of questions about the strength of the team. Suddenly, Crichton stopped pacing and turned to face Lester.

"Have you spent any time with Ricky at camp?" he asked.

Lester laughed. "Spent time with him? Well, we haven't gone shopping or anything like that."

Crichton wasn't in the mood to be humoured. "Have you talked to him?" he asked dryly.

"Well," Lester replied, "I've tried to talk to him, but he's such a quiet kid, it's tough, you know?"

"Okay," Crichton tried again, "how does he seem to you otherwise?"

Lester thought for a minute before answering. "He seems okay. His strength tests were all good. He's in decent shape."

"Yeah, yeah," Crichton interrupted, "the kid's a beast. We all know that. Where's his head at?"

"It's really hard to tell," Lester answered.

Crichton faced the window and, with his back to Lester, said, "Ronnie, stop beating around the bush and tell me the truth."

Lester sighed. "Okay, John. In my opinion, the boy looks scared to death."

Crichton walked back to his desk and sat down. "Maybe he just needs to get back on the horse."

Lester nodded. "I guess we'll find out tomorrow."

●

Eric Rollins had just turned twenty-four, and it was obvious from his appearance that he had spent the summer on a rigorous workout regime. He weighed 207 pounds, five pounds more than last year, but his body fat was lower. He had used the layoff to add speed and strength to his game. He looked good and felt good and, since he'd had the wires taken off his jaw, he never shut up. Eric was the happiest, most upbeat guy in camp.

Ricky Phillips, on the other hand, was a different story.

Last year, as a twenty-one-year-old, he'd been the unofficial leader of the team. There was even talk of making him the captain. This year, he was extremely quiet. He rarely spoke to anyone other than Eric, and if someone asked him a question, he'd often look to Eric for some sort of approval before answering.

The Sharks opened the exhibition season on the road in Los Angeles. They played well and won 3–1. Eric had a strong game, but Ricky seemed unable to get him the puck. To make matters worse, the fans let Ricky know they were not about to forget the Charlie Davidson incident. It was a sparse crowd at the Staples Center, par for the course for an exhibition game, but every time Ricky touched the puck he was booed loudly. Ricky tried to make light of it after the game when he talked to a reporter. He muttered something about it being a compliment to be booed on the road. What he didn't tell the reporter was that he had really been unnerved by the booing. Eric watched Ricky talk to the reporter out of the corner of his eye. He wasn't sure that the reporter believed Ricky's answer. He was, however, certain that Ricky didn't believe himself.

The next morning, as the players suited up for another workout, Crichton and Lester met again in the GM's office. Until the game in Toronto, Crichton's tenure as GM of the Sharks had been very smooth. The first move he'd made had been to hire Ron Lester as coach. The second had been to pull off the blockbuster trade with Florida so that he could draft Ricky. So far, every decision he had made had helped improve the hockey team. However, he was starting to get extremely worried about his star player.

"So, what did you think about last night?" Crichton asked Lester.

"I thought we played pretty well, you know, for the first game and all," Lester answered.

"I don't give a damn about the rest of the team. I know they played well. What'd you think of Ricky?"

"Honestly?"

"Honestly."

"I thought he stunk."

Crichton let out a deep sigh. "Me too."

Lester smiled at his old friend. "Come on, Johnny, it was his first game in six months. I'm sure he'll be fine."

Crichton stared off into space, deep in thought. "I hope you're right."

●

Ricky continued to stumble through the exhibition season. The team, meanwhile, seemed poised to have a very successful season. Eric was emerging as the team's leader and best player. If he was frustrated by Ricky's play, he never let on. When they were at the rink, Eric was always professional. At night, when they were alone together in the apartment, he kept things upbeat and positive. In fact, when the boys were away from the rink, Eric did his best to keep Ricky's attention away from hockey.

When the preseason ended, Ricky had no goals, no assists, no penalty minutes. He was plus-three, but that was due more to Eric's play than to his own. During road games, he continued to be booed every time he touched the puck. The home fans, to their credit, tried too hard to make things right for Ricky. At the HP Pavilion he was cheered heartily each time he stepped on the ice and whenever he had the puck. Eric wasn't sure whether the overly exuberant cheering was worse than the booing, but he knew that both were bothering Ricky.

The day before the Sharks were to open the regular season, Coach Lester finished up his meetings with each player. His last two were with Eric and Ricky.

Eric entered the coach's office and sat down confidently. Lester got right down to business. "How's your jaw?"

"Good, Coach."

"Any headaches?"

"None."

"How'd you feel you played in the preseason?"

"I thought I played well," Eric replied.

Lester studied his star player. "Yeah, you look stronger than last season."

"Thanks, Coach."

Lester continued to study Eric's face. Time to liven this meeting up, he thought to himself. "How's Ricky doing?"

Eric knew the question would come sooner or later, and he tried not to sound too rehearsed. "He's good, Coach."

Lester jumped on that. "Good? He's done nothing the entire preseason."

"Well, yeah," Eric stammered, "but it'll come."

"Eric, this is a business we're running here. I've got to put the best players on the ice that I—"

Eric cut him off. "Ricky Phillips is the best player. In fact," he continued, his voice increasing in volume, "he's the best player in this league."

Lester knew that Eric was getting upset, and he paused for a moment while he decided how to defuse the situation. "Listen, Eric. Ricky *was* the best player in the league, but he certainly isn't right now. At the moment, you're my best player, and I need a centreman who can get you the puck."

Eric looked shocked. "What are you saying, Coach?"

"I'm saying that if Ricky doesn't get his game together fast, I'm going to move him off of your line."

"Oh, Coach, give him a chance," Eric pleaded. "He'll come around."

"Eric, this is professional hockey, and Ricky's being paid a lot of money to produce. If he can't do it, I'll find someone who can."

Eric stood up and headed towards the door. "He'll come around. You'll see."

Lester smiled. "I hope you're right. Can you send him in, please?"

Eric walked out into the hall and found Ricky sitting nervously in a chair. Ricky brightened when he saw Eric. "How'd it go?" he asked.

"It went okay," Eric replied. Then a thought occurred to him. "Ricky?"

"Yeah?"

"How do you think you're playing?"

Ricky looked at the floor. "Not very well."

"Well, you need to show some confidence when you go into that meeting. Tell Coach that you feel that your game is coming around."

Ricky didn't think his game was remotely close to "coming around," but he smiled bravely at Eric. "Okay," he said. Then he knocked on the coach's door.

❂

Ron Lester's demeanour changed completely when Ricky walked into his office. He was mad at himself for being too open with Eric. He hadn't meant to dump all of that on the kid, but he guessed, deep down, that he was hoping that Eric might get through to Ricky. Lester had kids of his own who weren't much younger than Ricky, and he now decided to take a gentle but firm, fatherly approach with the troubled star.

He smiled and pointed to a chair.

He watched as Ricky sat down timidly and thought to himself, This kid isn't even close to being a hundred percent.

"How ya doing, Ricky?" Lester asked.

"I'm good, Coach."

Suddenly, Lester didn't know what to say. It was kind of like when you go to pay your respects to someone at a funeral parlour. Do you make small talk? Or do you get right to the point and tell them that you're sorry for their loss?

So, Ricky, he thought, when are you going to get your head out of your ass and play some hockey? Lester smiled to himself at his private joke, and Ricky seemed to relax a bit too.

It was Ricky who broke the silence. "Listen, Coach, I know I didn't have the best preseason, but I think my game is starting to come around."

Neither man in the room believed that statement, but Lester answered, "That's great, Ricky."

Ricky smiled and waited patiently for the next question.

Lester wasn't sure how hard he wanted to push the kid, so he ventured cautiously, "You know, Ricky, when the regular season gets going, we're going to need you to . . ." he paused, searching for the right way to phrase his thoughts.

"Get my head out of my ass?" Ricky asked.

Lester laughed. "Yeah, you just read my mind." Then he added, "Do you think you can step up your game?"

Ricky looked at the floor. "I hope so."

"It's just that, well, you've always been our best player. I'm just hoping that you can get back to before . . . well, you know."

"Before the night I killed Charlie Davidson?" Ricky asked.

Lester smiled sadly. "Yeah, Ricky. Before the game in Toronto. I'm sure many people have told you this, but you know that what happened to Charlie wasn't your fault, right?"

Ricky looked up at his coach. "Maybe it wasn't my fault, but it doesn't change what happened."

"No, it doesn't." Ron Lester didn't want to sound callous, but he did want Ricky to understand the situation. "Ricky?"

Ricky looked back at him. "Yeah?"

"Life goes on, son. You need to get on with your life. I need you to play hockey. Your teammates need you. You're the best player in this league. Show everyone that Ricky Phillips is back."

Ricky stood up and tried to smile. "I'll do my best, Coach." Then he turned and left the office.

Lester watched him leave and thought to himself that it would take nothing short of a miracle to get Ricky back on track.

CHAPTER FOURTEEN

The San Jose Sharks opened the regular season with three games at home. It was a nice way to begin, especially after they won all three. Eric led the way with four goals and two assists, which temporarily helped to end the discussion of moving Ricky off of his line. Ricky even managed to pick up an assist on one of Eric's goals when he dumped the puck on net and the goalie mishandled it. Eric arrived out of nowhere and buried the rebound.

The San Jose fans were great to the team, and especially to Ricky. When his name was announced over the PA for his assist, he got a louder cheer than Eric did for scoring the goal.

San Jose's next four games were to be played on the road. First, they flew into Detroit to play the mighty Red Wings, who had also started out 3–0. The game was fast paced and entertaining and was decided in a shootout, which Detroit won. Detroit has a very knowledgeable fan base, and their treatment of Ricky was surprisingly good compared with what he'd faced during the preseason. Maybe it was because of Detroit's proximity to Toronto—where, ironically, fan support for Ricky was at its highest level outside of San Jose. The Wings' fans booed him, but they booed Eric, too, and only when San Jose was on the power play and looked as though they might score. In spite of the loss, Ricky felt good about the game.

After the game, the team boarded a chartered bus and made the short drive down to Columbus, Ohio, where they were scheduled to play the Blue Jackets the next night. Ricky sat at the back of the bus and took part in a poker game. He laughed at the banter and could feel himself slowly beginning to unwind.

When the Sharks took the ice in Columbus for their pre-game warmup, they were feeling loose and confident. Some of the guys lined up near the bench and did some stretching, while other guys skated in circles and fired pucks at the net. Hockey players are taught at an early age to ignore the crowd and concentrate on what is happening on the ice. That's why it took a while before anyone noticed the little boy who was standing in the first row of seats, just to the left of the Sharks' net. He couldn't have been more than nine or ten, and he was wearing a Blue Jackets jersey and ball cap. He would have blended into the crowd except for the sign that he was holding proudly over his head. There, for the whole arena to see, in giant block letters, was the word MURDERER.

Tony Jamieson, the Sharks' backup goalie, was the first to notice it. He'd been taking shots in the net, and when he was finished he peeled out so that Marcus Johannsen, the starting goalie, could warm up. As he skated towards the corner of the rink, he looked up, and there was the sign staring him right in the face.

Oh crap, Jamer thought. He turned around to face the ice surface and tried to put his back to the boards to block the sign. The kid thought this was funny, and he moved slowly back and forth. Since he could see Jamer but Jamer couldn't see him, the kid always had the upper hand. Jamer reacted by doing a series of exaggerated stretches with his arms in an effort to block the sign with his goalie stick. Goalies have always been considered eccentric by their teammates. After all, what kind of person would willingly stand in front of a vulcanized piece of rubber that is shot at you at speeds of up to a hundred miles an hour while rather large men try to obstruct your view of the puck and invariably end up falling, sometimes accidentally and sometimes on purpose, on top of you? Therefore, Jamer's unusual warmup didn't warrant any special attention from his teammates.

When Marcus's turn in the net was over, he skated over to Jamer. When Jamieson didn't return to the net, Marcus said, "Hey, Jamer. Your turn."

"Look behind me," Jamer said.

Marcus looked up and cursed. Then he added, "Man, that is totally crossing the line.

"Don't worry," he told his backup. "I'll handle this."

He took his goalie stick and swung it hard against the glass. "Hey, you little shit! Take down that sign!"

Plexiglass is extremely soundproof, so while every Shark on the ice could hear Marcus's outburst, the little boy didn't. He was, however, amused by the reaction of the two goalies and continued to wave his sign.

Jamer shoved Marcus and said, "Way to go, genius. I was trying to be subtle. I didn't want Ricky to see."

Realization dawned on Marcus. "Oh, right. Sorry, Jamer."

By now, Ricky and every other player on the Sharks was skating into the corner to see what was bothering the two goaltenders. When Ricky saw the sign, he could feel the wind leave his lungs. He had to fight to catch his breath. He tried to tell his teammates not to worry about it, but he was already shaking and found that he couldn't speak.

The guys started banging their sticks on the glass and cursing the kid, who gamely went on holding his sign. Once again, Eric took charge. He spun and looked up at the game clock. Then he yelled out so he'd be heard: "Boys, there's only three minutes left in the warmup. Let's go to the dressing room."

The team turned and followed Eric to the room. Eric stormed into the tunnel looking for Ron Lester and spotted him standing outside the dressing room, reviewing his lineup card.

"Coach!" Eric yelled. "I need to talk to you!"

Lester knew something was wrong when he saw the entire team standing behind Eric. He motioned into the room with his head. When they were all in the room, Lester ordered the trainers and support staff to leave. Then he closed the door and turned to Eric. "What's up?"

"Some little kid's standing behind our net and he's holding up a giant sign."

Lester didn't get it. "So?"

"So, it says 'MURDERER' in giant letters," Eric answered.

"You've got to be kidding," Lester groaned.

"It's completely crossing the line!" Jamer yelled.

Eighteen guys joined the fray with various comments and curses. Only Ricky was silent. He was now shaking noticeably as he tried his hardest to keep his emotions in check.

Lester went to the dressing room door and called to one of the trainers. "Donnie!"

Donnie came running over. "Yeah, Coach?"

"Get me the head of arena security. Tell him we don't play until I talk to him."

Donnie disappeared down the tunnel.

Lester returned to the room. The boys were really upset and he needed to get them back on track. He looked around the room, and his eyes fell on Ricky.

"Ricky, you okay?"

Ricky looked up and tried to smile, but every guy in the room could see him shaking. "I'm okay, Coach," he answered quietly.

"He's not okay, Coach," Eric interrupted. "This is bullshit."

"I got it, Eric," Lester said, cutting him off. His eyes never left Ricky. "Let's just wait for security."

A few minutes later, two burly men in blue suits knocked on the door. The larger of the two approached Lester. "Is there a problem, Coach?"

"Yes, there is," Lester answered. "There's a kid standing behind our net holding up a sign that says 'MURDERER.'"

"Uh-huh?" the guard grunted.

"Well, we think that it's way over the line, and we want that sign gone."

The guard sighed. He clearly wasn't thrilled about the prospect of going out and having a confrontation with a little kid in front of eighteen thousand people. "Are you sure about that, Coach?"

Lester nodded his head. "If that sign doesn't go, we don't play."

Slowly, the guard turned towards the door. "Okay, Coach. We'll get rid of your sign."

As the dressing room door closed behind the security guards, Lester muttered to himself, "It's not *my* sign, asshole."

The two guards headed over to the section where the boy with the sign was sitting, quietly watching the Zamboni resurface the ice. The guards approached the boy and his father and asked quietly if they could have his sign. Other patrons in the area noticed and started yelling at them to leave the kid alone. The commotion caught the eye of one of the cameramen, and suddenly the entire scene was being played out on the video screens at centre ice. Eighteen thousand people began to boo as the guards slunk sheepishly away with the little kid's sign. A few minutes later, the boy's image was once again flashed on the screens, and the crowd cheered him as if he were a superstar forward.

Meanwhile, back in the visitors' dressing room, the Sharks could hear the crowd booing. Jamer leaned over to Marcus and whispered, "That doesn't sound good."

Donnie opened the door to the room and stuck his head in. "Thirty seconds, Coach."

Lester nodded and took a deep breath. "Okay boys, listen up. This wasn't exactly the way we wanted to start, but let's put all this crap behind us and get ready to play hockey."

There was a slight murmur of assent from the players, but they were definitely rattled by their bizarre warmup. Jamer sensed it and tried to rally the troops. "Let's go boys!" he yelled. The team jumped up and headed for the ice. Instantly, they were greeted by a loud symphony of boos, and the ice in the Sharks' end was quickly littered with garbage that came raining down from the stands. Marcus had to hunker down just inside his net to avoid the flying debris. The opening face-off was delayed for several minutes while the arena staff came out to clean up the mess.

Once the game was underway, the Sharks fought gamely but were clearly thrown off by the kid, his sign, the booing fans and Columbus's aggressive forecheck. The Blue Jackets won 4–0. Neither Ricky nor Eric was a factor in the game.

Not since that famous incident at Yankee Stadium in 1996, when a twelve-year-old boy interfered with a fly ball to right field during a playoff game, had a professional sports game been as dramatically affected by a young child. The Sharks were quite relieved to leave Columbus behind and head to Nashville for their next game, against the Predators.

Later that night, Darryl Phillips was lying in his bed, watching the sports highlights. He was trying to find the right volume so that the TV could be heard over Haley's snoring when suddenly the anchorman said, "And now to tonight's game between the Sharks and Blue Jackets . . ."

Darryl was just about to shake Haley awake, but something made him stop. The host laughed as footage rolled of a scrum in the stands. "This was the scene just after the Sharks got off the ice after warmup. Apparently, a young fan had a sign at the game that was less than complimentary towards Ricky Phillips."

The video then showed the arena crew cleaning up the ice. "This is the welcome that greeted the Sharks as they took to the ice," he relayed happily. He never did show any highlights of the actual game. He concluded by looking at the camera and joking, "Apparently, the fans of Columbus just weren't feeling the love for ol' Ricky tonight."

Darryl quietly turned off the TV and tried not to wake up Haley. He stared up at the ceiling and knew that sleep would not come easily tonight. He realized with a sudden clarity that his son's problems were not going to just go away with time. He had never felt sorrier for anyone than he did right now for Ricky.

●

The Sharks' mini road trip ended with a swing through Nashville and Colorado. They beat the Predators and lost to the Avalanche to end up with three points in the four games. Although they didn't encounter any more kids holding MURDERER signs, the treatment Ricky got didn't improve much. He was booed relentlessly every time he touched the puck, and much of the mainstream media continued to cast him as the villain.

The Sharks won their next three games in San Jose to remain undefeated at home. After ten games, they were an impressive 7–2–1. Eric was leading the team—and the league— in scoring, which was amazing considering his injuries last year and the fact that his centreman had only one point.

Ricky's lone assist had not been lost on Lester and Crichton. One morning before practice, the two men met in Crichton's office to discuss the team's progress. They were pleased with the team's record and thrilled with Eric's play. They discussed a few trivial details such as which one of the seven defencemen would be a healthy scratch for the next game and how they would set up their forecheck for the Calgary game as opposed to the Edmonton game. But both men avoided the real reason for their meeting.

Finally, Crichton got to the point. "Ronnie," he said, "what are we going to do with Ricky?"

Lester had spent ten games worrying about Ricky. Secretly, he really liked the kid and felt sorry for him. Hell, he thought, I've been in thousands of fights myself and I never hurt anyone. He was hoping that if he bought Ricky some time, the centreman might rediscover his game.

"Johnny," Lester started hesitantly, "we're seven, two and one."

Crichton wasn't in the mood to be placated. "Oh, come on, Ronnie. He has one point!"

"I know, but Eric—"

Crichton cut him off. "Eric's leading the damn league in scoring with a centreman who can't get him the puck."

Lester took a deep breath and continued. "What I was trying to say is I'm worried that if we move Ricky, Eric's production will fall off. He's like a big brother to the kid."

"If it happens, then we'll move him back," Crichton said. "Ronnie, be realistic. He has one point and no penalties in ten games. He's a non-factor."

"I was hoping he'd rediscover his game," Lester said sadly.

Crichton laughed bitterly. "You don't think I wasn't? I'm the guy that traded to bring him here. He's had three years to develop. He's just getting to the age where he could completely dominate this league and bring us a championship, and now his mind has gone for a shit."

Lester didn't answer, so Crichton continued. "You know what the difference between me and you is, Ronnie?"

"You were an all-star and I was a plugger?"

Crichton laughed. "Well, that too. But the difference between us is where we draw the line between loyalty and doing a job. You would place loyalty ahead of doing the job. That's why you're a coach and I'm a GM. I know you want Ricky to succeed; so do I. But it's obvious to me that he's lost his game. Until he finds it, something has to be done. I like Ricky, too, but I place the job ahead of loyalty."

Lester felt like he was defending his own son. "I really don't want to move him," he said.

"Okay," Crichton said. "Let me give you another example of the differences between you and me. Don't think for a second that I wouldn't fire you if I thought that it would help the team."

"Wh-wh-wh—" Lester stammered.

"Relax," Crichton smiled. "We're seven, two and one. You said so yourself. Your job is safe." He paused before adding, with a laugh, "For now."

Lester continued to fidget in his chair. Remind me never to become a GM, he thought.

"Did you watch the sports news last night, Ronnie?" Crichton asked.

Now Lester was completely confused. "Ah, yeah, I watched it."

"Did you see the bit with me on it?"

Lester thought back. "Yeah, some reporter asking you if there was any truth to the rumour that Ricky was on the trade block."

"That's the one," Crichton said. "And here's the part where I'll fire you."

Lester raised his eyebrows but didn't say anything.

Crichton continued: "If you breathe a word of this to anyone, you're gone."

Lester stared steadily at Crichton. "Well, you know me, boss. I'm loyal, right?"

"That's what I'm counting on," Crichton said. "Anyway, here's the truth. This reporter asks me if there's any truth to the rumour of a trade involving Ricky, right?"

"Right."

"I flatly denied it, right?"

"Right."

"Well, the truth is I shopped Ricky to every GM in the league last week. I asked them to be discreet, but obviously the word leaked out somewhere. You know how many teams responded?"

"How many?" Lester asked.

"Four. Four teams out of twenty-nine. The best offer I got was a fourth-line centre and a third-round pick." Crichton shook his head as if he still couldn't believe it. "The consensus around the league is that he's finished. So here's the deal, Ronnie. I can't trade a former Hart Trophy winner, the league's most valuable player, for a fourth-liner and a pick, so I'm asking you, as a friend, to move him to the third or fourth line. If you won't do that, then my only option will be to send him to Worcester. So, what do you say?"

"I guess I don't have any choice, do I?" Lester asked.

Crichton sighed. "No, Ronnie, you don't."

❂

Coach Lester called Ricky and Eric into his office before the team's eleventh game of the season. Eric was pretty sure he knew what was coming, but Ricky appeared to be oblivious.

Lester wasn't happy about having to make the change, and he tried his best to soften the blow for Ricky. "Boys," he started, "we've got a tough stretch of games coming up, and I think we need to make some changes."

"What kind of changes?" Eric asked.

"Well, Eric, I think we need to change the lines."

"Why?" the winger snorted.

"Come on, Eric. I think you know why."

"I do? We're seven, two and one and we're gonna shuffle lines?"

Lester could feel himself getting heated. This was a dirty job and Eric was definitely not making it any easier. "Eric, you have twenty points, Pierre Cartier has fifteen."

"Yeah, and that's good balance on the top two lines," Eric argued.

"Well, you know what, Eric? I'm the coach and I'm making the change."

"This is bullshit, Coach, and you know it!" Eric yelled.

"Eric." Eric and Lester were surprised to hear Ricky's voice. They had both forgotten that he was in the room.

"It's okay," he said. "I've had one point in ten games." He looked at Lester. "Where do you want me to play?"

God, I love this kid, the coach thought. "I'd like to try you with Bobby and Jacko," he said.

"Okay," Ricky answered. Then he turned to Eric. "Everybody knows that I'm struggling, but you and Pierre will be great."

Eric mussed Ricky's hair like a big brother would do. "So you're okay with this?"

Ricky nodded his head.

Eric smiled. "Okay. Make sure you go out and work hard tonight."

●

The change in lines had an instant effect on the team. Eric and Pierre clicked almost instantly and the Sharks improved what was already a frightening offence. Ricky was reduced to a third-line checker, and he did well at his new role. The Sharks rolled off five wins in a row to start the month of November. Ricky didn't muster any more points, but in the five games his line was plus three. As a shutdown line, they were doing well.

Partway through November, something unusual happened. Late in a tight-checking game against Vancouver, Ricky curled into the corner of his own end. One of the defencemen hit him with a pass and he took off out of his own end. He seemed to find another gear as he tore through the neutral zone and blew past the Canucks' defenceman. He cut hard for the net and buried a wrist shot high to the glove side that sent the water bottle flying.

His teammates mugged him behind the net; most of them seemed happier for him than he was himself. As he sat down on the bench, Coach Lester patted him on the back and asked, "Where the hell did that come from?"

Ricky looked at him and said, "I have no idea."

Lester realized from the look on the kid's face that, unfortunately, he wasn't kidding. The goal stood up as the winner and the Sharks continued to roll.

The Sharks played thirteen games in the month of November, and Ricky continued to play an effective role as a checker. Every once in a while he would show flashes of his former brilliance, but they were few and far between. After twenty games, Ricky had three goals and four assists and was plus-seven. However, every guy on the team was a plus. It would have been hard not to be when the team was 15–3–2.

Every time Ricky showed a moment of greatness, Lester hoped it would trigger something inside him so that he could get his old game back. However, they always appeared to be isolated incidences. Ricky would have a brilliant rush one shift, then be cautious and timid the next. As Christmas approached, Lester decided that reuniting Ricky with Eric might help spark his game, and he decided to use Ricky on the power play with Eric and Pierro. The opportunity came partway through December, when the Sharks took the ice at the HP Pavilion for a home game against the New York Rangers. It was the thirty-first game of the year, and the Sharks were running away with the Western Conference with an awesome record of 21–6–3. The Rangers were a young, aggressive team in the middle of a hotly contested Eastern Conference.

The game started out like many of the Sharks' games that year—fast-paced and entertaining—and by the end of the second period the Sharks were ahead 3–1. Early in the third period, the Sharks were buzzing in New York's end and their relentless forecheck led to a Ranger penalty.

Lester decided that now was the time to put Ricky back out with Eric. "Pierre! You and Eric!" Lester yelled. Pierre and Eric jumped the boards and headed out into New York's end.

Then, Lester called Ricky's name. Ricky looked up from his place on the bench. "Yeah, Coach?"

"Go play the right side for Pierre."

Ricky started to protest: "Coach, I haven't played right wing since junior."

Lester cut him off. "Just set up on the half-boards and cut to the net when the opportunity's there. Now go!"

Eric smiled when he saw Ricky come out onto the ice. Ricky lined up on Pierre's right side and got ready for the face-off to the right of the Ranger goalie. The linesman blew his whistle, and Pierre got ready to take the draw against

Sean Jacobs, the Rangers' best player—and their dirtiest. Sean was the type of player who enjoyed knocking the other team off their game; he proudly called himself an "agitator." This was the new name for what players referred to twenty years before as "rats." Anyone who has ever played hockey knows a rat. He's the guy who's all talk during a scrum, especially when the linesmen are there to break up the fights, but who will rarely fight fair or face to face.

The linesman dropped the puck, and Pierre and Sean tied each other up. Ricky instinctively hustled into the circle and chipped the puck back to a defenceman. He then continued through the circle and set up on the half-wall. The Sharks' defencemen played catch for a few seconds, giving Eric enough time to go down along the boards and Pierre to set up just to the right of the Rangers' net.

The Sharks made a series of quick, crisp passes that really got the Rangers' penalty killers spread out. The puck came to Ricky on the half-wall, and he fed a quick pass to Eric. He blistered a pass through the Rangers' box right to Pierre, who rifled a quick shot on goal. The goalie made a terrific save, but by now the Rangers' box had completely broken down.

Eric grabbed the rebound and fed a cross-ice pass back to the right D. The Rangers tried to adjust, but all four of them reacted to the pass. The Sharks defenceman passed back across the ice to Ricky, who was now wide open at the top of the left face-off circle.

Ricky took the pass and bolted for the net. He fired a low, hard shot on net and continued to the net to look for a rebound. The goalie made a nice save, but his rebound went right to Pierre, who banged home the loose puck. Ricky was just about to raise his stick to celebrate the goal when he was cross-checked hard from behind by one of the Ranger defencemen. The goal celebration quickly turned into a scrum as Ricky's teammates came to his defence.

Pierre slashed the Ranger defenceman across the shins. "Nice cheap shot, asshole."

The defenceman slashed him back. "Piss off, Cartier."

That was all Pierre needed, and he and the Ranger D dropped their gloves and went at it. The Sharks' two defencemen were happy to join the scrum, and they quickly paired off with two other Rangers.

Meanwhile, Ricky was face down on the ice, still smarting from the cross-check. Being hit from behind when you don't expect it is not unlike being in a car accident. Your body is propelled forward and your head snaps backward. The cross-check had been hard enough to knock the wind out of him, and he was still trying to catch his breath as he pulled himself up to his hands and knees. Eric saw that Ricky was hurt and skated towards him. Ricky turned his head to look at Eric when Sean Jacobs skated up behind Eric and shoved him hard from behind. Eric turned around, and Sean drilled him with a hard sucker punch right on the jaw. The punch staggered Eric, and Sean hit him a second time before Eric had had a chance to regain his wits and fight back.

You cheap-shot bastard! Eric thought as he dropped his gloves and grabbed hold of Sean. Not only was he angry at the sneak attack, but he was scared that he might have reinjured his jaw. He pulled back his right hand and hammered Sean square in the face.

By now, Ricky was resting with his left skate on the ice and his right knee on the ice. He was leaning on his stick and watching the various fights in front of him. As he watched

Sean hit Eric with another right hand, something inside him snapped. A morbid series of snapshots played before his eyes: Eric going face-first into the glass; a right hand hammering Charlie Davidson in the face; a pile of players falling on top of him; running down the hallway of the Air Canada Centre; the waiting room at the Toronto General Hospital; meeting Julie; three angry guys filled with hatred and holding pool cues; a little boy holding a sign that read MURDERER.

He was so confused. He didn't think they were playing Toronto tonight, but everyone seemed to be wearing Leaf jerseys. He looked to his left and saw the linesman separating Pierre from another player. That's strange, he thought. Why would the Leafs be wearing Ranger jerseys?

He looked around for Charlie, but he couldn't find him. I need to find Charlie, he thought to himself.

As the fights lost their momentum and were broken up by the linesmen, Ron Lester finally noticed that Ricky was still down, in the "take a knee" position that players use when resting while listening to a coach's instructions. Lester assumed he was hurt. Why else wouldn't he get up?

Lester called down the bench. "Donnie!"

"Yeah, Coach?"

"I think Ricky's hurt. You better go see."

"Got it." Donnie hustled across the ice to check on Ricky. When he got there, he dropped to his knees and put his arm on Ricky's back. "You okay, buddy?" he asked.

Without looking at Donnie, Ricky answered, "Eric's hurt bad."

"What?" Donnie turned in time to see the linesmen breaking up Eric's fight with Sean. Eric was cursing at Sean something awful and calling him a gutless cheap-shot artist.

Donnie laughed and turned back to Ricky. "Well, he seems okay to me." It was then that he realized that Ricky wasn't even looking at Eric.

"Eric's hurt bad," he repeated.

"He is?" Donnie asked. "What happened?"

"Charlie Davidson hit him from behind. He went face-first into the glass."

Oh shit, Donnie thought. "Okay, Ricky, you just hang on." With his left hand, Donnie traced an imaginary circle above his head. This was the signal to the bench to summon the team doctor, a local general practitioner who offered his services to the team in exchange for front-row seats. In three years, he'd never once had to go out onto the ice to help a player. As he walked across the ice, it seemed to him that Ricky didn't appear to be hurt.

"What's going on, Donnie?" he asked when he got there.

"I don't know, Doc. But something's not right," Donnie answered. "Ricky? Doc's here."

Ricky didn't acknowledge the two men. He stared at the boards, where something appeared to be holding his attention. "I need to find Charlie," he said.

"Charlie?" Dr. Welch asked.

"Charlie Davidson," Donnie told him.

"Oh boy," Doc responded. "Ricky, can you hear me?"

"Eric's hurt bad," Ricky muttered.

"Donnie, go get some players to help get him off the ice," Doc commanded.

Donnie turned and bolted for the bench.

"Ricky, can you hear me?" Doc asked again.

"What kind of place would allow a sucker-punching murderer to play a game of pool?" Ricky asked.

"I'm not sure," the doctor answered.

Donnie returned with two players, who stood by nervously waiting for instructions.

"We need to try to get him off the ice," Dr. Welch told them. Then he turned to Ricky and said, "Let's go, Ricky. We need to get off the ice."

"I need to see Charlie," Ricky answered.

"Okay, these guys will help you," Doc answered.

Ricky's teammates managed to get him to his feet and started directing him back to the bench. The crowd, which had fallen silent when Ricky was down, burst into applause.

Lester met him at the door to the players' bench. "You okay, Ricky?" he asked.

"I need to see Charlie," Ricky answered, then stumbled past Lester and down the hall to the dressing room.

Dr. Welch's eyes met Lester's as he hustled to keep up with Ricky. The look on his face told Lester all he needed to know. The coach knew he needed to concentrate on the game, but he wanted to bolt back to the dressing room to check on Ricky.

"Damn," he muttered to himself.

CHAPTER FIFTEEN

John Crichton sat in his private box at the HP Pavilion and watched the brawl unfold before him. As cooler heads eventually prevailed and things seemed to be getting back to normal, he noticed Donnie Lawson hustling across the ice. He leaned over the edge of the box and strained to see who it was that Donnie was rushing to attend to. When he realized that it was Ricky, he stood up and nervously jammed his hands into his pockets. He waited anxiously to see how seriously Ricky appeared to be injured. When he saw Dr. Welch making his way out onto the ice, he turned and ran down the hall towards the elevators. The doors opened and an elderly attendant smiled at him.

"Good evening, Mr Crichton."

"Dressing room!" Crichton snarled.

"Yes, sir," the attendant stammered and pressed the down button.

The doors opened and Crichton rushed towards the dressing room. What greeted him was a scene of pure chaos as half the team's support staff and the team doctor chased Ricky through the hallways of the arena and tried to calm him down while Ricky babbled something about needing to talk to Big Joe.

As Ricky ran past him like a delirious pied piper with his bewildered band of followers, Crichton grabbed Donnie and demanded to know, "What the hell is going on?"

"I have no idea, sir," Donnie replied. "Something is seriously wrong with Ricky, though."

"Who's Big Joe?" Crichton asked.

"The only Big Joe I know is the trainer for the Leafs," Donnie answered.

Realization dawned on Crichton. Oh no, he thought.

By now, Ricky had made it to the end of the hallway and was on his way back towards Crichton. "Big Joe said he was going to be okay! I want to talk to Big Joe!" he wailed.

"Hey, Ricky," Crichton called out. "I know where Big Joe is."

Ricky paused for a moment and looked around, not really seeming to see anything.

"Yeah," Crichton added. "He's in here. Follow me." Crichton turned and headed for San Jose's dressing room. As he did, he grabbed Donnie and dragged him along by the arm. "Your name's Big Joe," he muttered.

"What?" Donnie asked.

"Your name's Big Joe. All you've got to do is talk to him and calm him down."

Donnie didn't feel too sure about this idea, but he nodded and followed Crichton and Dr. Welch into the room.

Ricky came crashing into the room behind them. "I need to talk to Big Joe."

Crichton looked at Donnie and nodded. Donnie cleared his throat. "Hi Ricky. Are you okay?"

"Big Joe!" Ricky sounded relieved. "I came to see how Charlie's doing. Stu Porter met me at the door. I thought he was going to kill me." He laughed nervously.

Donnie looked at Crichton and shrugged his shoulders. Crichton glared at him. "Uh, yeah, Ricky, that Porter sure is a feisty one."

"He sure is," Ricky agreed. Suddenly, Ricky sat down on the bench. He appeared to be slowing down, but he was still very agitated. Crichton could see his right leg bouncing up and down like a jack hammer. "So Joe, is Charlie going to be okay? It didn't look good when they brought him off the ice."

Donnie wasn't sure how far he should continue this bizarre charade. He looked over at Dr. Welch, and their eyes met. Welch very slowly and clearly mouthed the words, "Tell him the truth."

"Uh, Ricky, Charlie's dead. He's been dead for several months now. You're in San Jose right now. We're playing the Rangers tonight."

Ricky's shoulders slumped and he leaned back against the wall. "I didn't mean to kill him."

"I know you didn't," Donnie answered.

The dressing room door opened quietly and two paramedics entered with a gurney.

"Ricky?" Donnie said.

"Yeah, Big Joe?"

"These guys are here to help you. They're going to take you to the hospital, okay?"

"Toronto General, okay? Then I can see Charlie?" Ricky asked hopefully.

"Ricky, Charlie's gone. Now let's get you some help," Donnie said.

Ricky ran his big hands through his hair and sighed, "Okay." It was the most coherent thing he'd said in the last hour.

John Crichton parked his car at the Regional Medical Centre of San Jose and walked towards the front entrance. He was in a foul mood. Last night he had watched his most valuable asset melt down in front of eighteen thousand people. He headed towards a bank of elevators and banged his thumb into the button for the fourth floor. The elevator doors opened and he walked quietly over to the nurses' station. A young, attractive nurse looked up at him and smiled.

"Can you tell me which room Ricky Phillips is in, please?"

"He's in room 402."

"Thanks."

"Sir?"

"Yes?"

"He's heavily sedated. He probably won't even know that you're here."

Crichton tried to smile. "Then I guess I'll just sit with him for a while."

Crichton walked down the hall and quietly opened the door to Ricky's room. He peeked in cautiously and, sure enough, Ricky was sleeping. He looked around the room and noticed that Eric was asleep in a chair. At that moment, all the rage that Crichton had been feeling started to ebb. Eric didn't care that Ricky was the best player in the NHL. He was here and had spent the night cramped up in a lousy hospital chair because his best friend was hurt. Suddenly, Crichton felt ashamed of his own behaviour. He was worried about losing Ricky Phillips, Calder Trophy winner, Hart Trophy winner and his team's ticket to the Stanley Cup when what he should have been worried about losing was Ricky Phillips, Eric Rollins's best friend.

Crichton walked over and gently shook Eric's shoulder. Eric sat up and rubbed his eyes.

"Go home and get some rest," Crichton said. "I'll stay until his folks get here."

Eric rubbed his neck and tried to stretch out the stiffness in his back. "Mr. Crichton?"

"What's up, Eric?"

"What's going to happen to him?"

Crichton thought about answering like a GM: Upper body injury. Oh, he'll be fine, he'll go home and rest up. We'll place him on injured reserve for a few weeks and he'll come back stronger than ever. He smiled ruefully at his private joke. Then he looked at Eric and he knew that this was more important than a hockey game.

"His folks are coming to get him and they're going to take him home."

"To see a shrink?"

"Yeah, to see a shrink."

"Will he ever play again?"

Crichton let out a long sigh. "I really don't know."

Part Three

FOUR MONTHS LATER

CHAPTER SIXTEEN

Ricky Phillips's car rolled smoothly through Toronto's morning rush-hour traffic. Heading south on University Avenue, he eased his car into the right-hand lane and turned onto Elm Street. He took another quick right onto Murray, then pulled into an underground parking garage. He had been making this drive for months now, and he was pretty sure that he could do it with his eyes closed. He parked his car, locked his doors and headed towards the stairwell. He walked briskly up one flight of stairs and entered the main lobby of Mount Sinai Hospital. He crossed the lobby to a bank of elevators and pressed the button. A few minutes later, he stepped out onto the fifth floor and walked down the hall. At the last door on the left, he turned the handle and opened the door. He stepped into a tastefully decorated waiting room, crossed the floor and sat down in a wingback chair.

"Good morning, Ricky," a pleasant voice called.

Ricky looked up and smiled. "Good morning, Mrs. Fitzpatrick."

"Dr. Barker is ready for you," Mrs. Fitzpatrick said.

Ricky stood, thanked her and headed back to the doctor's office.

For the first few months after Ricky had come home from his meltdown, he had seen Dr. Barker every day. This had been easy to do since Dr. Barker was the head of psychiatry at Mount Sinai, and Ricky had been admitted as a patient.

Ricky had developed an instant rapport with Dr. Barker, and they quickly got to the root of the issue: Ricky had never fully come to grips with Charlie's death. That was the easy part. Ricky felt guilty and responsible for Charlie's death, but he would be able to move past that. But as they delved deeper into Ricky's emotional turmoil, they discovered that there was something more, just below the surface, that Ricky couldn't quite put his finger on. Dr. Barker was pretty sure he knew what it was, but he wanted Ricky to express it in his own words. He felt that this was crucial to Ricky getting back on an even keel, but try as he might, Ricky couldn't quite figure out what it was that was bothering him. The two of them had simply taken to referring to it as "the tip of the tongue."

Ricky knocked on the door and waited. A few seconds later, the door swung open and Dr. Barker ushered Ricky into his office with a smile and a pat on the back. Automatically, Ricky walked over to a large, black leather chair and sat down. Dr. Barker sat down beside him in an identical chair and got right down to business.

"How are you doing, Ricky?"

"I'm okay."

"How was your week?"

"Good."

"How are your folks?"

"Fine."

"Mom?"

"She's good."

"Dad?"

Ricky paused. Dad was always the most difficult part of his sessions. How was Dad? Ricky cleared his throat. "Dad is frustrated."

Dr. Barker nodded sympathetically. "It must be difficult for him."

Ricky shrugged his shoulders and looked out the window. "I heard him talking to my mom one night. He said that he didn't know why you just didn't give me some fancy drug that would clear my head so that I could get back to hockey."

Dr. Barker smiled sadly. "Well, unfortunately, Ricky, it doesn't work that way." He paused and studied Ricky's face before continuing. "I had another phone call about you yesterday."

Sports reporters called all the time, hoping to get information on Ricky's condition. Dr. Barker always protected his privacy, and Ricky trusted him completely.

"Who was it this time?" Ricky asked.

"John Crichton." Dr. Barker watched Ricky stiffen at the sound of that name.

"What did he want?" Ricky asked nervously.

"I don't know. It was just a voice mail."

Ricky's shoulders relaxed and he let out his breath.

"I'll give him a call and when we meet next week, I'll let you know what he said, okay?"

Slowly Ricky nodded. His "tip of the tongue" feeling was back.

❀

John Crichton's intercom light flashed on his phone. He punched the speaker-phone button.

"What is it, Jessica?" he asked.

"Sir, there is a Dr. Barker from Toronto on line one."

"Thank you." Crichton picked up the phone and hit another button. "Dr. Barker," he said. "Thank you for returning my call."

"That's not a problem," Dr. Barker said politely.

Crichton was used to negotiations, and he was used to getting his way. He got right to the point. "Dr. Barker, I would like an update on Ricky's progress."

Dr. Barker paused while he thought of the best way to answer that question. "I'm sorry," he said. "I'm not at liberty to discuss a patient with anyone other than the patient."

"Okay," Crichton said. "Let me put it another way. I signed Ricky to a three-year, twenty-four-million-dollar contract. I think I'm entitled to know what's going on with my investment. The regular season's almost over. Will I have Ricky's services for the playoffs or not?"

Dr. Barker sighed and spoke slowly. "I'm not going to discuss his health with you. What I *can* tell you is that he won't play again this year because I won't give him the clearance to play this year."

It was the news that Crichton had been expecting but still didn't want to hear. There was a long pause before he asked the second question he was afraid to have answered.

"What about next year?"

"My best guess?"

"Sure, your best guess."

"Eighty-twenty."

"For or against?"

"Eighty per cent against," the doctor answered.

◉

The hockey season ended with the Sharks losing in the Western Conference final. Ricky continued to wrestle with "the tip of the tongue," but still couldn't figure out what it was. Spring gave way to summer, and Ricky felt the urge to get back to Muskoka to his cottage, his boat, the golf course and Popo. The summer moved along nicely, and Ricky appeared to be in good health both mentally and physically. His parents came up to the cottage regularly, but Darryl was under strict orders from Dr. Barker not to push the issue of hockey with Ricky.

Early in July, Eric Rollins came by for a visit. He and Popo golfed with Ricky during the day and even managed to get him to the bar at night. Ricky was relaxed and having fun. One day, the boys were sitting on Ricky's dock, trying to decide whether they'd go golfing or waterskiing, when Popo said, "Hey, Eric, there's a skate in Gravenhurst tomorrow. Are you interested?"

Ricky felt himself tense up as Eric answered, "Yeah, Popo that would be great." Then, without thinking, Eric said, "Ricky, are you going to skate?" One look at Ricky's face—which was as white as a ghost's—and he knew the answer. "Oh man, I'm sorry . . ." Eric started.

"It's okay," Ricky answered. The "tip of the tongue" was closer than ever.

Eric and Popo skated several times over the next few weeks. Each time, Ricky would sit quietly in his giant cottage and wait for them to come back. One day, when the boys were getting ready to go to the rink for a skate, Ricky got into his car and drove to Toronto for his weekly appointment with Dr. Barker. The meeting was not unlike any other that they'd had, as Ricky recounted his week for the doctor. However, each time that he mentioned Popo and Eric, he seemed agitated. Finally, Dr. Barker asked where the boys were.

Ricky found that he couldn't answer.

Dr. Barker repeated the question.

Finally, Ricky answered, "They're at the arena."

"Is that a problem?" Dr. Barker asked.

"No, I guess not," Ricky shrugged. "It's just that . . ." *Augghh!* There it is again! he thought angrily.

"Just what?"

Suddenly, Ricky's mind cleared and the thing that had been bothering him, the thing that was on the tip of his tongue, leapt to the front of his mind. Tears welled in his eyes, but he was smiling at the realization.

"What is it, Ricky?"

Ricky blinked at the tears and cleared his throat. "I don't want to play hockey anymore."

For the average person to say that they had had enough of something would probably not be a very big deal. But for the person whom *The Hockey News* had named the greatest hockey player alive just over a year ago, it was a life-altering moment. Ricky Phillips wanted to walk away from the game that had completely consumed his life for the past twenty years.

●

Two days after his revelation with Dr. Barker, Ricky drove Eric down to the airport in Toronto so that he could catch a flight back to Halifax. They had been friends long enough for Eric to know that Ricky wouldn't be much of a conversationalist on the ride down, but on this occasion, he was particularly quiet. Ricky hadn't yet told Eric about his meeting with Dr. Barker and was trying to think of what he was going to say to his friend. When they got to the departures area, Eric thanked Ricky for his hospitality. As they shook hands, Eric looked Ricky square in the eye. "Will I see you at camp?"

Ricky looked down at the floor, and Eric knew what the answer was going to be. Ricky looked back up at his friend and smiled a sad, shaky smile. "I don't think so."

"Are you ever going to play again?" Eric asked.

Ricky hugged his friend, then smacked him on the back. "We'll see."

●

For Ricky, the breakthrough with Dr. Barker felt like the weight of the world had been lifted from his shoulders. For him, it was a really simple concept: I don't want to play anymore. He was, however, smart enough to know that explaining his decision to either his dad or the Sharks would be anything but simple.

As Ricky suspected, his father was devastated, his agent was furious and the Sharks were not too thrilled with the idea either. He still had two years left on his contract and they certainly didn't want to pay sixteen million dollars to a player who wasn't going to play.

Ricky solved that by flying to San Jose and meeting with John Crichton. Not only did he sign a new contract with the

Sharks that allowed them to retain his NHL rights should he ever decide to make a comeback, but he also agreed to release them from all further payments by formally announcing his retirement. Then, just before he left the meeting, Ricky handed Crichton a cheque.

"What's this?" Crichton asked.

"It's what I owe you from last year," Ricky said.

Crichton looked at the cheque and almost dropped it. It was made out to the owners of the San Jose Sharks in the amount of four million dollars.

"You guys were really generous to pay me for the whole season, but I only played about half the year."

Crichton started to protest. "Ricky, this isn't necessary—"

Ricky cut him off. "Mr. Crichton, I know you guys took a chance when you drafted me and I always tried to play my hardest for you. The money isn't the issue. This is my way of trying to say thank you, to you and the club, for everything you've done for me and to say I'm sorry that I'm letting you down now."

Crichton didn't know what to say. It was the longest conversation he'd ever had with Ricky. What struck him was the new sense of maturity the player displayed. He hadn't come with his father or his agent, and Crichton was pretty sure that neither of those men knew that Ricky had just returned four million dollars to the team. Crichton's respect for Ricky and his understanding of what he'd gone through had just increased immensely.

"What are you going to do now, Ricky?"

Ricky smiled. "I'm really not sure, Mr. Crichton."

"Isn't that kind of scary?"

Ricky laughed. "No, Mr. Crichton, losing your mind is scary. This isn't so bad."

"Well, if you ever decide to play again—"

"I know, and thank you. You will be the first person that I call."

They shook hands, and Crichton watched as Ricky disappeared around the corner from his office. As he did, he was hit by a giant wave of disappointment. Ricky was, after all, the most talented player he had ever seen. Crichton knew that he should try to be happy for Ricky, but try as he might, he just couldn't. A feeling of rage was starting to bubble in his stomach. A huge piece of his Stanley Cup puzzle had just walked out the door, and he was certain that he would never see Ricky Phillips again.

●

Ricky held the golf ball in his right hand with the tee sticking through his fingers. He bent over and used the ball to help push the tee into the grass. He stood up and looked down the fairway. The sun had just appeared above the trees, but it hadn't yet burned the dew off of the grass. It was going to be a beautiful August day. He took a deep breath, then let it out gradually. He slowly pulled his club back, then effortlessly hit a laser straight down the middle of the fairway. At six foot three and 225 pounds, he had learned years ago that he didn't have to swing hard to hit the ball a long way.

"Nice shot."

"Thanks," he answered. "Think you can beat it?"

Popo laughed. "Not likely."

Popo hit his shot, and the two friends headed off down the first fairway. As was their custom, they played the first

167

few holes with little or no conversation. They were both still waking up and getting loose, and hitting decent shots was more important than conversation. By the fourth or fifth hole, the grass would be dry, the sun would be getting higher in the sky and the conversation would start to turn towards something other than lob wedges and five-woods. Girls were an important topic, especially to Popo, and Ricky liked to talk about engines, especially if they were attached to boats. Hockey was rarely, if ever, discussed. Popo still skated with the NHLers in Gravenhurst, but Ricky hadn't been on skates since his last game in San Jose.

After they putted out on the ninth hole, they grabbed a Gatorade and sat down on the bench at the tenth tee for a quick rest.

"I saw Dr. Barker yesterday," Ricky said.

Popo already knew this, but he nodded encouragingly so that Ricky would keep talking.

Ricky took a long pull on his Gatorade as he basked in the warmth of the Muskoka sun. He sat on the bench and watched Popo as he got ready to hit his tee shot.

"So what did he say?" Popo asked.

"Who? Dr. Barker?" Ricky asked.

"No, Santa Claus. Of course Dr. Barker," Popo replied.

"He says I need to get a job."

"Oh yeah?" Popo grunted as he pulled back his driver and hit a long fade down the right side of the fairway.

"Yeah," Ricky said as he got up off of the bench. "He doesn't think it's natural for a twenty-two-year-old kid to have as much money as I've got and not be working." He placed his tee in the ground and took a practice swing. "He says that there's more to life than golfing and going to the bar."

Popo laughed. "He has a point. Did he say anything about wakeboarding and chasing girls?"

"No. He just said he thinks that I should get a job. He says it will keep my mind active."

"You had the best job in the world. Why don't you just go back and play for the Sharks?" Popo asked.

Ricky shook his head. "No, I'm done with hockey."

Popo shrugged his shoulders in frustration. He couldn't understand why Ricky had ever walked away from the game. He shouldered his golf bag and started down the fairway.

Ricky grabbed his bag and hustled after Popo.

"Popo, do you like *your* job?" he asked.

"Well, it's certainly not like life in the NHL, but I guess it's okay," Popo answered. "You know how it is. I work hard in the spring, fall and winter so that I can afford to play in the summer."

Ricky seemed deep in thought as they walked along. Finally, he spoke. "Popo, I'm twenty-two years old. My whole life has been hockey. When we were with the Colts, I barely got through grade twelve. I guess I could get a job in hockey, but I don't want to be involved in the game anymore. Hell, I haven't even been on skates for almost a year." Finally, Ricky got around to what was really on his mind. "Popo, could you get me a job selling insurance?"

Popo laughed. "Are you serious?"

Ricky didn't smile. He just stared at his friend. "Yeah, I'm serious."

"Oh," Popo shrugged. "Sure, Ricky. I could get you a job. Do you want to work with me in Muskoka?"

"I dunno," Ricky answered. "Probably in Barrie, I guess."

"Okay," Popo said. "The company has offices all over Canada, so I guess you could work wherever you want."

"You don't mind talking to your boss?"

Popo shook his head. "No problem, Ricky. I'll set something up for you. You're still a big star. I'm sure that they'd be thrilled to have you."

Ricky smiled. "Thanks, Popo." Then he pulled out his wedge from his bag, addressed the ball, set his feet and hit a beautiful arcing shot that landed a few feet below the pin.

CHAPTER SEVENTEEN

Ricky finished out the summer at the cottage and, when the Labour Day weekend ended, he closed it up and headed back to his parents' place in Oro-Medonte.

Popo had helped to get him a job with the Canadian National Insurance Company and, as predicted, his boss was excited about the prospect of having Ricky come on board. For a person who had never held a regular, full-time job before, Ricky was quick to settle into the nine-to-five routine of an office job. He liked selling auto and house insurance, but he tried to avoid dealing with life insurance because it just felt too ironic, given the Charlie Davidson incident.

During his first few months in Barrie, he was so busy learning his new job that the days passed quickly. For the most part, he enjoyed his job, but as the year progressed he started to encounter some difficulties. To the people of Barrie, he was still Ricky Phillips, National Hockey League star. He couldn't leave the office to grab a coffee or a quick meal without having to sign autographs. Most people were polite and friendly, but almost invariably they would offer their condolences about Charlie and sympathize about what a terrible ordeal Ricky had gone through. Their hearts were always in the right place, but for a guy who was trying to move on with his life, it was one constant reminder after another.

The other thing that bothered Ricky was that a lot of his clients were middle-aged men, and as soon as Ricky had organized their renewal on their car insurance, they would ask if he minded if they stopped by the office with their kid for a quick photo. "He's a big fan of yours," was a compliment that he started to get tired of. But what could he do? So Ricky would smile and say, "Sure, bring the kid around! What's that? Sure, I'll sign a stick for him too! Why not?"

●

Ricky's twenty-third birthday came with very little fanfare. He kept to himself at the office and hadn't made any new friends. Most of the people he worked with were a lot older than he was, and they had families and other commitments. One of the receptionists, a girl named Cheryl, seemed to be about his age. She was attractive and very friendly, and he liked talking to her. He wanted to get to know her better, but she sported a ring on her left hand and he wasn't sure if she was engaged or maybe even married. At any rate, he didn't feel that he knew her well enough to ask. The bottom line was that he hadn't told anyone about his birthday, and they didn't know, so it was business as usual.

That night, his parents took him out for dinner in downtown Barrie. His mom was always happy to spend time with him and chatted away excitedly. If Ricky was happy, she was happy. It didn't matter to her that Ricky had walked away from hockey. All that concerned Haley was how her son felt, mentally and physically.

His dad, however, was a different story. It made absolutely no sense to him that someone would want to work in an office when they could play hockey for a living. He tried his best not to show his disappointment, but Ricky could feel his tension. He knew he was disappointing his dad, but Ricky felt good about his decision. After a few months in the insurance business, he knew that he wasn't going to stay in that line of work forever, but he was just as sure that he wasn't going back to hockey.

Darryl was quiet during dinner and didn't say a word on the drive home. The car was barely parked in the driveway when Ricky thanked his parents for the dinner and bolted for his room in the basement. Darryl stomped into the house and headed for his bedroom. He flopped onto his bed and grabbed the remote control. He began stabbing away at the buttons, flicking from one channel to another.

Haley watched him beat up the remote for a few minutes before she finally spoke.

"Did you enjoy your meal?"

"It was fine," he grunted.

"He knows you're upset with him, you know," she said.

"What? Who knows?" He was itching for a fight, and if he couldn't have it with Ricky, he'd have it with Haley.

Haley took a deep breath and started slowly. "Your son knows that you're upset with him."

"Good. Maybe then he'll go back to hockey."

"Look, I know you're angry—"

"Angry! Why would I be angry?" he yelled sarcastically. "My son was the best hockey player in the world, and because of a freak accident he's thrown away his whole career." Darryl was so engrossed in his ranting and cursing that he didn't hear Ricky coming up the basement stairs to grab a glass of water. He was so angry that he was close to tears. The last coherent thing that he said before firing off another series of curses was, "The damn accident wasn't even his fault. It was . . ." and then he stopped short.

"What, Darryl? Say it! Get it off your chest!" Haley demanded.

"It was Charlie's fault!" he yelled. "He was playing hurt, which he shouldn't have been doing, and he ran Eric from behind. Ricky was just defending his teammate and now his career is over! He could have had a Hall of Fame career, and now he's walked away from it!" Oh man, he thought, it felt so good to say that. He was so angry, but he felt that he could never have said any of that to Ricky.

Ricky stood completely motionless in the hallway, his heart pounding. He couldn't have moved if his life depended on it.

Haley waited a few minutes to let Darryl calm down before she continued.

"None of that matters, Darryl. It doesn't matter whose fault it was or how things have played out. All that matters is that your son loves you and your disappointment in him is written all over your face every time you're around him."

Darryl didn't answer but stared straight ahead at the television set.

"Darryl?"

"What?"

"Why don't you sit down and talk to him?"

Again, he didn't answer.

"Do you love your son less because he's not a star in the NHL?" she asked.

In the hallway, Ricky let out a breath that he didn't even know he had been holding. He felt as though he had been punched in the stomach, but he knew one thing for sure: he didn't want to hear the answer to that question. Quietly, he turned around and crept back down the stairs.

Darryl paused for a long time, and Haley thought he wasn't going to answer. Finally, he spoke. "I sure hope not."

●

Later that night, Ricky's birthday celebration continued while he watched TV by himself in the basement family room. Darryl came in and sat down quietly.

"Hey, Bud," he said nervously.

Those two words said it all. The ice was broken and both men relaxed.

Ricky smiled and answered, "Hey, Dad."

Before long, the TV was off and the two of them sat and talked for hours like a father and a son. Like a friend and his buddy.

●

Ricky came into work the next day in a very good mood. By the end of last night's conversation, his dad seemed to understand a little bit better why Ricky didn't want to play hockey anymore. Ricky himself couldn't quite articulate why he didn't want to play. The closest he could get to an explanation was that he had lost his love of the game. He wasn't satisfied with that, because he felt there was more to it than that, but for the moment it was as close as he could get to explaining his decision. He also felt that he was slowly coming to terms with Charlie's death and that that he was ready to start moving on with his life. It felt good to clear the air, and so he arrived at work feeling more relaxed than he had in months.

As he walked through the door, Cheryl looked up and smiled. "Good morning, Ricky. How are you?"

"I'm good," he replied. And before he could stop himself, he started babbling to her. "Last night was my birthday."

"Oh yeah?" she said. "Happy birthday."

"Thanks, thanks. It was my twenty-third."

"Yeah," she smiled. "I figured you were around my age."

"Oh yeah? Why's that?" he asked.

Cheryl blushed. "I used to watch you when you were with the Colts."

"I didn't know you were a Colts fan," he said.

Cheryl looked down at her desk and answered shyly, "I haven't watched them since you stopped playing."

Ricky was getting confused by the signals. If he didn't know any better, he would swear that Cheryl liked him. I need to figure this out, he thought, and before he had time to lose his nerve, he said, "So when's your big day?"

"Big day?" she asked, puzzled.

"Big day . . . wedding," he said, pointing to her ring.

"Oh, this?" she laughed, holding up her left hand. "This was my grandmother's. I'm not engaged. I just wear it because it helps to keep away the lecherous middle-aged men who come here to get their auto insurance renewed."

Ricky smiled a huge smile. "No kidding."

"No kidding."

"So," he said, gathering his courage, "would you like to join me for lunch today?"

"That would be very nice," she said.

❂

Ricky started to see Cheryl regularly, although they tried to be discreet about it at work. She was beautiful and poised and fun to be with, and he was happier than he had been since Charlie's death. Cheryl was a good athlete herself. She golfed in the summer and downhill skied in the winter. She had followed his career since he was in Barrie, and she knew all about his trials and tribulations at the NHL level. What Ricky liked was that she never brought up hockey. If Ricky wanted to talk about it, she was a great listener, but she never offered her opinion or her advice. And, best of all, she never once told him that she was sorry he wasn't playing anymore. As far as he could tell, Cheryl liked him for who he was and not because he was a former NHLer.

❂

As his first-year anniversary in the insurance business approached, Ricky still felt that he was at loose ends. He had the constant feeling that he was looking for an answer to a question. The problem was that he didn't know what the question was.

His personal life was going well. He and Cheryl were together constantly and he couldn't have been happier. His professional life was a different story. He enjoyed the

177

insurance business, but he was still treated as a novelty by people. He could almost feel their thoughts when they came to see him—That's the guy that killed that other guy in that hockey fight. He felt like a large fish in a small bowl, on display for people to gawk at.

One day, while he was sitting at his desk going over a memo, he happened to look at the top of the stationery. It listed all the towns and cities in which the company had offices. As he read the names, an idea began to form in his mind.

Vancouver, Edmonton, Calgary. He was familiar with those places from his days in San Jose. Vancouver's nice, he thought, probably not too different from San Jose. Edmonton and Calgary—both nice towns, but if I'm a freak show in Barrie, it would be ten times worse in those hockey-mad towns. Although, he thought to himself, maybe I would be more anonymous because of the larger populations.

Winnipeg. Too cold.

Marathon. Where the hell is that?

He read every name until he came to Halifax. I could maybe see Eric again, he thought, but he'd only be home in the summer.

By the time he had read the entire list, he knew he wanted to make a change, that he needed to get out of Barrie. Most of the people there killed him with kindness. Some were openly fascinated by him. He stood up and pushed in his chair. He was ready for some privacy.

❋

Ricky stood in front of his boss's desk and said, "Mr. Robertson, do you have a minute?"

"Sure, have a seat."

Ricky sat down and got right to the point. "Sir, I was reading your memo earlier and I noticed all the places on the stationery where the company has offices."

Mr. Robertson nodded.

"Well, I was wondering if it would be possible to get a transfer to one of those spots."

Again Mr. Robertson nodded. He was a tiny man who reminded Ricky a bit of Ben McMillan.

"I can help you with a transfer, Ricky, but I'd hate to lose you. Are you unhappy here?"

"No, I like the job. It's just that living in Barrie has been . . ." he struggled to find the right words to say what he was thinking.

"People still think that you're a big star, eh?" Mr. Robertson asked.

"Yeah, there's that, and some of them stare at me like I'm some sort of exhibit piece."

Mr. Robertson nodded. "I can imagine it's been a very difficult time for you these past few years."

"It's been a little crazy," Ricky said quietly.

"Well Ricky, a transfer to western Canada would be difficult because the west is booming and there's big money to be made out there."

"Money isn't an issue for me, sir."

"Well, I could try the east coast . . ." Mr. Robertson stopped. "Money isn't an issue?"

"No, sir," he looked at his feet, embarrassed. "I have lots."

"Hmm. Have you ever thought of Marathon?"

"I'd never heard of it until I saw it on the letterhead. Where is it?"

179

"It's way up in northern Ontario, about three hours east of Thunder Bay. It's a tiny pulp and paper town, maybe five thousand people. I was up there once for a meeting. It's a beautiful spot, nestled in a little bay right on the shore of Lake Superior. If you like the outdoors, you'd like it up there."

"Really," Ricky was turning this over in his mind. "What would it be like to get a transfer up there?"

"The Marathon office is always looking for people. Because it's such a small town, and because it's so remote, a lot of people don't want to go there. They want to go to Calgary and Vancouver, to where the action and the money are."

"Well, like I said, money isn't an issue for me," Ricky repeated.

"Okay, Ricky, if you're interested, let me know and I'll call the Marathon office for you."

"Thank you. If you wouldn't mind, could you give me a day or two to think about it?"

"Sure."

"If you do phone them, would it be possible to keep my name out of the conversation?"

Mr. Robertson didn't need to ask why. "Okay," he said. "I'll just say a young man named Richard Phillips is looking for a transfer."

"Richard," Ricky said, repeating the name to himself as if trying it on for size. No one had ever called him Richard, not even his mom.

"Thanks for your time, Mr. Robertson. I'll get back to you in a day or so."

●

Ricky sat in the middle of a crowded downtown restaurant and stared at his plate. He was afraid that if he looked up at Cheryl she would start to cry again, and they were both trying hard not to cause a scene. Ricky and Cheryl had been having a nice lunch until Ricky sprang his idea of moving up to Marathon on her. As he watched her across the table trying her best not to cry, he realized that he was starting to fall in love with her. However, he also knew that he really needed to get out of Barrie before he lost his mind—again.

Cheryl looked up at Ricky and took a deep breath. "What's the town called again?"

"Marathon."

"But I don't understand. Aren't you happy here?"

Before he could answer, two young men in business suits walked past their table. One of them noticed Ricky and poked the other one. They both stared openly at him as the waitress led them to their table. Ricky looked back at Cheryl.

"I'm happy with *you*. It's just that at work and around town I'm beginning to feel like people are constantly watching me and talking about me like I'm some kind of freak."

"So why Marathon?"

"I guess I just want to be anonymous for awhile."

"Ricky, it's Canada. People will recognize you anywhere."

"I dunno. It's been almost two years since I played. And if I go, I'm going to go by the name Richard Phillips."

Cheryl made a face at the "new" name.

Ricky laughed and said, "You think I'm crazy, huh?"

She nodded. "Completely nuts."

"Well, I've already gone crazy once, and I don't recommend it. I'm hoping this is something that makes sense." Ricky looked across the table at Cheryl and spoke earnestly.

"Cheryl, you mean a lot to me, but I really need to look into this. If I don't get out of Barrie . . . well, I don't know what will happen, but I know I need to make a change."

Cheryl put on a brave face and tried to smile. "Well, Ricky, I hope you find what you're looking for."

"Thanks," Ricky mumbled.

"And when you do, come and see me. You'll know where to find me."

CHAPTER EIGHTEEN

It took Ricky two days to make the drive to Marathon, but long before he arrived, he knew he had made the right decision. On his first night out, he stopped in Sault Ste. Marie. He grabbed a quick bite to eat and then walked along the waterfront while he watched a couple of giant ore carriers navigate through the locks. Being in the Soo brought back a slew of memories of his days with the Colts and the epic battles they used to have with the Greyhounds. As he gazed out at the water, he remembered the great delight that Ben McMillan used to take in sticking it to Skip Daniels. He realized that this was the first time in a long time that he had thought fondly about a hockey memory.

The next day, he left the Soo and headed towards Wawa. The highway meandered along, hugging the shoreline of Lake Superior. It was the most spectacular scenery Ricky had ever seen. By the time he reached Marathon, he was in love with northern Ontario. Even if I can't pull in a radio station, he chuckled to himself.

Mr. Robertson hadn't lied; it was a beautiful spot. The town was nestled in a protected bay dominated by high hills—"mountains" to the locals—which made for a very picturesque setting. The focal point of the town was the pulp and paper mill, located right at the water's edge. It didn't take him long to find the Canadian National Insurance Company's office. It was about two blocks up the hill from the mill. Ricky parked his car and walked in.

A receptionist, who looked like she was well past the mandatory retirement age, looked up. "Yes?" she said. It was more of a challenge than a greeting.

"Hi, I'm Rick—Richard Phillips. Is Mr. Coleman in?" Ricky asked.

The receptionist picked up her phone and rang Mr. Coleman, and a few seconds later a large, energetic man came bustling out of his office. He smiled when he saw Ricky and extended his hand. "Hi, I'm Fred Coleman." He paused while they shook hands, and he studied Ricky's face. "Have we met?" he asked quizzically.

Ricky reminded himself to stay calm. "I don't think so," he answered. "I'm Richard Phillips."

Fred continued to stare at him, but then merely asked, "Have you had any lunch?"

Fred took Ricky for lunch and then gave him the tour of the town. As they drove up the main street from the mill, they passed an arena.

"Do you play hockey, Richard?"

Ricky coughed. "Ah, no. No I don't."

Fred shrugged. "Well, we have a good minor hockey system here and a recreational men's league. We even have a pretty good junior team. But if you're not into hockey, the snowmobiling and ice fishing are great. And in the summer, the boating and fishing are as good as anywhere in the world," Fred said proudly.

They carried on up the road past the golf course that Ricky had passed on his way into town. Fred noticed Ricky looking at the course. "Do you play?" he asked.

"Yeah, I play a bit," Ricky answered.

"Well, would you like to join me for a round in the morning?"

"That sounds like fun," Ricky replied.

Ricky checked into a hotel room for the evening, and the next morning he hit the links with Fred Coleman. Fred turned out to be a pretty good golfer, but he was no match for Ricky, despite the rented clubs. As they putted out on the seventh green and walked towards the eighth tee, the golf course spread out before them and revealed a stunning view of Lake Superior.

"Wow," Ricky said.

"Uh-huh," Fred agreed. "I never get tired of that view."

"It's incredible," Ricky agreed.

Later, on the eighteenth green, Ricky dropped a nice putt to complete an impressive round of 75. With rental clubs on a course he had never played before, he had duly impressed Mr. Coleman.

Back at their cars, the two men shook hands.

"Are you sure we've never met?" Fred asked again.

Ricky laughed. "I'm sure."

"Have you found a place to stay yet?"

Ricky shook his head. "Not yet, but I'll have a look around today."

Fred nodded. "It won't be a problem. There are lots of places available. Are you okay to start work tomorrow?"

Ricky smiled. "Yup, I'll see you in the morning."

Fred jumped into his truck and headed back to the office, leaving Ricky to head into town to do some house hunting.

CHAPTER NINETEEN

Ricky was working at his desk when his intercom rang. It was Mrs. Montgomery, the not-so-chipper voice at the front desk. Ricky had dubbed her Methuselah because he was convinced that she was over a hundred years old.

"There's a man here that needs an auto quote," she said in her tired, bored voice.

"I'll be right out," Ricky answered.

He got up and walked out to the reception area. A young man about Ricky's age was standing near Methuselah's desk. He was dressed in work boots, jeans and a jean jacket, topped by a camouflage baseball cap. Ricky extended his hand and introduced himself.

The young man shook his hand. "Matt Holland." He studied Ricky's face. "Have we met?" he asked. "You look familiar."

"I don't think so," Ricky said. "I just moved here a few months ago."

"Oh yeah? Where you from?" Matt asked.

"Uh, southern Ontario," Ricky answered trying to keep things vague.

"Hmm," Matt replied, "what on Earth would make you want to move to Marathon?"

"I like the outdoors."

This seemed to satisfy Matt, and Ricky moved to change the subject before he could ask any more probing questions.

"So Meth—I mean, Mrs. Montgomery—says you need an auto quote."

Matt beamed. "Yup, just bought myself a new pickup."

Ricky smiled to himself. The biggest difference he had noticed so far between Marathon and Barrie was the number of pickup trucks. Apparently everyone in this town drove one.

"Congratulations!" he said. "Why don't you come with me and we can get started on your quote."

The two men headed back to his office, and Ricky asked Matt the pertinent questions about his truck and punched the numbers into the computer. The quote he gave Matt seemed to satisfy him because he smiled, stood up and shook Ricky's hand.

"So, how old are you?" Matt asked.

Man, we've got to work on this guy's tact, Ricky thought. "Twenty-three."

"Right on. I just turned twenty-five," Matt said. "Not a lot of young people up here, eh?"

"It's pretty quiet," Ricky agreed.

"So you like the outdoors, huh?"

"Yeah."

"Do you hunt?"

"Ah, no, I don't hunt."

Matt stared at him incredulously.

"Fish?"

"Yeah, I like to fish," Ricky answered. In fact, he'd never cast a rod in his life. He liked to wakeboard and water-ski, but that had to wait for Muskoka and the cottage. Lake Superior wasn't suited to those activities.

"Well, would you like to go fishing sometime?" Matt asked.

Ricky realized that maybe Matt was just a lonely guy in a small town.

"You work in the mill?" Ricky asked.

"Either the pulp mill or the gold mine up here. Yeah, I work in the mill."

"You get decent time off?"

"Yeah, it's good."

Ricky smiled. "Okay, then. Let's go fishing sometime."

●

Matt turned out to be a really good guy, and because he was born and raised in Marathon, he was dialled in with all the local people and activities. Before long, Ricky was one of the boys and was being included on poker nights and trips to the local watering hole. The locals found Ricky to be a bit of an oddity. He was friendly and polite, but very quiet. He claimed to have moved up north because he liked the outdoors, yet he didn't hunt. The first time that he took Ricky fishing, Matt reported back to his friends that it was very apparent that Ricky was a complete greenhorn. They had just ventured out onto Lake Superior in Matt's eighteen-foot aluminum boat when the questions started.

"This is a pretty small boat for this lake, isn't it?" Ricky had asked.

"It does the job," Matt replied.

"What if a storm blows up?"

"Then we'll go in."

"This is the largest lake in the world."

"So?"

"So, you come out here with only one engine. What if it quits?" Ricky asked.

Matt sighed. "Then we hope that the wind is blowing onshore."

Despite Ricky's apprehension and the very obvious fact that he had no idea how to cast a line, he really enjoyed himself. Before long, he was badgering Matt to get back out on the water. One day, he caught onto a huge lake trout, and by the time he'd fought it into the boat, the fish wasn't the only one that was hooked.

"This is awesome!" he exclaimed.

❀

A few weeks later, on a Monday morning, Ricky got in his car and headed west on Highway 17. Three hours later, he arrived in Thunder Bay. He was navigating from maps that he had downloaded from his computer. The first led him directly to a Ford dealership where three salespeople were sitting around, sipping their morning coffees. It had been a slow day. The two young salesmen looked at Ricky, sized him up as a tire-kicker and went back to their coffees. The third salesperson was an older woman. She put down her coffee and walked over to Ricky and smiled.

"Hi, I'm Janet. May I help you?"

Ricky nodded. "Yes, please. I'd like to buy a truck."

Janet nodded. "Anything in particular?"

"All I need is four-wheel drive and a towing package. Oh, and it needs to be black or silver."

One hour later, the dealership owned Ricky's car as a trade-in, and Ricky pulled out of their lot in a brand new silver-and-black Ford F-250. Janet left work early to take her kids out for lunch to celebrate the easiest sale she had ever made.

Ricky's next map led him to a large marina downtown. He parked his truck and got out and looked around. There, sitting majestically on a black trailer, was the most beautiful boat he had ever seen: a thirty-five-foot Fountain Center Console offshore fishing boat, equipped with triple 300-horsepower Mercury engines.

Black and silver, he thought. What a coincidence.

Ricky walked into the shop and looked around. A young kid who looked like he wasn't old enough to shave was standing behind the counter. He looked at Ricky and smiled.

"What's up?" he asked.

"I'm looking for Art."

"You're looking at him."

"I'm Richard Phillips."

Art slammed his hand off of the counter and grinned. "Holy crap! That is one beautiful boat. It arrived from the factory yesterday. Congratulations!"

"Thanks a lot. Have you run it?" Ricky asked.

Art nodded. "Runs like a top."

Art helped Ricky load up his boat, then taught him how to launch it, how to drive it, trim it, dock it and, most importantly, how to get it back onto the trailer. Three hours later, Ricky left Art with a rather large certified cheque and headed back towards Marathon with his new boat and truck.

●

The next day, Matt was sitting in his house watching TV when he heard a horn honking. There stood Ricky, grinning like a kid on Christmas Day. Matt walked down his driveway to where Ricky was standing in front of a brand new truck. Attached to the truck was an unbelievable fishing boat.

"What do you think?" Ricky asked, still grinning.

"About what? The truck or the boat?"

"Both."

"Well, I know what the truck is—it's beautiful—but I've never seen a boat like this," said Matt.

"It's called a Fountain," Ricky said. "It's supposed to be the best offshore fishing boat in the world."

"Who'd you kill to get a package like this?" Matt asked only half-jokingly.

For the first time, Ricky looked a bit embarrassed. "Oh, I have some money saved up," he said. "From before." He didn't elaborate on what he meant by "from before."

❂

Ricky skipped the next poker night so that he could get out in his new boat. Not surprisingly, Ricky and his boat were the main topic of conversation at the table.

"I checked out that boat on the Internet," said Johnny Crawford as he folded his hand. "It retails at a quarter of a million dollars."

"Don't forget the truck," said Robbie Montgomery. "That's a seventy-thousand-dollar hit."

Matt was deep in thought. "Internet, huh?"

"I bet he's a drug dealer," Johnny said as Robbie turned over his cards to reveal a jack-high straight.

Robbie laughed as he raked in his chips. "Really, who else would have that kind of coin?"

Matt didn't seem at all upset that his three aces had just been defeated. "Internet," he repeated more to himself than to anyone else. He pushed himself away from the table and stood up.

"Deal me out, boys. Johnny, can I borrow your computer for a minute?"

Johnny nodded. "What are you going to do? Try to learn how to play poker online?"

Matt shook his head. "No, I'm gonna Google something."

"Google what?"

"Not what—*who*. Richard Phillips."

●

Ricky was on the phone when he heard his office door open. He looked up to see Matt letting himself in.

"Methuselah said I'd find you back here," he whispered.

Ricky gave him the "one second" gesture with his hand.

Matt reached into his pocket and pulled out an object, which he tossed lightly towards Ricky. It spun through the air and landed right in the middle of his desk.

Ricky's eyes went from the item on the desk to Matt, who returned the stare.

"Sorry to cut you off," Ricky told the caller. "Can I call you back, please? Something's just come up." He paused, listened for a second, said "Thanks" and hung up.

He looked at Matt. "So what's this?" he asked, trying to seem nonchalant.

"What does it look like?" Matt said. "It's a Ricky Phillips hockey card."

"Okay, and . . . ?"

"Looks an awful lot like you, don't you think?"

Ricky picked up the card and examined it. His dad had had a print of this exact card enlarged to poster size and displayed behind his bar in the basement.

"I guess there is a slight resemblance, if you hold the card just so," Ricky said.

"Oh, cut the crap, *Richard*." Matt spit the name out sarcastically. "You and I both know that you're Ricky Phillips, former National Hockey League star."

Ricky leaned back in his chair and sighed. He ran his fingers through his hair and looked at Matt.

"How many people have you told?" he asked.

"What? I haven't told anybody anything. Look, man, I don't care what your story is. I just don't like being lied to." He turned on his heel and grabbed the door.

"Wait," Ricky said.

Matt hesitated, then looked back into the office.

"I'm sorry," Ricky said. "I moved up here to make a fresh start, and I was just looking for a bit of privacy, that's all. I didn't really think of it as lying."

"Misleading? Deceiving?" Matt offered.

"Fair enough," Ricky conceded. "But like I said, I was just looking for some privacy. When I was living in Barrie, I couldn't go anywhere without people staring at me, whispering behind my back or asking for an autograph."

Matt's hand still rested on the doorknob. He was genuinely pissed at Ricky and wasn't sure he was ready to let him off the hook just yet. Slowly, he let go of the handle. Then he took the seat in front of Ricky's desk.

"Look, Ricky—can I call you Ricky?"

Ricky smiled and nodded.

"Ricky, you've got us figured all wrong. Johnny, Robbie and I, we don't care that you're a celebrity. What we care about is whether or not you're a straight-up guy. We're pretty isolated up here, and because of that, friends become very important. And friends up here are very loyal. We're not going to bug you for an autograph. We're going to bug you to go fishing or play poker. You just need to be honest with us."

Ricky smiled. "I think I can do that."

"I don't think anyone in town will bug you when the truth gets out."

"I hope you're right," Ricky said. "So how'd you figure out who I was?"

Matt laughed. "Oh, you dumb shit. Have you ever heard of Google? You're all over it. Next time you go to live under some mysterious secret identity, you might want to try something a little more clever than going by Richard instead of Ricky."

Ricky's face flushed with embarrassment.

"Oh, and another tip might be not to drop three hundred grand on a new fishing boat when it's painfully obvious that you've never fished a day in your life."

Matt continued to lecture, and Ricky's face continued to get redder. By the time Matt told Ricky that the boys thought he might be a drug dealer, the two of them were laughing so loudly that Methuselah could hear them all the way out to her desk.

"Noisy little punks," she muttered to herself.

●

On the night of Ricky's twenty-fourth birthday, Marathon's biggest bar was packed. Matt, Johnny and Robbie had spread the news that there was to be a big party and that something special was going to happen. Although Ricky liked to go for a night out with his friends, be it in Muskoka or back in the day in San Jose, he had never been one to drink too heavily. Tonight, however, Matt had seen to it that Ricky was feeling no pain. Matt was an excellent pool player, and earlier in the evening he had challenged Ricky to a game of pool. The loser had to provide the coins for the next game and buy a round of drinks. Ricky lost, but his competitive spirit kept him coming back for more. As the night wore on, the bar filled up and Ricky found himself feeling relaxed and happy.

Suddenly, Matt climbed up on top of the pool table and yelled out, "Ladies and gentlemen! May I have your attention? Now, as most of you know, today is my friend Richard's birthday."

Matt was momentarily drowned out by some polite but confused cheers.

"Richard has something he wants to say to everyone," Matt continued.

"I do?" Ricky asked quizzically.

"Get up here, Richard!" Matt yelled.

Johnny and Robbie grabbed Ricky and hoisted him up onto the pool table. Ricky got shakily to his feet and looked questioningly at Matt.

Matt smiled and looked at the crowd. "Richard's not much of a public speaker, but that's okay. He has a prepared statement . . ." And with that he reached into his pocket and pulled out a sheet of paper.

"You're a bastard," Ricky whispered to Matt.

"Right back at ya, buddy," Matt grinned. "Now read."

Ricky tried to focus his eyes on the paper. "Ladies and gentlemen," he began.

He was immediately interrupted by a chorus of "What?" and "We can't hear you."

He took a deep breath and tried again. "Ladies and gentlemen," he slurred loudly.

Everyone cheered.

"My name is Ricky Phillips and I'm not a drug dealer."

"Hi Ricky!" everyone yelled.

Ricky put his arm around Matt and whispered, "I'm going to kill you."

Matt, who was trying very hard not to laugh, said, "You can kill me tomorrow. But right now, you need to read."

"I can't even see the page, you prick."

"Just stop your whining and read."

Ricky looked at his "statement" and continued. "My friends, I'm not a drug dealer. I am a hockey player whose real name is Ricky Phillips. I came to Marathon to escape the intense pressure that people in southern Ontario place on their celebrities."

"Aaaawww!" the crowd yelled sympathetically.

"Oh man—is *everyone* in on your little game?" Ricky asked Matt.

"Pretty much," Matt smiled. "Now keep reading."

Again Ricky looked at his paper. "My friends, I am very sorry that I tried to mislead you, and because of my dishonesty I would like to apologize by offering you all a drink on me."

A loud cheer erupted in the bar.

"Wait, everybody!" Matt yelled. "Richard's not finished."

"Have you seen my boat?" Ricky read.

"Yeah!" the crowd yelled.

"Well, I have another confession. I'm a pathetic fisherman."

Ricky hadn't heard a cheer like that since he played for San Jose. He waited for the crowd to quiet before he finished with the confession Matt had prepared.

"I would be honoured if the good people of Marathon would help me celebrate my twenty-fourth birthday and accept my sincere apology for misleading you. For the rest of the night, the drinks and wings are on me."

The bar exploded in a loud cheer.

Ricky had a terrific time that night. He lost every game of pool, made a bunch of new friends and, best of all, not one person asked him for an autograph.

❀

The next morning, with his head still throbbing from the night before, Ricky headed into the office. He talked to Mr. Coleman and asked him if he could have some time off.

Coleman nodded. "Yeah, Ricky, no problem. Things are a bit slow right now anyway."

"Thanks a lot," Ricky answered.

"What are you up to, if you don't mind my asking?"

Ricky smiled. "I'm going to take some buddies on a fishing trip. We should be gone about a week."

Suddenly, Coleman jumped up. "Oh, that reminds me, Ricky. Mrs. Montgomery has finally decided to retire. She'll probably be gone when you get back. We're taking a collection so we can get her a nice gift. Would you care to contribute?"

Ricky reached into his pocket and pulled out some crumpled bills. He smoothed out a hundred-dollar bill and handed it to Coleman.

"Is this enough?" he asked.

"Um, I was actually thinking more like twenty," Coleman answered.

Ricky laughed. "Keep it. Tell ol' Methuselah to get herself something nice."

Coleman grinned and smacked Ricky on the back. "You have a great time fishing."

●

Early the following morning, Ricky rumbled through town in his truck, with his boat in tow behind him. First, he picked up Matt, who jumped into the truck and handed Ricky a coffee.

"So, you going to tell me where we're going?"

Ricky put the truck in gear and headed off to pick up Robbie and Johnny. "You'll see," was all he said.

Once he had all three of his travel companions in the truck, Ricky headed along the shoreline past the mill. The road wound around the bay to the far side of the natural harbour. Located there was a nice boat ramp.

After they launched the boat and parked the truck, Ricky started to idle out of the bay, past the mill and into the open water of Lake Superior.

Ricky looked at his three friends. "You ready?" he asked.

The three of them nodded, a little bit hesitantly. They had no idea where they were going. All Ricky had told them was to bring an overnight bag and their fishing gear.

Ricky brought the throttles up, and the boat leaped up onto plane. After several minutes of cruising along at fifty miles an hour, it became obvious that Ricky wasn't going to stop anytime soon.

Matt leaned over towards Ricky and yelled above the roar of the engines and the wind, "So where are we going?"

"Wawa."

"What?"

Ricky laughed. "Not 'what.' *Wawa*."

"But that's over two hundred kilometres away!" Matt stammered.

Ricky nodded. "Yup. We should be there in about two hours."

Matt shook his head and smiled. "Wow, Ricky, I don't know what to say. This is really generous of you."

Ricky turned suddenly serious and looked at Matt. "You guys," he said, nodding his head to the stern of the boat where Robbie and Johnny were sitting, "have been really good to me. This is just my way of saying thanks."

Matt smiled. "Well, thanks again."

Ricky nodded and hammered down on the throttles. The boat jumped up out of the water and accelerated even harder. Ricky let out a whoop. "Hey, Matt!" he yelled.

"Yeah?"

"Better make it an hour and a half."

❂

Ricky and his friends spent the next week slowly fishing their way back to Marathon. For three guys who'd lived their whole lives in northern Ontario and thought that they knew fishing, this truly was the trip of a lifetime. When they finally idled back into Marathon, the boys were tired and smelly but had thoroughly enjoyed their time. They had caught some nice fish, told some stories—where the truth was always optional—and shared some laughs.

That night, Ricky backed his boat up into his driveway and staggered into his house. The water was still dripping off of the bottom of the trailer when he collapsed gratefully onto his bed.

❂

The next day, showered, shaved and refreshed from a solid night's sleep, Ricky came bounding into work. He had completely forgotten about Methuselah's retirement. He threw open the front door and stared at the new receptionist. Gathering himself, he walked over to her desk as she stood up to introduce herself. Ricky grabbed her by the shoulders and pulled her into a bear hug and kissed her full on the mouth.

"Wow!" she said when they broke their embrace. "Do all northerners greet each other this way?"

Ricky smiled and apologized. "I'm sorry," he said. "I'm Richard Phillips. My friends call me Ricky."

The girl smiled back at him. "Back home, my friends call me Cheryl."

CHAPTER TWENTY

Ricky took Cheryl out for lunch and they spent the time catching each other up on their lives. Cheryl told Ricky that she realized right after he left that she wanted to be with him. So she had emailed Mr. Coleman and asked him to keep her in mind if an opening ever came up in Marathon. He replied to tell her that his receptionist was contemplating retirement and he would keep her updated. About a week before Ricky left on his fishing trip, Cheryl found out that she had the job. She asked Mr. Coleman not to tell Ricky because she wanted to surprise him. The week that Ricky was out on his fishing trip, Cheryl moved to Marathon, found herself a nice little basement apartment and started working for Mr. Coleman.

Ricky looked at her and smiled. "Well, it certainly *was* a surprise."

After lunch, Ricky gave Cheryl a quick tour of the town and introduced her to his friends. He found Robbie and Johnny, but no one had seen Matt. They returned to the office only to find him sitting in the lobby. Ricky introduced Cheryl to Matt, and then the two boys headed down the hall to Ricky's office.

"Wow," Matt said. "Slightly better looking than Methuselah."

Ricky laughed and opened up the door to his office. "So what's up?" he asked as he sat down at his desk.

"Just wanted to thank you again for the fishing trip," Matt answered.

"My pleasure," Ricky replied.

"I have one favour to ask you, too."

"What's that?"

"I want you to play hockey with us."

Instantly Ricky shook his head. "No. Sorry, but I don't play anymore."

"Ah, come on, Ricky. It's just pickup here at the rink on Wednesday nights. No refs, no scoreboard. Some of the guys can really play and some are just out for the beer after the game."

Again Ricky shook his head.

"Just promise me you'll think about it," Matt implored.

Ricky looked at his friend, who was now giving him his best puppy-dog eyes.

Slowly, Ricky smiled. "We'll see."

●

When Ricky got home from work that night, he went straight to his computer and sat down. He started to compose an email message.

Dear Dr. Barker:

How are you doing? It's been a long time since I've written to you but I guess that's a good thing, isn't it? Anyway, life is pretty good up here. The scenery is beautiful and I've made some good friends.

Cheryl has moved up here, too. Anyway, the reason I'm writing to you is because a friend of mine has asked me to play some pickup hockey with him. I just wanted to know what you think. I look forward to your reply.

Sincerely,
Ricky

●

After work the next day, Ricky came home and headed straight for the kitchen. He turned on the oven to preheat it. Cheryl was coming over for dinner, and he planned on dazzling her with a frozen pizza.

While the oven was heating, he went into the living room and turned on his computer so that he could check his email. He had three new messages. One was from Popo, one was from his mom, and the third was from Dr. Barker. He clicked on Dr. Barker's email first.

Hey kiddo:
Terrific to hear from you. I'm glad things are going well for you in Marathon. I'm happy to hear that Cheryl is up there. She seems like a great person.
Ricky, if you want to play hockey again, I think that is wonderful. I think pickup hockey would be a great way to reintroduce yourself to the game.
Write anytime you want.
Sincerely,
Albert Barker

Ricky read over the email a couple of times. *I wonder what he meant by 'reintroduce myself to the game,'* he thought. However, his thoughts were interrupted by the ringing doorbell. He got up and went to the door to let Cheryl in. He gave her a kiss hello and then led her to the kitchen.

"Boy, are you in for a treat," he said. "I hope you like frozen pizza."

"Oh, it's my favourite," she said playfully.

Ricky smiled. "Well, then, for a delicacy of this magnitude, I really think you should pitch in and earn your keep. Do you want to clean lettuce or slice tomatoes?"

Cheryl took the knife from Ricky and said, "I'll do the tomatoes."

Ricky started to methodically clean some lettuce, while Cheryl started in on an unsuspecting cucumber. He stood with his back to Cheryl, looking out the kitchen window, and said, "I sent an email to Dr. Barker yesterday."

He tried to sound casual, but Cheryl could hear the tension in his voice. "Oh yeah?" she said as encouragingly as she could.

"Yeah," he answered. "Matt has asked me to play pickup hockey with him on Wednesday nights."

"Uh-huh . . ."

"Yeah, I just wanted to know what he thought."

"And what did he say?"

"He says he thinks that if I want to play again, that it would be okay."

"That's good," Cheryl said.

Ricky plunged his hands into the water again and said, "Cheryl?"

"Yes?"

"What do *you* think?"

Cheryl put down her knife and walked over to Ricky at the sink. She put her arms around his waist and rested her head on the back of his shoulder.

"Ricky, you don't need my permission to play hockey."

Ricky turned around so that he could see her. "I know," he said. "I was just wondering what you thought."

Cheryl looked up into his unusually serious face.

Ricky forced a weak smile. "It's just that . . ."

"What?" she asked.

"It's just pickup, right?"

Cheryl reached up to kiss him. "It's just pickup," she answered. Then she held him close and waited for the fear to ooze out of his body.

❀

Fall descended rapidly on northern Ontario. The nights got longer and colder and people started to prepare for another long winter. Ricky had his boat winterized and put into storage.

On a cold Wednesday night in early October, Ricky did something that he hadn't done for what felt like a very long time: he packed his hockey bag. Actually, he first had to buy a bag and then all the equipment to go in it, because he no longer owned any gear.

He was surprised by how nervous he was as he drove to the rink. He actually considered blowing off the idea and going to look for Cheryl. As he parked his truck, he gripped the wheel with both hands. He took a deep breath and exhaled slowly. Memories of his first skate with the Colts all those years ago came back to him. Remembering how scared he was that day made him smile. "It's just pickup, Ricky," he said to the image in the mirror. Then, before he could change his mind, he opened the door and jumped out of the truck. He grabbed his bag and stick and tried to appear confident as he made his way to the entrance of the arena. As he walked into the main lobby, he saw the blackboard listing the dressing room assignments. There, below two peewee teams at 7:30 and a bantam girls' practice at 8:30, he read DRESSING ROOM #4: THE PYLONS.

He felt himself beginning to relax. Arenas are the same wherever you go. The aromas of stale coffee and arena french fries mixed with the ammonia smell from the ice-making unit greeted his nose. In a dusty old display case, pictures of past championship teams and individual heroes were displayed alongside trophies from this tournament and that.

The concession stand was operated by an elderly lady in a blue smock. Her hands shook when she counted your change and she called everyone who placed an order, from the smallest tykes to the largest midgets, "dear." Ricky was convinced that he had seen this very same lady in every small town rink he'd ever played in. As he walked past her, she smiled.

Automatically, Ricky smiled back. "How ya doing?" he asked.

"I'm good, dear. How are you?"

He almost laughed at her response, but recovered in time to say, "Fine, thanks."

She smiled again and told him to enjoy his skate.

Ricky walked down the hallway to the dressing rooms. Everything was so natural to him—the smells, the sounds, the people. He felt the way you do when you are driving towards your hometown after being away for a long time. As you get closer, you start to pull in the local radio station and your senses start to get bombarded with sights and sounds that you had all but forgotten about. When he got to dressing room four, he leaned on the door and shouldered his bag in through the doorway. There were only a couple of guys there, but one of them was Matt. He smiled when he saw Ricky.

"Hey, Buddy. I wasn't sure you'd make it."

"I'm only here for the fries," Ricky answered. "I hear they're pretty good."

"The fries are great . . . the coffee sucks," Matt said.

Ricky threw his bag down beside Matt's and then sat down on the bench. He greeted each guy as they began to trickle in. Most of them he knew by sight, if not by name. The players he didn't already know, he introduced himself to.

The familiarity of the dressing room came back to him quickly, and he realized how much he had missed it. From the NHL to the most humble beer leagues, the dressing room was the place where teams bonded as friends and teammates. The banter flowed easily and you had guys that teased and poked fun and guys that took the ribs.

Johnny Crawford was one of the only guys that still used a wooden stick. He sat in the corner and lovingly gave it a tape job. When he was finished, he stood up and leaned on it and checked its flex.

One of the guys noticed him and called across the room, "Hey, Johnny, you get that thing at Esso?"

Without missing a beat, Johnny answered, "Free car wash, too." Then he added with a smile, "Besides, with hands like these, I don't need some fancy stick."

"With hands like those, you should be a mason," called back his heckler.

"Why's that?" Johnny asked innocently.

"Because your hands are made of stone."

The boys laughed, and Ricky found himself smiling at Johnny's expense.

When they went on the ice, Ricky took a few hesitant strides while his body tried to readjust and muscles that he hadn't used for two years slowly came back to life.

Matt seemed to be in charge, and after a short warmup he yelled, "Let's go!" Guys scurried around and threw the extra pucks in the nets, and then the guys in white jerseys headed to one bench while the coloured odds and ends headed to the other.

Ricky was heading towards the bench when Matt called him.

"Ricky, you centre me and Johnny."

Ricky turned around and said, "It's okay, I'll start on the bench." He didn't want to step on anybody's toes.

"Don't be stupid," Matt replied. "Get out here."

Ricky came back and stood at centre ice.

"You guys ready?" Matt called to the other team.

They nodded their heads and Matt shot the puck down into the coloured team's end, and, just like that, Ricky's two-year hiatus from the game was over.

His first few shifts were a struggle. His legs felt tight, his passes were off and he couldn't believe how quick the pace was. When he came to the bench after his first shift, he sat down and rested his forehead on the edge of the boards. He was pretty sure he was going to throw up.

"You okay?" Matt asked.

The feeling subsided as Ricky sucked in huge gulps of air.

"I'm good," he gasped.

"Don't feel too bad," Matt said. Ricky was too busy fighting for breath to know that Matt was making fun of him. "The pace is probably quicker here than it was in your last league."

"It sure feels like it," Ricky managed between breaths.

As the hour wore on, however, Ricky began to get his legs back. At the same time, the pace of the game began to slow, as it often does with a bunch of older guys who aren't in the shape that they once were. At one point, Ricky's line was buzzing in the other team's end. Ricky found himself in the left corner, almost on the goal line. When the defenceman came out to challenge him, Ricky deftly put the puck through his legs and stepped around him. His body was now below the goal line, but as a right-hand shot he was able to hold the puck in front of the line. Then he rifled a shot that went straight up and lodged the puck into the top of the net.

The goal had the effect of stunning both benches into silence. Granted, the defenceman was an elementary school teacher and the goalie was a mill worker, but everyone on the ice knew that only a player of exceptional skill could have made that shot.

As the goalie turned to try and whack the puck out of the netting with his stick, the silence was broken by someone on the coloured team's bench.

"Holy shit!" he yelled.

Johnny laughed as he skated by Matt. "Did you see that shot?" he asked.

Matt shook his head. "I saw it, but I don't believe it."

As the clock approached 10:30, Ricky was starting to feel pretty good. His breath was back, his legs felt good and he was having fun. He jumped the boards with Matt and Johnny as Team Multicolours threw the puck into Ricky's end. He circled low into the left corner and then took off. A defenceman hit him with a pass as he cut to the middle of the ice near the blue line. He took the pass and accelerated. One defence-man/millworker was left to beat, and Ricky blew past him along the wall. As he hit the blue line, Ricky wound up and unloaded a slap shot. The goalie didn't move until after the shot had ricocheted off of the crossbar and careened high up into the netting behind the glass.

Once the goalie realized he was still alive, he skated towards Ricky and tried to swing his stick at him.

"Are you crazy?" he screamed.

"Huh?" Ricky didn't know what was wrong.

"There's no slap shots, asshole!" the goalie yelled. "I've got to go to work tomorrow, and I'd like to go in one piece."

Matt arrived and stood between them.

"Easy, Jimbo," he said. "He didn't know."

Jim slowly calmed down and mumbled, "That's okay."

Matt turned to Ricky and laughed. "Nice shot, genius."

"Sorry, I didn't know about the slap shots."

"That's okay. By tomorrow he'll be telling everybody that he robbed you with his glove."

Johnny patted Ricky on the shin pads. "Yeah, but first he'll have to go and change his underwear."

●

With each passing week, Ricky's conditioning improved and his hands came back. He got to the point where he could score at will. For a few weeks he did just that, and then he began to feel the need to seek out new challenges. He made it his goal to set Johnny and Matt up as many times a game as he could. Matt would usually convert the chance, but he quickly realized why Johnny was the brunt of all the "no hands" jokes. Ricky was determined to see Johnny score, but it didn't seem to matter how many times he set him up, Johnny would find a way to miss.

One night, towards the end of December, the boys were sitting in the dressing room after a skate, enjoying the finer points of beer league.

Matt called over to Ricky: "I'm putting together a tournament team in January. Do you want to play?"

Instantly, reflexively, Ricky shook his head.

"Aw, come on, Ricky, I've gone to this tournament five years in a row and I've never made it out of my pool. With you playing, we could win the whole thing."

Ricky's impulse was to refuse again, so he was surprised to hear himself answer, "Where is it?"

Matt saw the opening and pounced. "It's in Thessalon. It's a lot of fun. Sixteen teams from all over northern Ontario. You even get the odd team from southern Ontario. Some of the teams are really serious, but most of them are just there to have fun."

Ricky gave a noncommittal "Hmmmh."

"I guarantee you'll have a good time. Think about it, okay?"

Ricky shrugged and took another sip of his beer. "We'll see," he said.

CHAPTER TWENTY-ONE

Over the Christmas holidays, Ricky and Cheryl flew home. Darryl and Haley picked them up at the airport in Toronto and drove them back to Barrie to spend a few days with their respective families. Ricky and his dad spent a lot of time together in the basement just talking. Darryl was fascinated by the fact that Ricky had started playing hockey again and peppered him with questions. Ricky downplayed the whole thing and assured his dad that it was no big deal, it was just pickup. The night before he left to return to Marathon, Ricky finally told his dad that he was thinking of playing in a tournament. Darryl wasn't sure what the big deal was.

Ricky shrugged his shoulders and looked at the floor.

"What's wrong?" Darryl asked.

"I dunno," Ricky answered. "It's just that I'm worried about having another meltdown."

For once, Darryl didn't know what to say. Finally, he thought of something. "I'm sure you'll be fine."

Ricky looked at his dad. "Easy for you to say. You've never gone nuts in front of eighteen thousand people."

Darryl grinned. "Look on the bright side, Ricky."

"What's that?"

"If you melt down in Thessalon, there won't be eighteen *people* there, let alone eighteen thousand."

Slowly, Ricky smiled. "That's real encouraging, Dad. Thanks for that."

Darryl smiled. "No problem. We should have these talks more often."

●

On the first Friday in January, Ricky left work early to start the long drive down to Thessalon. After Matt's constant goading, a talk with Cheryl and several phone calls home to his dad, he had finally agreed to play.

Accompanied by Matt, Robbie, Johnny, their hockey bags, sticks, luggage and enough beer to supply a good-size wedding, Ricky pulled out of Marathon at two in the afternoon and headed south on Highway 17. Six hours later, they arrived in Thessalon in time to grab a quick bite and check into their hotel. Then it was off to the rink to get ready for their first game, which was scheduled for nine o'clock.

On the way down in the truck, Matt had explained the tournament format: sixteen teams were grouped into four pools; you were guaranteed three games because you played each of the other teams in your pool; the winners of each pool played off in two semifinal games, with the winners advancing to the final. Games consisted of two twenty-minute periods; in the event of a tie, you played a five-minute sudden-death overtime period, followed by a shootout, which was also sudden death. The teams that made it to the semifinals won back their entry fees. The winning team won back its entry fee plus fifteen hundred dollars. The way Matt figured it, if they won, that would pretty well cover most of their expenses for the weekend.

When they got to the rink, Ricky was surprised to realize that he didn't know a lot of the guys on the team. He thought the team would be made up mostly of guys from the Wednesday night skate. However, the only players from Wednesday nights were Matt, Robbie and Johnny. The guys Matt introduced him to had some serious hockey credentials—three guys, including the goaltender, had played junior for the Marathon Renegades, while a fourth had played collegiate hockey at Lakehead University in Thunder Bay.

Ricky was really jittery as he got ready for the game. It had been a long time since he had felt the adrenaline pumping like it was just now. When they took the ice for a brief warmup, Ricky noticed that his legs were really stiff from the long drive. He did his best to get loose, but he knew it would be several shifts before he found his legs. As they skated around, he kept stealing glances at the opposition, a team out of Sault Ste. Marie.

He skated past Matt and observed, "They look quick."

"They should," Matt answered. "They won this tournament last year."

Ricky let out a sarcastic laugh. "No way!"

"Yup, just my luck," Matt said. "Drive six hours to draw the defending champs."

If Ricky thought that the pace was quick on Wednesday nights, he was sadly mistaken. This was good, fast hockey. It took him two or three shifts to adjust. What corrections he did make were primarily defensive, because the Soo controlled the play for most of the first period. Apparently their legs were a little fresher than those of Team Marathon.

The only saving grace for Marathon was that Matt had made an excellent choice of goaltender. He was the only reason it was just 1–0 for the Soo at the end of the first period. After using the first twenty minutes to adjust to the pace and work out the kinks from his legs, Ricky elevated his play in the second period and Marathon began to take the offence to the Soo. Early in the period, Ricky scored on a bullet of a wrist shot from the slot. Then he put any thoughts of a goaltenders' battle to rest when he scored three more times late in the second period. Marathon won the game 4–1 and was pulling away at the wire.

After the game, the boys were sitting in the dressing room having a beer when the door opened. One of the tournament organizers entered and handed Matt the game sheet.

"Who's Ricky Phillips?" he asked.

"Right here," Ricky answered.

"Here's your prize," said the man.

"Prize? What for?" Ricky asked.

"Player of the game." He handed Ricky a plastic bucket, then turned and left the room.

Ricky took the bucket and began to rummage through it. It contained a T-shirt, a puck and a nice new skate rag, all branded with the tournament logo. Under the skate rag, he found coupons for free food and beer at the booster club upstairs, as well as a free skate sharpening.

The other players were admiring his prize pack when Ricky said, to no one in particular, "I haven't won a prize in a hockey game since the All-Star Game in Atlanta."

"What'd you get for winning?" someone asked.

"A Chevy Tahoe," he answered.

The room went suddenly very quiet.

Ricky looked around at their startled faces and mumbled, "But this is nice, too."

●

After the game, the team went up to the booster club to celebrate the win and tell a few tales. Ricky was sitting quietly, sipping his beer from his plastic cup and listening to the boys banter back and forth.

At one point, someone said to Robbie, "What's with that thing on your face?"

Robbie, who was very thin on top, had been trying without much success to grow a goatee. He rubbed his chin thoughtfully and said, "The way I see it is if I can grow some hair on my face, then maybe my head will catch on."

"Why not just take some from your back?" one of the boys asked.

Everyone except Robbie laughed, and the conversation moved on. They were discussing where to go for some food before heading back to the hotel when a man came up behind Ricky and asked, "Is this a private party, or can anyone join in?"

Ricky jumped up and turned around, and there stood Ben McMillan. Ricky was so excited that he grabbed his old GM in a huge bear hug. The boys were exchanging startled, quizzical glances when Ricky made some hasty introductions. Then he turned to Ben and said, "Mr. McMillan, please, join us."

Before he could even take a seat, Ricky asked him, "So what are you doing here?"

"Same thing I've always done," McMillan answered. "I'm watching hockey games."

"Are you still with the Colts?" Ricky asked.

"I retired a few years ago as the GM. Now I just scout."

"How long have you been up north?"

"Almost two weeks."

"See anyone you like?"

"There's a big kid, defenceman out of Elliot Lake. He's pretty green, but he might turn into a player," McMillan answered.

Robbie interrupted. "Sorry to butt in, Ricky. We're gonna grab a bite to eat. Do you wanna come?"

Ricky looked at McMillan, who was starting to stand up. "You go on with your friends," he said. "It was nice to bump into you, Ricky."

"Wait," Ricky said. "Mr. McMillan, do you have a minute?"

"Sure."

"Can I buy you a beer?"

"Are you kidding?"

Ricky laughed and turned to Robbie. "You guys go on ahead. I'll meet you back at the hotel." He went and bought two more beers, then returned to his seat with McMillan.

"So," he asked, "how did you know it was me?"

"They have a centreman here in Thessalon that I wanted to have another look at. I was looking for the rink attendant to see if he knew when they played again, when I noticed this guy bury a wrist shot in the top corner."

Ricky grinned.

"'I'd know that shot anywhere,' I said to myself, so I stayed and watched to the end of the game."

McMillan took a long pull on his beer, then looked at Ricky. "So now you know why *I'm* in Thessalon, Ontario. The big question is, what are *you* doing here?"

Ricky looked at his old mentor. "What do you mean?"

"What do I mean?" McMillan echoed. "Ricky, you should be in the NHL."

Ricky laughed. "NHL! Mr. McMillan—"

"Ben," he interrupted.

"Okay . . . Ben. I haven't played hockey for almost three years."

"Doesn't matter."

"What do you mean it doesn't matter?" Ricky asked.

"Just that: it doesn't matter. I watched you play tonight."

Ricky shook his head as he cut him off. "You watched me play in a beer-league tournament. It's a long way from The Show."

Now Ben shook his head. "Ricky, I've been scouting hockey a long time. What I saw tonight was a guy with big-league skills. You can still play in The Show if you want to. I don't give a rat's ass about the calibre of the tournament or the other players. A scout spends all his time looking for that one diamond that's hidden amongst all of the hockey rough. You were the diamond when you were sixteen, and you're still the diamond at . . ."

"Twenty-four," Ricky interjected.

Ricky downed the rest of his beer and tried to decide how much further he wanted this conversation to go. McMillan was watching him calmly, as though he knew it was Ricky's turn to speak.

Oh, what the hell, Ricky thought. "Ben," he asked, "how much did you hear about my last game?"

McMillan cleared his throat before answering, uncomfortably, "I heard you had a nervous breakdown."

Ricky smiled sadly. "That's putting it mildly. My shrink said I suffered from a severe case of post-traumatic stress disorder and I completely disassociated myself from reality. It took several months on some pretty heavy drugs and daily therapy sessions before I came back."

McMillan nodded his head sympathetically.

Ricky took a deep breath and continued. "I've come to grips with Charlie's death. I've even rediscovered my joy for the game. I'm having a lot of fun with these guys. My biggest concern is that if I play at a higher level, or if it got too rough again, that I might snap."

"Ricky," McMillan said, "men's rec leagues can get pretty rough."

Ricky looked into his empty beer cup. "I doubt that it's like The Show, though."

McMillan smiled sagely. "I wouldn't be too sure about that. Guys are serious about their hockey at any level."

"Well, so far it's been pretty tame."

McMillan stood up and held out his hand. "I hope you're right."

Ricky stood and shook McMillan's hand. "It was really great to see you."

McMillan smiled. "I'll see you tomorrow morning. I want to watch you play again before I hit the road. Now go on and catch up to your friends."

"Okay," Ricky said. "I'll see you in the morning."

❂

At eight o'clock the next morning, Team Marathon took the ice for their second game. Ricky was in a lot better shape than most of the guys, who had stayed up late drinking and were now paying a heavy price, but he was still tired. He had gone to bed early, only to find himself tossing and turning. He'd spent most of the night thinking about his conversation with Ben McMillan.

When their opponents came out onto the ice, it was painfully obvious that they, too, had overindulged. The two teams warmed up in absolute silence.

Ricky skated past Matt and asked, "Where are these guys from?"

Matt answered groggily, "Can you keep your voice down, Ricky? They're from Blind River."

Ricky smiled impishly. "Tough night?"

"Just a little."

"I thought you said that you wanted to win this tournament."

"I do," Matt protested. "I just forgot at four o'clock this morning. You should have reminded me."

"I would have, but I was sleeping," Ricky answered.

"That's a good idea, Ricky. I'm going to go lie down on the bench and sleep. You take these guys on for a while."

The referee blew his whistle, and Matt let out a groan. Ricky laughed and skated to centre ice for the face-off.

Blind River had no answer for Ricky's speed and energy. He scored four times in the first period, and by the time the buzzer sounded, Marathon was up 5–0. Early on, Blind River realized they were in over their heads, and Marathon's speed, combined with their lack of sleep and sore heads, put them in a very bad mood. They stopped skating and resorted to hacking and whacking. Consequently, the game got very dirty.

Ricky was still pretty new to rec-league hockey, and he was unfamiliar with the etiquette. Late in the second period, he came flying through the neutral zone and unleashed a howitzer at the goalie. The puck just missed his head and slammed off the glass behind the net. The puck hit so hard that it bounced all the way back out into the neutral zone. Marathon cleared the zone, and one of the defencemen hit Ricky with another pass. This time, he flew naively down the left side and cut hard behind the net. He looked up just in time to see Blind River's biggest player flying at him.

Instinctively, Ricky dropped his shoulder and caught the would-be assassin square in the chest. The attacker bounced off of him and landed flat on his butt. Ricky never broke stride and cut out in front of the net, where he neatly deposited a backhand past the goalie for his fifth goal of the game. Ricky raised his stick to celebrate the goal just as the Blind River player got back to his feet and came flying at him for a second time. Ricky saw him just in time and brought his hands down to cover his face. The Blind River player tried to throw a series of gloved punches at Ricky. The rest of the players joined in to break up the ruckus.

"Have you run up the score enough yet, asshole?" the Blind River player snarled.

"Oh, suck it up, Alice!" Ricky shot back.

Matt grabbed Ricky and steered him away from the scrum.

"Ricky!" he yelled. "Take it easy!"

When Ricky looked at Matt, he was smiling. "It's okay, Matt. I feel good."

"What?"

"I feel good. I don't think I'm gonna go nuts."

"Nuts?!" Matt repeated. "I don't care about your mental state, you idiot. I just don't want you to fight."

Ricky was still smiling at him.

"Listen to me: if you fight, you'll be kicked out of the tournament."

Just then, the referee skated over. "Sixteen, let's go!"

"What for?" Ricky yelled angrily.

"Two for roughing."

Matt grabbed Ricky by the jersey and pushed him towards the penalty box. "Get your ass in that box and sit there. When your penalty's done, get over to the bench and sit there till the end of the game. These cement heads just want to get you kicked out."

Ricky skated over to the penalty box and sat down. It was like sitting in an old, comfy easy chair. He was elated. He had knocked a player down and he had got right back up. And what's more, no one had gotten hurt. He looked around the penalty box and smiled to himself, "There's no place like home."

●

After the game, Ricky was the first one changed. He was hoping to see Ben McMillan before he left. He walked out into the heated viewing area but couldn't find him, so he made his way over to the concession stand and bought a Gatorade. Then he went to the window and watched the start of the next game. He was standing there when he heard a voice behind him say, "Nice game."

He turned around and smiled at McMillan. "Thanks," he said. "I thought I'd missed you."

McMillan smiled. "Had to hit the can one more time before I hit the road."

Ricky nodded. "Where you off to now?"

"I'll pick my way home," McMillan said. "I'll stop in Espanola and Sudbury, maybe Parry Sound, but I better get going. I've been up here longer than I planned."

Ricky nodded again and said, "I'll walk you to your car."

The two men walked in silence until they got to McMillan's car. Ben turned and smiled at Ricky. He held out his hand and said, "It was really great to see you."

Ricky shook his hand, then summoned the courage to ask the question that had been weighing on his mind since last night.

"Did you mean what you said last night about, you know, me playing in The Show?"

"Skill-wise?"

"I guess so."

"Skill-wise, you could play right now."

Ricky didn't respond, so McMillan went on. "Ricky, you've always been able to do things that other players couldn't. You skate beautifully, you've got great hands and you've got great size."

Ricky smiled at the compliment.

McMillan got in his car and started it. While the engine was warming up, he rolled down his window. He looked up at Ricky and smiled. "Ricky, my last piece of advice is this: if you are thinking of making a comeback, you'd better not wait too long. Father Time has a nasty way of sneaking up on us. I know you've had a tough time, but you'll never forgive yourself if you decide when you're forty that you should have tried again."

Ricky nodded.

McMillan put his car in gear. "Make the comeback, Ricky. I know you can play at that level." Then he pulled out of the parking lot and drove away.

Ricky was still standing there long after McMillan's car had disappeared from sight.

Huh, he thought to himself. I wonder.

●

After a very quiet afternoon spent trying to catch up on sleep lost the night before, the boys took the ice for their game against a team from Manitoulin Island. With two games now under their belts, they were starting to gel nicely as a team. They had good goaltending, decent defence and a lot of skill at forward. And then, of course, there was Ricky. He seemed to get better with every shift. He added three more goals in the Manitoulin game to give him twelve in three games. Marathon won easily, 6–2, to advance to the semifinal.

On Saturday night, the boys arrived at the rink for their third game of the day. They had drawn a team from Sudbury in the semifinal. Matt appeared to be extremely jittery.

"You okay?" Ricky asked.

"Yeah," he answered rather gloomily. "It's just that I was looking at the results of the four pools, and I think they have the two best teams paired up in the semi."

Ricky laughed. "Is that all that's bothering you?"

Matt nodded.

"Well, look at it this way: once we beat Sudbury, we'll have an easier time in the final."

Matt's sense of trepidation proved to be well founded. Sudbury had a smooth-skating, disciplined team. They also had done some advance scouting because they double-teamed Ricky on every shift. He told Matt and Johnny to go to the net and he'd find them, but by the end of the first period their line had failed to generate any scoring chances. The period ended 0–0 and the scoring chances were about even.

Early in the second period, Sudbury scored on a fluky shot that bounced in off a Marathon defencemen's skate. Ricky's line continued to struggle, but Marathon's second line scored halfway through the period to tie the game.

On the next shift, Sudbury broke out of their end nicely, fed their right winger on a long outlet pass, and he buried a shot high on the stick side to regain the lead. The score stayed that way until the end of the game. With a minute and a half to go, Marathon had a face-off deep in their own end. Ricky won the draw back to his defenceman, who outlet it to Johnny on the right half-board. Two Sudbury skaters were marking Ricky, while the other three retreated to the neutral zone. Johnny looked like he wasn't sure what to do.

"Go! Go!" Ricky yelled.

Johnny started to move up the right side. When he got to the red line, Ricky screamed, "Dump it in!"

Johnny flicked the puck high in the air and Ricky took off after it at full speed. The Marathon goalie bolted for the bench and a sixth attacker jumped onto the ice. The puck landed on edge and took a funny hop, which the Sudbury defenceman had difficulty handling. The second that it took him to regain control was long enough for Ricky to get there and quickly strip the defenceman of the puck. Ricky then turned away from the D and was promptly hammered into the boards by two Sudbury checkers.

So much for non-contact, he thought as he battled to control the puck. With three players on him, Ricky knew there should be teammates open everywhere. The three Sudbury players were trying to pin Ricky and the puck against the boards and force a face-off. Desperately, Ricky pushed himself away from the boards with his hands and kicked the puck down into the corner. The puck went right to Johnny, and the three Sudbury players converged on him instantly.

"Johnny! Back!" Ricky yelled.

Johnny, who seemed only too happy to get rid of the puck, instantly passed the puck back to Ricky. The result was that the three Sudbury players were caught scrambling, and for the first time in the entire game Ricky was left unchecked. He used the time to take a quick look around the ice. He spotted Matt all alone on the left hash mark and ripped a pass over to him. Matt one-timed the pass and got a good shot off. The Sudbury goalie slid across and made a fantastic save, but he couldn't control the rebound. The puck deflected to the goalie's left side, where it landed on a patch of open ice. The first person to arrive was Johnny, who had started to the net after passing the puck to Ricky. Johnny slapped desperately at the puck, and it fluttered past the helpless goalie and landed in the back of the net. It was Johnny's first goal of the winter, and he jumped in the air as if he had just won the Stanley Cup.

The two teams faced off at centre ice and the remaining seconds wound down without further incident. The overtime was spirited, but neither team managed to muster a quality scoring chance. Both teams headed back to their benches and got ready for the shootout.

Matt grabbed some water and splashed it on his face while he tried to catch his breath.

"Ricky, if I win the coin toss, do you want to shoot first or let them shoot?"

Ricky was leaning on the boards and breathing heavily. He shrugged. "It's a tough call. If you go first and score, the pressure's on them. If you miss, they have a huge advantage because they can win it with one shot."

The ref blew his whistle and called for the captains. Matt went over to the referee and returned a few seconds later.

"I lost the toss and they're shooting first," was all he said.

The player who had scored both of Sudbury's goals skated out to centre ice. The ref blew his whistle and the shooter started towards the net. Marathon's goalie came out to challenge. The forward gave a little fake with his head, but the goalie didn't bite. The forward now had no choice but to try and deke. He pulled the puck hard to his back-hand just as the goalie sprawled back towards the net with his legs. The forward flicked a hard backhand that beat the goalie cleanly. The puck rang loudly off the goalpost and landed harmlessly in the corner of the rink. The Marathon bench erupted in a loud cheer.

"What a beautiful sound!" Matt yelled. "Okay, Ricky, get out there and win this thing!"

Ricky got up off the bench and stepped out onto the ice. "You got it, Coach," he smiled.

Ricky skated towards centre ice and looked at the ref. He had already decided that, unless the goalie came out a ridiculously long way, he would shoot.

"You ready?" the ref asked.

Ricky nodded his head and the ref blew his whistle.

Ricky skated towards the puck and picked it up. As he moved towards the blue line he veered off sharply towards the right boards. He looked up to see the goalie trying to adjust his angle. Ricky picked up speed as he hit the top of the circle and cut to the middle of the ice, where he pulled the puck to his backhand. The goalie moved to his right and tried to stay with Ricky. The instant that the goalie moved, Ricky drew the puck back to his forehand and released a lightning-fast wrist shot. The puck bulged the twine in the top corner before the goalie could even react. Ricky circled into the corner and raised his stick to celebrate. Team Marathon was headed to the final.

●

Saturday night's celebration was somewhat more subdued than Friday's had been. Matt was suddenly in drill sergeant mode, reminding everyone to watch how much they drank and to be sure and get some rest.

One of the guys let out a sigh. "Come on, Matt. We came here to have fun."

Matt nodded. "Yeah, yeah, and I want you to have fun, but I want to win, too. I've been coming here for five years, and this is the first time I've had a chance to win."

"Don't worry," someone else answered. "It's in the bag."

And it was. On Sunday afternoon, Marathon beat a team from Huntsville, 4–1. Ricky had two goals and an assist. After they collected their winnings and said their goodbyes, Ricky, Matt, Johnny and Robbie loaded up the truck and hit the road for the long journey back to Marathon.

The time passed quickly thanks to the banter and Matt's repeated choruses of "We Are the Champions." Ricky was his usual quiet self. He enjoyed the banter and had grown to love the scenery of the north shore of Lake Superior, but he was also deep in thought. Although it would be a long time before he could ever share his thoughts with anyone else, Ricky was starting to contemplate a comeback.

CHAPTER TWENTY-TWO

The rest of the winter went by quickly. Matt entered the team in two more tournaments and they won both. The boys introduced Ricky to snowmobiling and ice fishing. He enjoyed both, but not nearly as much as he enjoyed fishing in the summertime, because of his view that all activities were improved by the involvement of a boat.

As the northern winter slowly began to release its hold on the area and grudgingly gave way to spring, Ricky's sense of restlessness increased. Shortly after the team's return from the Thessalon tournament, Ricky had taken out a membership at the local gym. He wanted to increase his cardio and his strength, but found it very difficult to do on his own. After a couple of weeks of half-hearted workouts he talked to the owner of the gym, and by the end of the conversation, Ricky had hired him as his personal trainer. The seriousness of his workouts increased, and so did the results. By the end of March he had increased his best-ever bench press by five pounds; by the end of April he was riding the stationary bike longer and harder than he ever did in San Jose.

One day, Ricky came home from a particularly exhausting workout, flopped down on the couch and picked up the phone. He punched in a number and waited.

"Hello?"

"Hi, Dad."

"Ricky! How are you?"

"I'm good."

Darryl always knew when something was on Ricky's mind. "Everything okay?"

"Yeah, yeah. I've just been thinking, that's all."

"What about?"

Ricky hesitated before answering. For some reason, he was embarrassed. "I've been thinking about making a comeback."

Now it was Darryl's turn to hesitate. "Comeback?"

"What do you think?" Ricky asked nervously.

Darryl recovered quickly and laughed. "Well, you *were* the MVP of the Thessalon tournament. I'd say you have a shot."

Ricky laughed too. "Real funny, Dad."

Suddenly, Darryl turned serious. "Let me tell you a story," he said. "When I was seventeen, I made the Junior A team in Orillia. We were really good—went all the way to the national final. The next year, the team management were determined to win the whole thing. They brought in a bunch of hotshot twenty-year-olds, and three games into the season I was a healthy scratch. That's how I ended up playing in Barrie for Ben McMillan. Leaving Orillia was the hardest decision of my life. Orillia versus Barrie is the small-town equivalent of Toronto versus Montreal. I felt like Benedict Arnold when I went down to try out for the Colts."

Ricky laughed, and his dad continued with his story.

"Did I ever tell you that I had a Gordie Howe hat trick in my first game with the Colts?"

Darryl was never shy about sharing stories from his glory days. Ricky smiled and said, "Oh yeah, Dad, you've told me many times."

Darryl was still laughing when he had a sudden realization. "You know what?" he asked Ricky.

"What?"

"I just realized that the highlight of my hockey career came when I was seventeen. I was washed up by eighteen."

Well, that's a cheery thought, Ricky thought to himself.

Darryl seemed to read his mind and nodded at his end of the phone. "You never know when something that you love will come to an end."

Ricky thought about this, then said, "Well, I better go, Dad. Thanks for your time."

"Ricky?"

"Yeah, Dad?"

"You'll never forgive yourself if you don't at least try. You've been out of the game for a long time. Maybe you'll make it, maybe you won't. But you have to try. Make the comeback—I think it's awesome."

Ricky thanked his dad and hung up the phone.

●

Early in May, Marathon was greeted with an unusually warm, sunny day. Ricky wasted no time in launching his boat and getting out on the water. The lake was incredibly calm, and he and Cheryl enjoyed a relaxing day bobbing out on the water, trolling listlessly in and around the islands that dot the shoreline west of Marathon.

As he was watching his bobber sit uselessly on the surface of the lake, Ricky suddenly said to Cheryl, "Are you happy here?"

"Uh oh," Cheryl answered. "What are you up to now, Ricky?"

Ricky kept staring out at the water. "I want to go back to my cottage for the summer."

"Uh-huh. And are you planning to come back in the fall?"

He flicked his rod and muttered, "I don't think so."

Cheryl slammed her rod off of the side of the boat. "Ricky, you've got to be kidding!" she yelled.

"Keep your voice down—you're scaring the fish," Ricky tried to joke.

Cheryl didn't think he was funny. "Keep my voice down?! Are you crazy?"

Ricky laughed. "No, in fact. I think I'm doing better."

Cheryl was *not* in the mood to be humoured. "I don't get you, Ricky. First you decide to move to the middle of nowhere. Now you want to move back? I just got here. Got myself a job. Got settled, met some friends and now you want to leave again."

Humour hadn't worked, so now Ricky opted for the safe approach: silence. He stared out over the water and kept his mouth shut.

"*Ahhh!*" she yelled. "Men are so frustrating!"

Ricky smiled but kept his head down. It was safer that way.

"Okay, I give up. What do you want to do next fall? No, wait, I know: you're going to move to Whitehorse and sell real estate!" Cheryl said sarcastically.

"No," Ricky answered. For the first time, he looked away from the water and looked at Cheryl. "I'm thinking of trying to play hockey again," he said quietly.

His answer caught Cheryl so far off guard that she found herself momentarily speechless. Suddenly, it all made sense—the crazy workouts at the gym, his refusal to eat junk food.

"You're going to try a comeback?" she asked.

He nodded. "What do you think?"

Cheryl sighed. The anger was ebbing out of her and she was suddenly feeling tired. "I think you were born to play hockey, and if you want to play again, then I think that's wonderful." She smiled and rubbed his back.

"So what's your plan?" she asked.

Ricky shrugged his shoulders. "I dunno. I don't really have one. I thought I'd skate in Gravenhurst this summer, and if I feel like I'm keeping up I'll phone Mr. Crichton and ask if I can walk on with San Jose."

"Walk on?"

"San Jose still owns my rights, so if I were going to play, I'd have to try out with them."

"Oh," Cheryl answered. "So Ricky, this plan that you don't really have ... does it include me anywhere? Or am I going to stay in Marathon and work for Mr. Coleman?"

"I dunno," he said. "I guess that's up to you."

That wasn't the answer she was looking for, and she frowned.

"Oh hey," Ricky said. "Look, I've got a bite."

As he started to reel in his line, Cheryl noticed that the rod wasn't bending. "Must be a heck of a big fish," she muttered.

"I think it's a doozy," Ricky said as he struggled gamely

to reel in the line. He finally pulled it in, and sure enough, there wasn't a fish on the end.

"That's funny," he muttered. "I was sure I felt something. Maybe my bobber is too heavy."

He took the plastic red-and-white bobber and shook it, and something rattled inside it. Carefully, he pulled the two halves apart and looked inside.

Cheryl was peeking over his shoulder, trying to see what he was doing. "What is it?" she asked.

He turned around to face her and showed her the small object inside the bobber. "I don't know . . . you tell me."

The scream Cheryl let out could probably have been heard halfway to Wawa. She threw her arms around him and gave him a huge hug.

"Easy! Easy!" Ricky warned. "Don't drop it."

"Don't drop it?" she repeated incredulously. "You've had my engagement ring dangling in two hundred feet of water inside a ten-cent bobber for the last hour, and now you're worried about me dropping it?"

Ricky laughed and put the ring on her finger. "Is that a yes?" he asked.

Cheryl gave him a kiss. "Yes, it's a yes, you big cement head."

❀

Ricky and Cheryl met with Mr. Coleman to tell him they wouldn't be returning in the fall. Mr. Coleman took the news very graciously.

"I always knew you'd go back to hockey, Ricky," he said.

"Why's that?" Ricky asked.

Mr. Coleman shrugged knowingly. "I just couldn't see you doing a nine-to-five job for the rest of your life." Then he shook Ricky's hand and hugged Cheryl.

"I'll follow the Sharks with great interest next year."

"I wouldn't get your hopes up," Ricky answered. "I have no idea if I'll make the team."

Mr. Coleman smiled. "You'll make it. I've seen you play."

"You did?" Ricky asked. "When?"

"When you were with the Sharks. I'm a big hockey fan, *Richard*," he said coyly.

Ricky blushed. "You mean you knew who I was all along?" he asked incredulously.

Mr. Coleman laughed. "The seventy-five you shot with rented clubs on the first day we met was a bit of a giveaway." Then his eyes got puffy and he cleared his throat. "Good luck."

"Thanks," Ricky said.

Mr. Coleman gave Cheryl a kiss on the cheek and said, "Now get out of here. Northern men aren't supposed to cry, and I don't want you to see me break the tradition."

●

Matt, Johnny and Robbie came over and helped Ricky and Cheryl finish up their packing. Surprisingly, this goodbye proved to be easier than the one with Mr. Coleman. One reason was that the boys were really excited for Ricky. They were also fascinated by the concept that a guy who had played pickup hockey with them in Marathon this year could be playing in the NHL next year. Finally, they all knew they would see each other again.

"You're coming to the wedding, right?" Ricky asked.

"Just tell us where and when," Johnny answered.

Robbie nodded his bald head eagerly.

Matt shook his head. "We'll see you well before that."

"Oh yeah? When?" Ricky asked.

"Wherever you get us tickets. Minnesota or Detroit would be great road trips. We'll fly, too. You just get the tickets, we'll look after the rest."

Ricky hugged his friends.

"Tickets . . . that's all I have to do?"

"Well, beer would be nice too."

Ricky laughed, got in his truck and honked his horn in farewell. Then he and Cheryl pulled out of the driveway and headed off towards their next adventure.

Part Four

CHAPTER TWENTY-THREE

Chris Popovich groaned, rolled over and half-consciously swung his arm at the alarm clock to silence it. Instantly, he was asleep again. Nine minutes later, the damn thing went off again. He grudgingly pushed himself up to a sitting position, silenced the alarm and rubbed his eyes. For years he had been getting up earlier in the summer than he did during the work year, and it had never been difficult. But this year had been tough. He was exhausted. Ricky was completely wearing him down.

When Ricky first got back to Muskoka, he had dropped three bombshells on Popo. The first was that he was engaged, the second that he was going to attempt a comeback and the third that he wanted Popo to be his personal trainer.

"I'll pay you," Ricky had offered.

"Don't be stupid," he had answered. "I don't take money from friends."

"I just thought it might help to motivate you."

"I'll help you because you're my friend, Ricky. Don't worry about my motivation."

That conversation had taken place over a month ago. Popo had thought that Ricky was dreaming to think that he could play in The Show again. Sure, he was a former Hart Trophy winner, but he hadn't played for almost three years. It wasn't as if he had gone to some league in Switzerland or Germany and kept playing. He hadn't played—period. Come to think of it, over the past three summers, Popo couldn't remember Ricky even mentioning hockey.

Then there was the question of Ricky's mental health. The last game he had played in, he had gone nuts. So the guy moves up north, plays a couple of games in some loser beer league and suddenly he thinks he can play in the NHL. Not wanting to hurt his friend's feelings, Popo had agreed to help him with his training. He figured that they'd last a week or two and Ricky would give up. He figured Ricky had a better chance of discovering that Elvis was alive and working at the local video store than of returning to the big league. But Ricky had been relentless, and slowly he had worn Popo down and made him a believer.

Now, each morning when Ricky picked him up, he was on a bicycle. No more tranquil morning rides in the ski boat over to the golf course. Now Ricky would jump off of the bike, hand it over to Popo and then lumber off down the road. Popo would curse under his breath, get on the bike and set off after Ricky. Ten kilometres later, Ricky would end his jog and smile at Popo. Then he'd get back on the bike and say, "See you at the gym in an hour," ride the five kilometres back to his cottage, shower, and then head over to the gym.

Later that day, while he was standing behind the bench press, spotting Ricky while he lifted a ridiculous amount of weight, Popo said, "Tell me again why we can't play golf in the morning anymore."

"Because," Ricky grunted as he pushed the bar up.

Popo caught the bar and helped Ricky place the weight back on its support.

Ricky sat up and rested on the bench for a minute. "The golf is my mental training this summer. It's easy to play golf in the morning when you're fresh. It's harder after a 10-k run, a full workout and an hour on the stationary bike."

Popo shook his head in a way that said, "You're nuttier than I thought."

Ricky smiled. "Popo, when do you make mistakes in a hockey game?"

"When you're tired."

"Right. And when do you take stupid penalties?"

"When you're tired."

"Right. So after a full day of working out and I'm tired, I have to really concentrate on the golf. It's easier to make mistakes—choose the wrong club, swing too hard, make dumb decisions. Playing golf when I'm tired is great mental training."

"I think not playing golf in the morning is dumb and mental," Popo muttered.

Ricky looked at his friend. "Chris," he said.

Popo twisted his head to look at Ricky, who *never* called him Chris.

"If you're uncomfortable helping me, you don't have to do it."

Popo looked down. "It's okay, Ricky. I'll help you."

"Would you prefer that I pay you? Make it more of a business relationship."

"You couldn't afford me," Popo said.

Ricky laughed. "How much?"

Without thinking, Popo said, "Two grand a week."

"Done," Ricky said.

"Forget it. I don't want your money."

"You don't think I can come back, do you?" Ricky asked.

Shit! Don't ask me that, Popo thought. "No, no. It's not that, Ricky."

"What, then?"

Popo sighed. "I dunno. You've certainly made a believer out of me with your conditioning. I guess . . . I dunno, maybe when we skate next week, we'll get a better indication of where you're at."

Ricky nodded his head. "Fair enough," he said, adding, "Tell you what: I'll make you a deal."

"What's that?" Popo asked.

"If I make the Sharks lineup, I'll pay you two thousand dollars a week for services rendered. If I don't, you've helped me out for a summer simply for being my friend."

Popo smiled. "Sounds like I win either way."

●

Popo took the ice at the Gravenhurst Arena and skated around slowly, trying to get loose. Then he went over to the bench and lifted his left leg up onto the top of the boards. He leaned his head down as far as he could towards his knee. When he had done this on both legs, he turned around so that he was facing centre ice. Then he got down on his hands and knees and slowly stretched out his groin muscles. For the next month he would skate twice a week with a collection of incredible players, and he wanted to make sure he was loose. He didn't want to get hurt, because the hockey he played in the summer blew away the pickup he played in the winter.

While he stretched, he looked around the rink. Skating past him were seven current NHLers, three more who were retired, four guys who played in the American league, two who had played in the O, and two guys who had earned educations on full hockey scholarships in the United States. That left him and his wrecked knee . . . and his buddy who hadn't been on the ice for three years. Well, he thought sarcastically, he *did* play in the Marathon National Beer League. Oh man, we are so screwed.

Just then, Ricky stepped out onto the ice. Popo watched him keenly, waiting for the first glimpse of . . . what? Rusty hands or mental instability. He wasn't sure which would be worse. But as Ricky moved around the ice, he looked different. He looked relaxed and confident.

After a brief warmup, the scrimmage started. On his first shift, Popo was fighting for the puck in his own zone. He came up with the puck and spun around in time to see Ricky take off up the middle of the rink. Popo hit him with a pass just as the opposing D pinched in hard on Ricky. In one motion, Ricky received the pass, put it through the defenceman's feet, stepped around him and took off. He bolted through the neutral zone and went one on one with the next D. He blew past him like he wasn't there, went in on the goalie and sniped one high to the glove side.

Ricky turned and headed back to the neutral zone while the other team brought the puck back up the ice.

Popo skated up to him and said, "Where'd that come from?"

Ricky smiled. "I learned it in Marathon."

By the end of the skate, Ricky had scored three more times and Popo was looking forward to tomorrow morning's workout. My friend's going to play in The Show, he thought to himself. Popo was now a believer.

●

John Crichton sat in his office and did a slow burn. He prided himself on always being in control of situations, but he had just been caught completely off guard and now he was furious with himself. A few minutes earlier his phone had rung. Casually, he'd picked it up.

"John Crichton," he muttered.

"Hello, Mr. Crichton," said a pleasant voice at the other end. "This is Ricky Phillips."

What the hell? Crichton thought. "Ricky!" he said, gathering himself. "How are you?"

"I'm good, sir. How are you?"

"I'm good. Jeez, Ricky, it's been a long time. To what do I owe the pleasure?"

"Well," Ricky said, "I was wondering if I could come to tryouts?"

Crichton never hesitated. "Sure you can, Ricky. That would be great." Crichton could feel Ricky relax all the way through the phone line.

"That's awesome, Mr. Crichton, thank you. So, when do I report?"

"Well, you've already missed rookie camp," Crichton said, "but you can come and take your physical on September 12, and camp opens on the fifteenth."

"I really appreciate the opportunity, Mr. Crichton," Ricky said.

Crichton was still feeling caught off guard by the suddenness of Ricky's call. All he could muster was "No problem, Ricky."

"Okay, then. I guess I'll see you in September," Ricky replied. Then he hung up and, just like that, the ghost from the past was gone.

Five minutes after the phone conversation ended, Crichton still hadn't moved. The flashing of the light on his intercom snapped him out of his funk. Crichton picked up the phone.

"Yes?" he said curtly.

"Sir, Coach Lester is here to see you," his receptionist responded pleasantly.

Crichton ran his fingers through his hair and sighed. "Tell him to give me five minutes."

He stood up and walked to his window. He stood there for a long time and looked aimlessly out the window, his eyes seeing nothing in particular, his mind racing. Damn it, John. You've got to learn to think quicker on your feet, he thought to himself. Then he laughed bitterly and shook his head.

"'Sure Ricky, come on out to camp,'" he muttered in a mocking tone. "'Waste everybody's time, take up a spot. And then I'll have the pleasure of cutting you.' Shit! How could I have been so stupid?"

Ron Lester opened the door and smiled. "Talking to yourself, Johnny?"

Crichton spun around, embarrassed. "What do you want, Ron?" he asked gruffly.

"Now, what could possibly have you so riled up this early in the morning?" Lester asked.

Crichton turned back towards the window and leaned on the sill.

"You'll never guess who just called me: Ricky Phillips."

"Oh yeah?" Lester smiled. "How's he doing?"

Crichton glared at Lester and walked over to his desk. "How's he doing? He wants to come to camp."

"That's great," Lester answered. "It'll be good to see him."

Crichton flopped angrily into his chair. "Great?! Are you serious? He's just going to take up space and waste everybody's time!"

Lester had worked with Crichton long enough now to know that there was no point trying to reason with him when he was wound up. He knew that if he kept quiet, Crichton would vent at him and get it out of his system. Letting out a sigh, he sat down in the chair across from Crichton's desk.

As if on cue, Crichton started in on him. "Do you honestly think that I haven't kept tabs on him?"

Lester remained impassive. He didn't even blink.

"He hasn't played for three years. He's been selling insurance in some little jerkwater town in northern Ontario."

Now it was Lester's turn to get angry. He leaned forward in his chair and stared Crichton down. "I've kept tabs on him too. And I'm from northern Ontario. That 'jerkwater town' is called Marathon."

Crichton returned his friend's stare, then softened slightly and replied, "Look, I'm not trying to piss you off. I'm just mad at myself."

Lester shrugged his shoulders. "I don't see what the big deal is."

Crichton raised his left hand with four fingers extended. "One," he began, dropping a finger, "he hasn't been on skates for three years.

"Two," he dropped another finger. "He's going to waste everybody's time. Three, last time he played, he went nuts. Four, I don't want to be the guy to cut him." He looked sadly at his closed fist.

Lester raised his right fist. Slowly he opened up his four fingers. Then he extended his thumb. "You forgot number five," he said.

"What's that?" Crichton asked.

"What if he's really good?"

Crichton shook his head. "For the last three years, we've been a solid team. Twice we've made it to the conference final, but we could never take that last step. Do you have any idea how many times I've thought that Ricky could have been the missing piece to the puzzle?"

Lester shrugged his shoulders. "Maybe he still can."

Again Crichton shook his head. "It'll never happen. There's no way he can play at this level again."

"But what if he can?"

Crichton slammed his hands on his desk and stood up.

"Listen to me, Ronnie! Ricky Phillips will not play again for this team. Three years ago he screwed me—"

Lester glared at Crichton and answered slowly and evenly. "*Screwed* you? Are we talking about the same kid? The one who returned four million dollars to the team because he didn't complete the season?"

"That's not what I meant," Crichton said defensively.

"That's what you said," Lester challenged. "The kid had a nervous breakdown."

Now Crichton could feel himself getting really rattled. He'd always respected Ricky for returning the money, but he would have gladly paid Ricky ten times that amount if he could have just stayed healthy and helped deliver the Sharks the Stanley Cup. He felt torn. He knew that he should be happy for Ricky. He should welcome him back and encourage the comeback attempt. But a part of him still felt that Ricky had let the team down. Let his teammates down and betrayed Crichton's loyalty.

Suddenly, a thought occurred to Lester that sent a chill down his spine. "Johnny . . . If he's good enough to make the team, you'll give him a spot . . . right?"

Crichton let out a deep breath. "There's no way he'll be good enough."

"But if he is?"

Crichton turned around and went back to his window. With his back to Lester, he answered: "Ricky Phillips will not play for this team. If he's horrible, I'll have the shitty job of cutting him. If he's okay, I'll put him on waivers and maybe someone else will pick him up and he can make a fresh start somewhere else. If he's really good, I'll sign him to Worcester."

"So," Lester said to Crichton's back, "you'd sacrifice the good of this team because you're pissed off about something that happened three years ago that was beyond the kid's control in the first place."

Crichton turned around and looked at his friend. "Ronnie, be reasonable. There was a time when this kid was the missing piece of the puzzle, and to be honest with you, I'll never be able to forgive him for walking away from the team. But my feelings aside, there's no way he could step back in and play at that level again. It's just not going to happen. He's going to come to camp and waste everybody's time. Then, whether I like him or not doesn't matter; I'm still going to have to cut a former Calder Trophy winner."

Lester got up and walked towards the door, then turned to take a last look at Crichton. "He won the Hart too." Then he left and closed the door behind him.

❂

Popo stood in the middle of the eighteenth fairway and stared at the green. He was still 150 yards away, and it had taken him two shots to get this far. His whole round had been a disaster. He'd stopped counting his score on the fifteenth, and he doubted he'd break a hundred, even if he could stick one close here and one-putt for par.

His whole summer of golf had been a washout. Ricky's new workout regime had nearly killed him, and he wasn't even the one doing the actual working out—he was merely supposed to be helping keep Ricky motivated. But the days were so long and the workouts so intense that by the time they hit the golf course in the afternoon, Popo was too tired to focus on his game. Last summer, he had consistently golfed in the seventies. This year, the best round he'd managed to put together was an eighty-three. He was still muttering to himself when he pulled out an eight-iron and walked over to the ball. He hit a nice shot that came to rest within ten feet of the pin. He shouldered his clubs and looked up and to his left about fifteen yards, where Ricky was getting ready to play his second shot. He watched as Ricky hit an effortless pitching wedge that nestled in nicely, six or seven feet from the pin.

"Bastard," Popo muttered under his breath.

They walked up the fairway together towards the final green.

"This whole concept of tiring yourself out so that you'd have a harder time concentrating on the course doesn't seem to have affected your score any," Popo said.

Ricky smiled. "No, but I *am* really tired when we come out here. I have to make quite an effort to stay focused."

Popo lined up his putt and managed to drop it to at least end with a par.

"Nice putt," Ricky said. Then he stepped up and knocked down his putt for a birdie. They walked off the green, grabbed their bags and headed towards the parking lot.

"So when do you leave?" Popo asked when they got back to their vehicles.

"My flight's at noon tomorrow."

"Nervous?"

Ricky nodded his head. "Terrified."

Popo smiled. "You'll be fine. There won't be a guy in camp that can touch your fitness level. You've worked your ass off this summer."

"Thanks," Ricky said. "I couldn't have done it without your help."

Popo shrugged. "I was just along for the ride. You're the one who has made this happen."

"Yeah, I feel good," Ricky acknowledged. "I'm just worried about embarrassing myself on the ice."

Popo held out his hand and Ricky shook it. "It'll never happen. Ricky Phillips is back," Popo said. "But I do need to know one thing before you go."

"What's that?" Ricky asked.

"What'd you shoot today?"

Ricky laughed and opened the door of his truck. He got in

and rolled down the window. Looking at Popo, he smiled, "I'll tell you if you tell me."

"I stopped counting," Popo said.

Ricky backed out of his parking space and said, "Too bad for you." He rolled forward slowly until he was alongside Popo again. "Listen," he said. "I don't know what to say—"

"Forget it," Popo interrupted. "I was glad to be able to help."

Ricky looked at his friend and smiled. "Thanks, Popo."

"What'd you shoot today?"

Ricky laughed and accelerated hard towards the exit of the parking lot.

Popo got in his car. Suddenly, his cell phone rang. He started the car and grabbed the phone.

"Hello?" he said.

"Sixty-eight," said the voice on the other end of the line.

"I hate you," Popo said. Then he closed his phone and backed out of his parking spot.

CHAPTER TWENTY-FOUR

Ricky parked his rental car and walked towards the main entrance of the HP Pavilion. He'd had very little sleep the night before. On the plus side, unlike his first big tryout with the Barrie Colts all those years ago, he hadn't thrown up. Now he was just plagued by self-doubt, and it took tremendous willpower to urge his legs to keep moving forward and not turn and bolt for the car and the airport.

He walked into the main concourse and saw an efficient-looking woman sitting at a desk. He looked around for a familiar face, but he didn't recognize anyone. He walked over to the woman and she looked up and smiled.

"Are you here for the physicals?" the woman asked.

Ricky nodded nervously.

"Okay," she said. "If you'd just sign in here, then you can head down the main concourse and you'll find a change room. The physicals are being conducted in the large room at the end of the hall."

Ricky signed his name and thanked the lady. Once he was changed, he walked towards the room where the physicals were being held. He was greeted by a hive of activity. Six or seven physiotherapists were putting guys through their paces—seeing how high they could jump, how much they could lift, how many sit-ups they could do.

One of the physios walked over to Ricky. "Hi," he said, "I'm Mitch."

"Ricky Phillips," Ricky answered.

"Nice to meet you, Ricky. Would you like to get started?"

Ricky nodded, and Mitch led him over to a stationary bike. "First thing I need to do is take your resting heart rate and blood pressure," Mitch said.

Ricky nodded and got onto the bike. After Mitch had taken his initial readings, he produced a long, flexible tube to which he attached a new face mask, which he then slipped over Ricky's face.

"This will measure your VO$_2$ level. When you start pedalling, you'll see the needle move. Your job is to keep it between here and here," Mitch said, indicating a range on the gauge on the bike. "At the end, I'll tell you to go as hard as you can for the final two minutes."

"How long's the ride?" Ricky asked.

"Half-hour," Mitch answered.

Ricky started pedalling and moved the needle into the acceptable range effortlessly. After twenty minutes, his breathing was still nearly effortless. As Mitch watched Ricky, he caught the eye of one of the other physios with a "hey, check this guy out" nod of his head. At the twenty-eight-minute mark, Mitch yelled at Ricky, "Okay now, go as hard as you can!"

Ricky nodded and hammered on the pedals. The bike groaned under the exertion that Ricky put on it and the needled was pinned to the end of the gauge.

When the ride was over, Mitch took Ricky's pulse and said, "I'm just checking to see how long it takes you to recover."

Ricky nodded and took a sip of water. He hardly seemed winded. Mitch then put him through a series of tests: vertical jump, sit-ups and crunches, the core stability ball, throwing a medicine ball. As he worked out, the other physiotherapists in the room had started to watch him out of the corner of their eyes.

The final test was the bench press. As they walked over to the bench, Ricky asked Mitch what the heaviest lift had been so far.

"Three fifteen," Mitch answered. "You get one warmup lift, and one lift on your maximum weight. What do you want to start at?"

"Three hundred," Ricky answered.

Mitch shook his head. "No, not your maximum. What do you want to warm up with?"

"Three hundred," Ricky repeated.

Ricky lay down on the bench, popped the weight off the bar and brought it down to his chest. Then he effortlessly lifted it and put it back on the rack. He sat back up and rested on the bench.

"Okay," Mitch prompted, "how much do you want for your actual lift?"

Ricky thought for a second, then answered, "Three seventy."

Mitch set the weight at 370 pounds, then got behind the bench to spot. By now, everyone in the room had stopped what they were doing to watch Ricky as he got ready to try the lift.

Ricky sat back on the bench and popped the weight up. He held it for a second, then lowered it to his chest. With a grunt, he powered the weight back up. It had looked easy.

As he sat back up, Mitch asked, "Why do I get the feeling you could have lifted more?"

Ricky smiled. "I could . . . but I wanted to make sure I'd be successful."

Mitch smiled and told him he was free to go. After he had left, one of the other physios came over and said, "Who was the Schwarzenegger wannabe?"

Mitch shrugged. "Kid named Ricky Phillips. His scores are off the charts."

The other physio smiled wryly. "Yeah, but maybe he can't skate."

❀

On the opening day of training camp, Ricky shouldered his bag and pushed through the door of dressing room number three. He would be skating with guys who had played last year for the farm team in Worcester, as well as the young draft picks who would probably be sent back to their junior teams at the end of camp. The main nucleus of the Sharks wouldn't report until the end of the week.

The players took the ice and skated around and stretched while they waited for the assistant coaches who would be running the workout. An hour later, John Crichton opened the door to the team's private box and sat down beside Ron Lester. He handed Lester a cup of coffee.

"Thanks," Lester said.

Crichton looked down at the ice surface to watch the scrimmage. His coffee hadn't cooled enough to sip before he saw a player break out of his own end, take the puck the length of the ice and score.

"These the Worcester guys?" Crichton asked.

Lester nodded.

"That was a nice goal," Crichton said. "Who was that?"

Lester smiled and blew on his coffee. "Wouldn't believe me if I told you."

"No shit!" Crichton exclaimed. "Ricky?"

Again Lester nodded. "Have you seen the results of the fitness testing yet?"

"Not yet."

"Guess who has the highest VO$_2$ rating in camp," Lester challenged.

"Really?"

"Really," Lester answered. "His scores are unbelievable. He lifted 370 pounds. He's in better shape than he ever was when he played for us before."

Crichton looked down at the ice. "Still doesn't change anything."

"Johnny," Lester said.

"What?"

"He's in better shape than Eric, and *he's* always the fittest guy in camp."

"I don't care," Crichton said. "He will not play for this team."

"Johnny."

"What?" Crichton asked angrily.

"He just scored again." Then Lester smiled sagely and took a sip of his coffee.

●

After the workout, Ricky was leaving the arena through the main entrance when he saw Eric Rollins, heading towards him.

"Ricky Phillips," he said. "I *heard* you were in town."

Ricky held out his hand and grinned. "Hi, Eric."

Eric shook his hand. "Were you going to let me know you were here, or were you planning on hiding out through the whole camp?"

Ricky laughed. "Well, us lowly scrubs aren't allowed to bother the captain of the team."

"Scrub? I watched your workout. You looked great."

"Thanks," Ricky said.

"Where are you staying?" Eric asked.

"The Fairmont, around the corner on Market Street."

"Why don't you come and stay with me?" Eric suggested.

Ricky shook his head. "Thanks, but I don't want to impose. Besides, I have no idea how long I'll be here."

"You'll make it," Eric said confidently.

Ricky shrugged. "I'll give it my best shot. Hey, listen, I may not want to bother you for a place to stay, but I *would* like to buy you dinner. Are you interested?"

"Sounds great."

Later that night, over steaks and beers, the years fell away and the two quickly rekindled their friendship.

●

The Sharks' camp promised very few surprises. After all, they were a perennial contender, and changes to the lineup would be minimal. The only major source of intrigue was the comeback attempt of Ricky Phillips.

One of Ricky's biggest concerns as he got ready for the regular season was how he would be greeted by opposing fans when the Sharks went on the road. His comeback attempt had received very little media attention in the San Jose area. The team had not gone out of its way to publicize Ricky's return, and with the National Football League season in full swing and baseball gearing up for its postseason, sports fans had too many other things to worry about. *The New York Times* and *The Toronto Star* were the only newspapers to dispatch reporters to cover the story.

His first exhibition game was against the Columbus Blue Jackets, and Ricky knew that if he was going to be treated harshly, it would be in the city where he had faced the little boy with his MURDERER sign. The first time he picked up the puck, he realized he was holding his breath, waiting for the boos to start. However, the tone of the crowd didn't change and the game went on unremarkably. Ricky took a deep breath, relaxed and had a three-point night.

With each passing game, the number of reporters covering the Sharks got a little bit bigger. *Sports Illustrated* ran a feature that revisited the whole issue of fighting in hockey. Like it or not, Ricky was being thrust back into the spotlight. It didn't affect his play, though, and as the preseason schedule wound down, he was leading the Sharks in scoring, with five more points than Eric and six more than Pierre Cartier, although they hadn't played in all the games because they had already made the team.

As opening day approached, Ron Lester and John Crichton were faced with a dilemma: What were they going to do with Ricky? After the last practice session, Lester walked down the hall to Crichton's office and knocked on the door.

"Come!"

Lester opened the door and walked in, taking a seat across the desk from the general manager.

"What's up, Ronnie?" Crichton asked.

"We need to announce our roster for opening day," Lester answered.

Crichton nodded. "Okay."

Lester stared at his boss, who seemed to be missing his point. "Okay. Well, we're set everywhere but centre."

"Right."

"I want Ricky."

"You can't have him."

"Why the hell not?"

"I'm assigning him to Worcester."

Lester could feel his blood starting to boil. "Why?" he asked.

Crichton stared back. "Because I said so."

Lester's shoulders sagged. He and Crichton had worked together for a long time and had usually gotten along pretty well—as well as a GM and a coach can, anyway. He tried to reason with his boss. "Johnny, he's leading the team in scoring. He's back! The Hart Trophy–winning guy is back."

Crichton sighed. "Look, Ronnie, I'm not convinced that he is. That's why I want him to play in Worcester. If he's gonna go nuts again, I want it to be down there, not in San Jose."

Lester met Crichton's eyes and looked steadily at him. "You're just sending him down because you're still mad at him for costing you a shot at the Cup."

Crichton never blinked. "That might be part of it, but I still don't think he's ready. So he's played well for ten exhibition games—big deal. Let's see if he can maintain it game in and game out. Let's see how he handles the travel and the hotel rooms."

261

Lester shook his head. "I hope you know what you're doing."

"Look, if it makes you feel any better, I signed him to a two-way contract. We can call him back anytime we want."

"I want your word that if he continues to play well, you'll give him a shot," Lester said.

"You have my word," Crichton answered.

Lester got up and left the office. It was the first time since he'd joined the Sharks that he wasn't sure he believed John Crichton.

❂

After practice, Eric asked Ricky if he wanted to grab a bite to eat.

"I'd love to, Eric," Ricky replied, "but I should get back to the hotel and pack my stuff."

"Why?" Eric asked. "Have you found a place to stay?"

Ricky shook his head. "I've been assigned to Worcester."

"What?" Eric slammed his hand off the seat of his stall. "That's horseshit! You've been the best player in camp. Do you want me to go and talk to Lester?"

"I don't think it was Lester's call," Ricky replied.

"Crichton?"

Ricky nodded. "I signed a contract with him yesterday. Little bit less than my last contract," Ricky said sarcastically. "He says that if I play well for Worcester, he'll call me back up."

"Do you believe him?" Eric asked.

Ricky shrugged. "He's always treated me fairly. He was good to me before, when . . . well, you know."

262

Eric stood up and shook Ricky's hand. "Shit, man," he said. "I was just getting to know you again after three years and now you're leaving."

Ricky smiled. "I don't plan on being gone long. Don't worry, I'll see you soon." Then he picked up his equipment bag and walked out the door.

●

One day late in November, Lester was sitting in his office with two of his assistant coaches, discussing the drills they wanted to run in that day's practice, when Lester's secretary knocked on the door.

"Sorry to interrupt, Coach," she said. "But a FedEx package just arrived. It's marked 'Urgent.'"

Lester jumped up and grabbed the package. "Thanks, Shirley, that's awesome." Then he turned to his two assistants. "Can you guys run the practice for me?"

The two men nodded. "What's so important about the parcel, Ronnie?" one of them asked.

"If I'm right, it's the video of Worcester's game last night against Hershey."

An hour later, Lester knocked on John Crichton's door. "Come!"

Lester walked in and headed straight to the audio/video equipment in the corner.

"Shouldn't you be out on the ice right now?" Crichton asked.

Lester was bent over the DVD player. "Freddie and Scotto are running the practice. I needed to watch this. I'm a little pressed for time."

"Watch what?" Crichton asked.

"Worcester's game in Hershey." He stood up and started fiddling with the remote. "I'll cue it up to the part I want, and then I'll explain. I told Coach McAllister to let me know immediately if it ever happened."

"If *what* ever happened?" Crichton asked. He was clearly enjoying the intrigue.

"This," Lester said and pressed Play.

Crichton looked at the screen as Lester provided a running commentary.

"This is early in the first period of last night's game."

Worcester was lined up for a face-off in Hershey's end.

"That's Ricky at centre?" Crichton asked.

Lester nodded as they watched him win the draw cleanly back to a defenceman. The D pounded a shot on net, which the Hershey goalie juggled. The loose puck caused a huge scramble, and the Worcester forwards crashed the net. The goalie eventually smothered the puck just as a Hershey defenceman hammered a Worcester forward with a cross-check.

"Now watch this," Lester said, as a typical hockey scrum ensued with guys pushing and shoving. Crichton could see Ricky skate in and shove the D who had just cross-checked his teammate.

"Look!" Lester said, suddenly animated. "He doesn't want to fight, but he's there for his teammate. See how he's got his gloves up?"

The footage continued to roll as the Hershey defenceman dropped his gloves and swung a hard right that caught Ricky square on the chin. Ricky dropped his gloves and swung back just as hard. The two of them traded several blows before

Ricky jerseyed the D and pounded him with three more good shots. Had the linesman not broken it up, he would have landed several more.

"Good thing they broke it up when they did," Lester said proudly. "Ricky was thumping him."

Crichton looked at Lester. "Okay, so he was in a fight. Did he then run around the rink looking for Big Joe?" he asked sarcastically.

"Actually, no. That's why I wanted you to see this." Lester said. "I've watched it a few times, and you can tell that he didn't want to fight, but he did when he had to."

"Huh," Crichton grunted.

"Johnny," Lester said. "Worcester won the game 3–1 and Ricky had a goal, an assist and a fight."

"A Gordie Howe hat trick," Crichton said more to himself than to Lester.

Lester nodded his head and smiled. "A Gordie."

"Huh," Crichton grunted again.

"Listen, Johnny, the reason I was rushing to show you this is because we fly to Detroit tomorrow to start a four-game road trip. We're four points behind the Wings and Ricky could really help us."

Crichton took the remote from Lester and rewound to the fight. As he watched it again, Lester continued: "He's leading the American league in scoring by a country mile and he just had a fight. He's not gonna go nuts. I'm telling you, he's back."

Crichton never took his eyes off of the screen. "Where's Worcester now?" he asked.

"Hamilton. They play the Bulldogs tonight."

For a long time, Crichton didn't answer. Finally, he spoke.

"It's just a few hours from Hamilton to Detroit," he mused. "Do you want to call McAllister, or do you want me to?"

Lester smiled. "I'd be thrilled to."

●

The Worcester Sharks were sitting in their dressing room at Copps Coliseum, having just come in from the pre-game skate.

Coach McAllister entered the room and said, "Ricky, can I see you for a minute?"

Ricky got up and walked over to the coach. "Yeah, Coach?"

McAllister looked at the floor. "Ricky, I'm afraid that I'm gonna have to scratch you from tonight's lineup."

Ricky's face fell. "Am I suspended for the fight last night?"

McAllister shook his head.

"Shit, Coach. My fiancée and parents drove down to watch me play. What am I gonna tell them?"

"Ask them if they can give you a lift down to Detroit."

"Huh?" Ricky hadn't yet made the connection. "What's in Detroit?"

McAllister looked up and grinned. "Coach Lester wants you in the lineup for tomorrow's game. Congratulations, Ricky, I know how hard you've worked to get back to the NHL. You deserve it."

Ricky was so stunned that he didn't know what to say. He stammered a thank you to McAllister and shook his hand. "Did Coach Lester say how long I'd be up for?"

McAllister laughed. "The way you've been playing, I would think that you'll be there until the end of your career. And with the shape you're in, that should be about twenty years. Now go on and see your folks about that ride to Detroit."

EPILOGUE

Joe Louis Arena in Detroit is home to a very loyal fan base. At centre ice, the word Hockeytown is painted over the giant Red Wing logo; it's a moniker the locals are very proud of. At 6:00 P.M. the stands were already starting to take on their distinctive red and white appearance as spectators dressed in team jerseys started to arrive well in advance of the 7:30 opening face-off. By the time the Sharks and Red Wings took the ice for warmup, the arena was almost full. By the time the puck was dropped, it would be a near-continuous sea of red and white. The majority of jerseys the crowd wore sported the names of the present-day Wings stars, but even today, decades after his retirement, one could still find thousands of people wearing Howe's number nine. Scattered about there were also a few Yzermans and Proberts, and one or two Sawchuks and Abels.

Sitting among the faithful, three rows from the back of section 119, were six people who stood out like the proverbial sore thumbs. Darryl Phillips, who sat in seat number one, had insisted that all six of them would wear brand new San Jose Sharks jerseys with PHILLIPS emblazoned across the shoulders above the number 16. Earlier in the day, he had gone into the Red Wings store in the arena and purchased the jerseys. Three of them were for people he had never even met before, but they were friends of his son and that was good enough for him. The bill for the six sweaters had come to just under a thousand dollars. Darryl wasn't the type of person to spend his money extravagantly but, as he explained to the sales clerk, his son had just been called up to the Sharks and was playing in his first game. If Ricky knew where they were sitting and happened to look into the crowd, Darryl wanted him not just to be able to feel their support; he wanted Ricky to be able to *see* it.

Sitting beside Darryl in seat number two was his wife, Haley. She sat serenely amidst the sea of energy that was emanating from the other twenty thousand people. She was just happy to be in the same building as her son. She was proud and a little nervous, but mostly she was happy—happy for her son because he was finally back doing what he was born to do.

Seat number three was occupied by Ricky's fiancée, Cheryl Rogers. She was finding it difficult to contain her emotions. She was so proud of Ricky that she was sure she was going to cry at any second. She was also blown away by the sheer size of the arena. She had never been to an NHL game before.

Next to her were three men who had spent the last eight hours crammed into the cab of a pickup truck. Last night at around nine o'clock, Matt Holland, occupant of seat number four, had received a phone call.

"It's Ricky," said the voice at the other end of the line.

"Where are you?" Matt had asked. "I can barely hear you."

"I'm on the 401 headed towards Detroit. I'm playing for the Sharks tomorrow night. Do you want tickets?"

"You bet," Matt had answered.

Ricky didn't need to ask how many; he just knew Matt would need three.

As soon as Matt hung up, he immediately phoned Robbie Montgomery and Johnny Crawford. There was no hesitation on the part of either one about going, and first thing in the morning they had piled into Matt's pickup truck and hit the road for Detroit. Now they were sitting beside Mr. and Mrs. Phillips and Cheryl and were maintaining a steady, although slightly intoxicated, chant:

"Ric-ky Phil-lips! Dun-dun, dun-da-dun! You're a py-lon! Dun-dun, dun-da-dun!"

A fan in the seat beside them, who was wearing a Red Wings jersey, finally interrupted them and said, "You fellas *do* know that to call a hockey player a pylon is an insult, right?"

Johnny happily explained that the player whose name they were chanting, who had just been called up to the Sharks, had played on their pickup team, the Pylons. They were all here to support him. Word spread through the section that number sixteen for the Sharks was playing in his first game and that the six people in the Sharks jerseys were his friends and family.

Suddenly a voice cut through the crowd from the back row. "Hey, isn't Phillips the guy that killed that other guy in that fight?"

Oh no, Cheryl thought. Darryl cringed and Haley looked down at the concrete floor. None of them wanted to acknowledge the question.

Matt stood up and turned around to face the questioner. "He didn't kill anybody. It was a tragic accident. But yeah, that was him." There was an icy edge to his voice.

The Detroit fan nodded and said, "I thought I recognized your jerseys. He's been gone a long time. It's good to have him back. He was a hell of a player."

Matt raised his cup of beer in a toast. "He still is."

Just then, the arena lights dimmed and a giant Red Wings logo began to dance around the rink. The crowd erupted as the public-address announcer heralded the arrival of the hometown heroes.

At the other end of the rink, the visiting team took the ice almost unnoticed. The six people seated in section 119 craned their necks as they tried to pick out their boy.

"Do you think he's scared?" Cheryl yelled to Haley.

Haley nodded as she stood and clapped. "Terrified." Then she turned to Darryl and asked, "Do you think they'll play him?" She looked up at his face, and in spite of the darkness she could see the tears coursing silently across his cheeks. He was trying to clap along with the crowd and wipe his eyes at the same time. He turned to her and smiled. "It doesn't matter, does it? He's already won, whether he plays or not."

The game turned out to be one of those nights where everything went right for the home side. After two periods, Detroit led 6–2. Late in the third, with the game well out of reach, the Sharks were buzzing in Detroit's end. Ricky Phillips was out for one of his rare shifts when he cut through the slot and buried a wrist shot in the top corner.

As is the custom when the visiting team scores, the rink went relatively quiet—except in section 119, where six people wearing Sharks jerseys were jumping up and down and screaming. Their enthusiasm was infectious, and slowly the applause began to spread through the section.

It was a loud enough ovation that they could hear it in the broadcast booth. The Wings' colour commentator noticed the commotion and pointed it out to the play-by-play man. "Once again the Detroit fans show their class and their knowledge of the game. That's a nice ovation they're giving to Ricky Phillips to welcome him back to the league after all this time."

The camera panned across the section and found the six people in their Sharks jerseys who were still cheering madly.

"Well," the play-by-play man answered, "it looks like it wasn't all Red Wings fans."

❋

Two weeks after the game in Detroit, Chris Popovich pulled into his driveway, got out and walked back to his mailbox, and absent-mindedly pushed down the flag on the side of the box. He opened the lid and reached inside. He rifled through the mail as he walked back to the house. Mixed in amongst his bills and flyers was a letter with American stamps. His eyes moved to the return address, and he realized it was from Ricky. As he walked through the front door of his house, he tore open the envelope. It was a card with a picture of the San Jose Sharks on the front. He opened it, and a piece of paper fluttered out and fell to the ground. The inside of the card contained only two words:

Thanks, Popo.

He bent down and picked up the paper. As he realized what it was, he grinned. It was a cheque for twenty thousand dollars. Popo looked down at the memo line and laughed. Ricky had written:

> *For services rendered. Treat yourself to some golf lessons.*

ACKNOWLEDGEMENTS

George Eliot once said, "It is never too late to be what you might have been." I've always known that I wanted to be a writer; I just never realized how little I knew about the process of developing a novel. I owe a huge debt of gratitude to the following people who helped me learn along the way.

Gord Henderson provided invaluable advice and introduced me to my agent, Michael Levine. Michael has handled all my nervous, panicked, overzealous questions with humour and poise.

Thank you to all the good people at HarperCollins, especially my editor, Lynne Missen. Lynne has a wonderful ability to see a concept and improve on it, all the while making it feel like it was my idea. Thanks to Lloyd Davis for helping me solve my timeline dilemmas and for making the National Hockey League's collective bargaining agreement understandable.

To the East Oro Public School graduating class of 2010: thanks for listening to the early draft and for providing realistic, thoughtful feedback.

Thank you to my boating buddies Steve MacDonald and Tom Shoniker and to my golfing partner, Dave Jamieson. Steve taught me about the effects of concussion and head trauma and what would have realistically happened to Charlie. He also provided insight into post-traumatic stress disorder. Tom used his legal background to help determine if Ricky would have faced criminal charges in the wake of the Charlie Davidson incident. Dave imparted his vast knowledge of both professional and international hockcy and provided insights into the way players, especially goalies, think.

To my extended family in Orillia, Ajax, New Jersey and beyond: the encouragement and the Sharks jersey have been wonderful.

And finally, to Janet, Lindsay, Nick and Luke: this would not have been a journey worth taking had you guys not been along for the ride.